THE BOOK OF URANIA

By Brendan Myers

ARCANA ELEMENTS

Arcana Elements is an imprint of Arcana Creations.

Cover design by Pat Bellavance with art elements under license by Can Stock Photo. Additional editing by Pat Bellavance.

Legal Deposit, Library & Archives Canada, October 2021

ISBN 978-1-9993954-9-0

www.arcanacreations.com

Acknowledgements

My first thanks goes to the students in my Science History and Methods class at Heritage College, from 2017 until today, who gave me the inspiration and the good-natured nudging to write this novel.

As if they could hear me, I'd like to thank all the philosophers and scientists whose lives I explored while researching and writing. I sometimes imagined they were here in my room, looking over my shoulder as I was writing. I hope I did right by them.

Finally, I am grateful to the people who read early drafts and showed me the way forward over the hurdles and ditches that cross every writer of historical fiction: especially Jean-Louis Trudel, and my partner Andrea Lobel.

Yes, this book is what a love letter looks like.

Table of Contents

Prologue   1

Book One: Nicolaus   5

Book Two: Tyco   51

Book Three: Giordano   97

Book Four: Johannes   143

Book Five: Galileo   163

Book Six: Isaac   221

Author's Notes   243

Brendan Myers

Prologue

Open your window and look far and near,
Who knows what wonderful things will appear!
Climb to the rooftop and look near and far,
Who knows how looking will change who you are.

§ 1.

The ninth sister sat at the end of the table, surrounded by her family, waiting for someone to notice her. For the last two or three centuries, the family held its annual reunion at the same ancient temple, near the summit of the stony mountain. Ivy climbed its cracked pillars. Most of its walls and roof had fallen away, leaving it open to the air. By evening, the trees and stones on the plateau became twilight shadows, and the temple glowed with golden warmth from the oil lamps and torches. Nymphs laid the bowls of olive oil and wine on the table, and satyrs in the corner tuned their lyres and drums. The sisters praised each other's doings since the last gathering, and shared scandalous news, while scooping up roast mutton and boiled vegetables with salty flatbreads and dipping them in olive oil. Whenever the satyrs played something that seemed to call for dancing, most of the sisters would rise to caper and swing about the table. The mountains echoed with their laughter; but the ninth sister only smiled and sipped her wine.

"Calli, when you were working with Dante," one of the sisters asked another, "why did you tell him your name was Beatrice?"

"It's the name of a girl he loved when he was nine years old," said Calli, as she closed the book she had read to everyone. "So, I knew the name would get his attention. He used my real name in the beginning of his *Purgatorio*. Very sweet of him to do that."

"He's created probably the best epic poem since the *Aeneid*," the mother declared. "You should be proud."

1

"Oh no, I disagree," said another sister. "*The Golden Ass* is better. For one thing, it's simpler. Anyone can identify with it. And for another, it's funny. *The Divine Comedy* is many good things, but it's painfully serious. I can barely read ten lines at a time."

"That's a curious thing to hear you say, Terri," said the mother. "It's what I'd expect to hear from Thalia."

Thalia, who drank her wine from a wooden beer mug instead of a decorated earthenware bowl, said, "*The Divine Comedy* was definitely not funny." The comment produced the laughter she wanted; she grinned to hear it.

The ninth sister said, "Have any of you read the new philosophy coming from Florence, in Tuscany?" When no one said that she had, the sister explained some more. "There's a boy there, trying to revive the tradition of Plato and Aristotle, and fit it together with Christianity, Kabbalah, Hermeticism, Islam – he's very ambitious. And only twenty-one years old! He wrote this book – would you like to hear some of it?"

Some of her sisters expressed mild interest, so she opened the book. "Here's what he thought about human nature – he writes this part as if it's a message from the gods to the very first human beings – he says, *We have made you a creature neither of heaven nor of earth, neither mortal nor immortal, in order that you may fashion yourself in whatever form you choose.*"

Thalia said, "You can always trust Urania to be more serious than Dante." Another wave of laughter was her reward.

Then Clio leaned in front of Urania. "But there was something else I wanted to say about *The Divine Comedy* –"

Hands and arms fluttered in front of Urania's face again, as Clio passed judgement over all Italian poetry. Urania sat low in her seat, saying nothing: only smiling when it seemed necessary. She cleaned her plate with her flatbread and shared a few scraps with the dogs. When the main course of the meal finished, she gathered her satchel and wandered out of the temple, to the belvedere overlooking the valley, and in the distance the Gulf of Corinth. Mars shone red and bright for her in the west; Jupiter took his place between the bright stars Aldebaran and Alnath, nearly perfectly overhead. She made a quick and imprecise measure of each planet's angle from the horizon, turning her hands palm over palm. Then she let her senses fly across the earth, searching for anyone else who might have wandered a few steps away from their people, to pose questions to the stars.

A voice in a crowded city beyond the Ionian Sea, hundreds of leagues away, caught her ear. It spoke of a new way to read her book. A smile curled on the edges of her lips.

Mother Mnemosyne noticed her absence from the table. "Urania!" she called, as she stepped outside. "Come, we're going to play kottabos. You'll miss all the fun!"

In the temple, Urania could see her sisters flinging the dregs of their wine-bowls at a small statuette at the centre of the table, attempting to knock it down. The sisters alternated between praising a thrower's aim or laughing at someone who got splashed in the face.

"I was thinking," said Urania, "Everyone in the family is some kind of artist. They're all poets, writers, musicians. Terpsichore is a dancer. I'm *none* of those things. I shouldn't be surprised that they weren't interested."

"You're their older sister," Mnemosyne assured her daughter, offering her hands. "And my beloved first-born daughter. Now, tell me about your new philosopher. What was his name?"

Urania shook her head. "See, not even you were listening," she said. She climbed on top of the stone railing of the belvedere.

"Where are you going!" Mnemosyne called out. She stepped closer, to catch her daughter if she fell. But Urania raised her arms and launched herself into the sky.

Brendan Myers

Book One: Nicolaus

§ 2.

**Rome, The Papal States,
1514.**

The cobblestone streets of the Eternal City chattered with priests and petitioners, the injured and the sick seeking healing, merchants selling pilgrimage medals and indulgences. Though they scrambled shoulder to shoulder across the entire width of the street, they parted to ease the passage of two men, one of them a dark-haired, round-faced cleric with a white tunic under a dark brown cloak, and the other a bishop whose attire was modest but whose skull cap and crozier told everyone what his rank was.

"You have far less to worry about than you think, my friend," said the bishop to his companion.

"But the Holy Father himself will be there," said the cleric, worried.

"He's been our pope for only a year," the bishop said. "He's as keen to impress the world, as you are to impress him. Hence, he summoned this council."

"He's not going to like what I have to tell him," the cleric said, as he took off his hat to wrangle it in his hands. "Nobody will."

"Try to remember why you were invited to the council in the first place," the bishop reassured him. "You have total command of the highest realms of mathematics and theology. You read Greek enough to translate Byzantine poetry. You could be revered as the greatest philosopher of our age. Yet you chose instead to care for the sick among the poor: a sign of deep Christian virtue. I can think of no one better qualified to speak to this council."

The cleric put his hat back on to show his modesty, but he still smiled. "Too much honour, my lord Bishop. Nonetheless, all my expertise can only confirm what you already know – that there is something wrong with the calendar. All I can add is the unhappy conclusion that there's nothing we can do about it. I feel like I'm walking to Calvary."

"Well, Nicolaus, if that's how you feel, then let me be the friend who walks beside you on the way," the bishop said, patting his companion on the shoulder.

They turned a corner and found themselves in the square before the front portico of the Lateran Basilica. A soldier in the distinctive yellow and blue uniform of the Swiss Guard rushed to their side. "Bishop Tiedemann Giese," he said. "As soon as you take your seat, we can begin."

"This is Doctor Copernicus of Toru?, he is advising the council today," said the bishop, as he motioned for the guardsman to allow Nicolaus to enter with him.

"At your service, doctor," said the guardsman, as he leaned his pikestaff aside so the two men could pass.

Nicolaus put his hand on the door and paused. The bishop was three steps ahead before noticing that his companion wasn't following. He turned and cocked his head to the side to ask for an explanation.

"Maybe you can give me a signal if you think I'm about to say something foolish, in front of the Holy Father," the trembling cleric asked. "Scratch your ear, or something."

The bishop laughed. "Trust yourself, and trust your intelligence. You'll do fine," He took his friend's hands, and led him across the threshold.

Urania, who had been following them a few steps behind, knew the guard wouldn't let her follow them into the basilica. She explored around the side and found a corner where no one would notice her leap to the roof, as easily as a cat jumps on a table. There she found an unguarded door in the cloister, and she stole her way inside. Exploring within, and avoiding the priests and other busybodies, she found a hiding place in the organ loft, where she could watch her new favourite philosopher address the council.

§ 3.

"I contend, sirs, that we don't know enough about it, to make a proper decision," said Nicolaus Copernicus, standing at a podium in the centre of the great basilica. His words caused a small stir among the rows of long-bearded, black-robed men seated in the pews to his left and right. The statues of the saints in their niches looked down on him; sunlight filtered by passing clouds and entering through the windows made the saints appear to disapprove of the scholar's stern pronouncements, no less than his grey-haired audience.

"Surely, the matter is not complicated," said Pope Leo the Tenth, whose silk white robe and red mini-cape were embroidered with Biblical quotations and trimmed with gold fringe. Beside him, Bishop Giese made a pained expression that the pope wouldn't see. He was the only bishop in the assembly not wearing an elaborate silk cape and embroidered mitre.

"I'm sorry to tell you that it is," said the man at the podium. "Our calendar governs more than what day we plant our crops in the spring and what day we harvest them. It governs what day is a Sunday, and what day is a solstice and an equinox, and thereby governs what day we celebrate our Lord's death and resurrection. And so, what appears a simple matter like calendar reform touches upon delicate questions of theology and salvation."

"We know this, Doctor Copernicus. Mind who you are speaking to," said the pope.

Nicolaus took off his hat and twisted it in his hands. "I beg forgiveness, your holiness," he said. "I feel the weight of eyes beyond this room watching us."

Urania, hiding in the organ loft, grinned. "You have no idea how right you are," she whispered to herself.

"May it ease your burden to know," the pope continued, "that the decision is ours, and not yours. You are here only to provide us with an expert opinion."

"Well then," said the expert at the podium, "it is my expert opinion that we do not know enough about the exact positions and movements of the sun and moon to create an accurate reform of our calendar."

Murmurs and whispers arose from the rows of bishops and cardinals in the pews on each side of him. One of them reached the doctor's ears: "The calendar doesn't need reform anyway. It was good enough for Julius Caesar, it is good enough for us."

Urania, watching from above, smiled, but shook her head.

"We all agree we don't know everything," said the Holy Father. "We are only men, imperfect and sinful. All the same, do we not know *enough*?"

"I contend that we do *not*, sir," Nicolaus repeated. He scratched the back of his head. "Do you realize," he said, "that with the biggest quadrant in this country, we still cannot fix the sun with enough precision to find the exact moment of equinox? And so, we do not know enough to calculate the discrepancy between our calendar year and the actual solar year – which we know is *not* three hundred and sixty-four days. Serious calendar reform requires greater precision than we have the *techné* to measure. Without that precision, we lose time. Slowly. A minute here, a minute there. Small steps that may not seem significant, one day to the next. But over the years those lost minutes add up to whole days. And then, everyone's lost."

Bishop Giese, looking for a way to save his friend's face, said, "Is it only that we haven't the *techné*? Or is there something else?"

Nicolaus paused before answering, as he considered whether to tell the whole truth or only some small part of it which would not create a stir. Twisting his hat again, he said, "The letters of Saint Paul, and the ancient masters of philosophy, both teach us that God set the earth upon its foundations, never to be moved, and that Man is the measure of all things." He took in a deep breath to give himself courage before continuing. "And yet when we measure the heavens with the tools of man – the quadrant, the astrolabe, and the triquetrum – we find that the planets do not follow the smooth and perfect circular motion which we should expect to see in a divinely ordained, mathematically perfect universe."

The assembly knew it and nodded their grey heads to show him so.

"Such perfect motion would be observed from the equant point," Bishop

Giese said.

"Yes," Nicolaus agreed, "but each planet has its own equant point, different from the rest. To my mind, this makes the cosmos – scattered. Without elegance, without unity. I can't live with that. It somehow seems... how shall I say it? Beneath the dignity of God to create such a messy universe."

"It is also possible," the pope suggested, "that the divine harmony you speak of is forever beyond the grasp of mere human reason. Hence, the necessity of faith, which is the substance of things wished for, the evidence of things not seen."

"That's not good enough for me," the scholar replied, his voice raised. An angry stir rose from his audience to match. Someone called for him to be removed from the stand for daring to contradict His Holiness as well as Scripture. Others demanded that he should be stripped of his academic credentials, and then stripped of his shirt and flogged. One of the bishops at the head table rose to his feet to wave an angry finger and howl about the punishments in hell that awaited those who rejected the faith or rebelled against Holy Mother Church.

Realizing the mistake he had made, Nicolaus put his head down, muttered an apology that no one could hear, and stepped down from the podium.

Bishop Giese leaned back, stroking his chin. Before Nicolaus got too far away, he thought of something that might restore his friend's confidence. He rose and cut through the din with a commanding voice: "Doctor Copernicus! I have one more question."

The council calmed itself enough to hear the bishop's next words.

Nicolaus turned around to face the council again. "Yes, my lord Bishop?" His eyes held only the faintest drop of hope.

"In your good judgment, what would it take to correct the errors?" he asked. "To bring reason and faith back into agreement?"

"It would take an observatory the size of this basilica," the scholar replied, knowing that many churches already doubled as observatories, and that the pope could pay for a bigger one if he wished. "But even if there was such a thing: it would take a new way of *thinking*, a new way of *seeing*. I must confess, I do not yet know what that would be."

The pope shook his head. "You came so well recommended. The famous Nicolaus Copernicus, *qui magnus mathematicus est.*" He dismissed Nicolaus with a wave of his hand.

Nicolaus acknowledged the jibe with a defeated nod and stepped away again.

Urania, charged with admiration for the way Nicolaus spoke his mind, dared to raise her head a little higher, risking being discovered, to watch him walk away. Then she retreated from the loft, to follow him into the city again.

$$§ 4.$$

The only light in the guest room that Nicolaus rented for his visit to Rome came from the cluster of candles on the desk, and another on the nightstand beside a votive image of Saint Catherine of Alexandria, patron saint of philosophers. Nicolaus laid as many sheets of rag paper on the desk as would fit, to sketch mathematical diagrams. Beside them was a slate chalkboard on which he wrote calculations. Sometimes he would pause to sharpen his chalk and his charcoal, the better to draw precise lines; sometimes he stepped to the window to contemplate the sky. A row of long low clouds dawdled overhead, slightly grey compared to the midnight blue behind them, making the stars appear more distant. Then he would shake his head, and wander back to the desk, to erase the chalkboard or shake the charcoal off the rag-paper, and start again.

Returning from one such contemplation, Nicolaus found a woman holding up his chalkboard, admiring his work. She wore a traditional Greek peplos: a simple Mediterranean gown, sleeveless, fastened around the waist with a cord, and at the shoulders with gold clasps. A sky-blue himation draped over one shoulder and hung down to her opposite hip.

"*Kháìre, didáktoras* Copernicus," she greeted him.

"*Kháìre,*" he replied. He was annoyed by her uninvited intrusion yet intrigued by her use of ancient Greek to say hello, as well as by her unusual dress. He took the chalkboard away from her and asked, "I'm sorry, but this is my room for the night. Are you another guest in the house?"

"I heard your presentation at the council today," said Urania. "You're very brave, doctor Copernicus. Anyone else in your position would have told them whatever they wanted to hear. You told them the truth."

"You were listening?" said Nicolaus.

"I'm a scholar, like yourself. And a friend, if you'll have me," she answered. "My name's Urania."

Nicolaus tilted his head, to glance at her from the side. "Urania," he said. "The Greek goddess of mathematicians and astronomers was called Urania." He regarded his visitor for a few heartbeats, then he moved to the door, to hold it wide open for her. "But I am a canon of the Church. I should not remain alone in the night with a woman who is not my wife," he told her.

"You were discussing calendar reform today," she asked him. "I can help you."

Nicolaus almost laughed. "Can you calculate the epicycles for all five planets, with enough accuracy to predict them for the next hundred years?"

"I can show you how to calculate the planets with no epicycles at all."

Now Nicolaus did laugh. "If you were listening to today's council, you heard the Holy Father himself say why we need them. There's no other explanation for why the planets stop in their courses and then move backwards, for weeks at a time."

"There *is* another explanation," Urania assured him. "With no epicycles. No equant points. I think you already know what it is. You read it in the books of Aristarchus, and al-Bitruji, and Nicole Oresme. They were friends of mine too, as it happens."

Nicolaus regarded her for a moment, then said, "An educated woman is *very* unusual in these modern times. So, where did you take your holy orders?"

Brendan Myers

The muse said, "Nowhere."

"Come now, we both know the only place a woman can get an education is in a convent," Nicolaus said. "So where is yours? Somewhere in Greece, I surmise?"

"I do live in a temple. But it's not a monastery. It's near the summit of Mount Helicon, northwest of Athens."

Nicolaus grinned. "Your namesake is said to have lived there. But who is the patron saint of your abbey? Who is your Mother Superior? The Church is like a small town; I might know her."

Urania said, "My mother's name is Lady Mnemosyne."

Nicolaus sighed, though his smile grew more patronizing than amused. "The nine muses are allegories, not gods. And you still haven't told me what you're doing here."

Urania said, "I'm here to help."

Nicolaus sighed. "I'm sorry *mein frau*, but after what I said at the council today, if I'm ever to show my face among my fellow clerics again, I have to find and solve a bigger problem than calendar reform. Something quite beyond intellects of women, however well schooled you might be. Now if you don't mind," He gestured toward the door again.

"Are there no women among the wisest of the gods?" she reminded him, with a slight sharpness in her voice. "Athena? Minerva? Saint Sophia? My own mother?"

"Allegories for knowledge, not gods," he said. "To speak of them as gods is paganism."

"But women, all the same," said the muse. She noticed the votive icon on his bedside table and said, "The patron saint of philosophers, too."

"I do not have time for this," Nicolaus said, his patience thinning. "So unless you can square the circle, double the cube, or trisect the angle, I have no use for your help." He gestured toward the door again.

But instead of moving to the door, Urania moved to the window. "What would the path of the sun in the sky be like, if the Earth rotated around its poles, and the sun remained in place?" she asked him.

"I'm going to find the landlord," said Nicolaus, and he marched out of the room.

"It would look exactly the same to us, wouldn't it?" she called after him. "The sun would still appear to rise in the east, and set in the west."

Nicolaus re-entered the room, making small respectful steps, as if the room was no longer his. "It would," he admitted to her.

"Suppose, then," she continued, as she drew several circles on a clean sheet of rag paper, "the sun did not rotate about the Earth, but rather the Earth and all planets rotated about the sun. What would the movements of the planets look like?"

"Difficult to say," said Nicolaus, still resisting her suggestion, but curious at the same time. He gravitated toward the window, to contemplate this question under the inspiration of the stars.

"As the Earth moves in its path toward one of them," said Urania, "wouldn't it look like that planet was slowing down? And as the Earth passed it by, wouldn't it look like that planet was –"

"Standing still," said Nicolaus, as he caught on to what she was saying. "Then going backwards for a while. Exactly as we see them do."

"And have you noticed," Urania continued, "that Mercury and Venus never travel far from the Sun?"

Nicolaus smiled. "Yet the others travel the full circumference, around and back again."

Urania held up her completed diagram for him to examine. It showed the sun at the centre, orbited by eight planets, the third of which was also orbited by a moon, the fifth was orbited by four more moons, and the sixth was surrounded by a ring.

"That's because Mercury and Venus are inside the orbit of the Earth, and the others are outside," she said.

Nicolaus took the diagram and examined it. His mouth made the shapes of the words he was thinking. He took off his hat and scratched the back of his neck.

"No epicycles," said Urania. "No equant points."

"Uniform circular motion, around a single divine centre," Nicolaus observed with admiration.

"They're not quite *perfect* circles," Urania mentioned.

Nicolaus pointed to the two outermost circles and asked, "What are these? Two extra planets beyond Saturn? And what is this cloud of things beyond the last one?"

"Would you like to see them?" she asked with a girlish grin.

Nicolaus put the diagram down and asked, "But why is there no wind? If the Earth moves through space, then there should be a terrible gale, all the time."

"The air moves *with* the Earth," Urania said.

"What, through the whole universe?"

"When you climb a mountain," the muse explained, a tired sigh escaping her nose, "you can feel the air getting thinner, colder, yes? If you could climb high enough, you would eventually find the air so thin you could not breathe it. Higher than that, there's no air at all."

Nicolaus grinned at his foolishness. "Of course you're right; I should have known. Beyond the sphere of the moon, everything is made of ether."

Urania made a pained smile. But before she could say more, Nicolaus remembered another objection. "Still, the sphere of the fixed stars always remains the same distance from the Earth," he said. "That's how we know the Earth doesn't move. If it were otherwise, half of the sky would swing toward us for half the year, and away from us for the other half. *Ergo*, the Earth does not move. Even the ancients knew that."

Urania looked up, as if she could see the stars through the roof of the building. "We knew a great many things that have since been lost."

"Why do you say 'we'?"

Urania let her smile serve as an answer. She turned to his diagrams and said, "There's another possible reason why you don't see the stars swinging toward you and then away again."

"Indeed. It might be that the stars are too far away for us to see their relative motion," Nicolaus agreed. "But if that were true, then the stars would have to be many thousands of times the distance from the Earth to the sun. A hundred thousand times more distant. At the very least."

"Very good, Nicolaus," Urania praised him.

"But that's an impossible distance! Surely God's creation cannot be so vast *and so empty* at the same time! Why would God have created so much *nothingness...*"

He paused to feel the gaze of the infinite falling upon him from the space between the stars, and from Urania's encouraging smile. Specks of starlight appeared in the darkness of her hair.

"But what if He *did*?" Nicolaus wondered aloud. "What if the cosmos is so much greater than even the best of us can imagine? Didn't Augustine himself say that God is greater than the greatest thing you can conceive?"

Now Urania's smile grew wider and more childlike. She took his hands and offered to him again: "The cosmos *is* greater than most people imagine. Would you like to see it?"

Nicolaus saw that one of her eyes was flecked with gold like the sun, and the other with silver like the moon. He looked around the room, and comfortable and spacious as it was for a guest house, it now seemed very small. With her hands grasping his, he could imagine the space outside, carrying him forth from the city walls, to a height where the whole city lay open to him in a single glance. Soon it was joined by the lesser lights of nearby villages at night, and then framed by the east and west coasts of the green Italian peninsula. A heartbeat later, they were above the clouds.

Nicolaus felt all his muscles bulge with the hot thrill of vertigo. "How high are you taking me!" he cried, as he squeezed her hands.

"All the way to the stars!" Urania answered, with glee.

Nicolaus tightened his grip on her hands as she pulled him aloft, ever higher. He saw the horizon of the Earth bend into a sphere, with the crescent of the morning sunrise glowing in the atmosphere far to the east. The outline of continents appeared only as a faint black shadow looming upon the deep blue expanse of the ocean. Towns, cities, and settlements pricked the darkness like distant candles. Soon they were high enough to perceive the Earth as a sphere. The stars surrounded them above and below, as did the bright belt of the Milky Way. Then the Earth receded to the distance until it was one star among many, in a bottomless cosmos.

"Have we stopped moving?" Nicolaus asked.

"We are moving faster than a gale force wind at sea," said the muse.

"But it looks like we're going nowhere," Nicolaus said. "And where is the Earth?"

"It is still nearby," Urania assured him. She pointed at a blue-white point of light, almost indistinguishable from the surrounding stars.

"No, that cannot be," Nicolaus said. "That star, that speck of dust in space, is the whole of the Earth?"

"Compared to the whole of the cosmos," the muse explained, "the whole system of the sun and his planets is smaller than a flax seed in the ocean."

"That cannot be," Nicolaus said, his voice trembling, his eyes closed. "If we are that small, then how much smaller is the meaning of our lives! How could anything we do matter? And where in all this nothingness is God? No, no, I cannot believe this!"

"Hold on, Nicolaus, there is so much more to see –"

"I don't want to see it. Take me back, take me back!" Nicolaus howled. He kicked his legs, feeling around in the empty space for something to stand on. He pulled himself up her arms and grasped her shoulders, as though she were a lifeboat in the sea, crushing her to save his life.

The muse stroked his face and said, "We're home now, you're safe."

He blinked his eyes and found himself back in his room in the guest house. He scrambled away from her, and gripped the post of his bed frame, tight enough to whiten his knuckles, as though he would drown if he let go. His breath quickened and his eyes grew fierce with astonishment. Then he noticed the diagram of the cosmos that Urania had drawn for him. He calmed his breathing and relaxed his grip on the bedpost. He stood, and examined the diagram again, marvelling at its simplicity and elegance. Urania, framed by the window and by a few silver starlets floating in the air about her, shared her most loving smile. Her hands remained open, inviting. Her hair billowed in a gentle breeze.

"Who are you?" he asked, his voice trembling with awe. "Are you a seraph? A messenger from heaven?"

"You know who I am," she said. "You've been looking for me for most of your life. I've been looking for someone like you, too."

"Looking for – me?"

Urania slid closer and said, "Looking for someone who can understand me, the way I think you can."

A new thought entered Nicolaus' mind. He grasped a rosary from his nightstand and brandished its crucifix toward her. "You're not an agent of the devil's party? You cannot touch me if you are."

Urania lowered his rosary with a gentle gesture, careful to give him no further cause for fear, but also to show that she could touch him, and so could not be a devil. She gestured for him to sit in a nearby chair, and she sat on the desk beside him.

"I'm a philosopher," she reassured him. "And no less human than you. Though I am a little older than I look. And I know things that take many lifetimes to learn."

Nicolaus relaxed himself; his sense of wonder returned. "Ah-ha! You're an antediluvian," he said, grinning, proud of having figured her out. "A survivor of the great flood, a passenger on Noah's Ark. The scriptures tell of men from that age who lived for nine hundred years. And longer! Are you the same spirit who visited Scipio? Boetheus? Plutarch? *Homer*?"

Urania smiled. "If you say so," she said, choosing not to disagree.

His rosary still wrapped around his wrist, Nicolaus examined Urania's sun-centred diagram of the cosmos again. "Uniform circular motion, around a single centre. A divine harmony," he marvelled.

"You wanted a new way of thinking, a new way of seeing," Urania said, smiling with him. "Here it is."

Nicolaus admired the diagram for another moment. Then he said, "Tell me more."

* * *

Khàìire, philia mou. Hello, my friend.

Yes, it's me. I decided to insert a few letters between some of the chapters. To clarify the important things, to straighten the record. Is that the phrase – to straighten the record? This language of yours, this English – it is not my first language. I am still unsure of it.

I'm taking a terrible risk, making these letters. There are laws among my people, very old laws, that say we are not allowed to reveal ourselves to you. Not our true selves, that is. If I break them, I would be taken to live in some faraway place, surrounded by a thousand miles of thorn bushes and fog. Or a wall as high as a mountain, made entirely of skulls. Or underground. Underground! Hell would not frighten me if it were only a lake of fire. But if it were underground, where it is always night, but the stars never shine, and morning never comes.

So, keep these letters secret. Between us. Between friends. If anyone asks, say that they're works of fiction. If you can do that, then I should be safe.

I want you to know me. I want my words recorded – my voice heard. I want my story told.

My first meeting with Copernicus seems like a good place to begin it. Especially because of what happened next.

§ 5.

Later that night, Urania sat on the roof of the same basilica, looking across the road to the windows of the house where Nicolaus had rented a guest room. She could see him at a table, working out several complex mathematical problems on a long sheet of rag-paper. She smiled, pleased to see something happening in the world which she had inspired. She poured some wine into a clay chalice for herself and drank a silent toast to him.

Behind her stood a tall man in a purple Roman toga. "Lovely little flame you lit in that man's mind," he said.

Startled, Urania turned around, then relaxed when she recognized him. "How did you know this was *my* doing?" Urania asked.

The man smiled and shrugged. "The influence of an Olympian is obvious to another Olympian, if not to anyone else," he said.

Urania nodded. She poured some wine for her visitor. "*Khâìire*, Julian Augustus," she toasted him.

"*Bibendum! Et vivet in bonum, Ourania*," he replied in Latin. They drank together, then watched Copernicus at work for another short while.

"Why did you do it?" he asked her.

"I wanted my sisters to see how philosophy can be beautiful, no less than music and poetry," she replied. "And I saw that man's potential. With him, I can *prove* the point."

"You would need him to do something quite magnificent, to prove a point like that," Julian said, with no small trace of annoyance in his voice. "But he is a mortal man. Mortals cannot do what we can do."

Urania nodded toward Nicolaus and said, "I saw that man do something that none of the gods have tried to do since the Mythic Age."

Julian folded his arms. "What did he do."

Urania looked up and said, "He tried to imagine the true distances of interstellar space."

Julian paused, as he grasped the significance of what Urania told him. Then he said, "And how far did he see?"

"Not far," Urania admitted. "It frightened him; he pulled away."

Julian laughed. "Ah, such is the nature of mortal man. They build great cities like this one; they launch their armies and their merchant fleets across the world; they struggle for knowledge and for glory. But they always fail to reach it. Oh, often they fail with grace, and finesse. It's a credit to their spirit that they can turn their failures into art. But still, they fail. That is their *hamartia*; they cannot do otherwise. If you try to show them the cosmos, as it truly is, they will not know how to see it; they will fail again."

Urania's attention drifted back to Nicolaus, still working on his papers. "Our ancestors were like them, once. I want to help them."

"Our ancestors were great souls," Julian countered. "Heroes and spiritual achievers. There will never be another generation like them."

Urania faced him and said, "Why not?"

"Why not!" Julian sputtered. "Every generation is bound to its fate. Our ancestors were bound by fate to become the gods. These mortals today are bound to strive for greatness and to fail. That is all there is to that."

Urania sighed, lowered her eyes, and said, "I sometimes think fate is whatever my father says it is, and nothing more."

The aged Roman looked to the sky for a moment, then said, "How much do you know about Prometheus the Titan, and the little game he played with your father, back in the Mythic Age? Inspiring humanity to make their own fire?"

Urania said, "I know that my father ended it by nailing him to the side of that mountain. And sending that creature every day, to eat his liver."

"Your father is king of the gods," said Julian. "A loss in a contest like that would disturb the natural justice of the world. He *had* to do it."

Urania contemplated this. Across the ancient plaza, Nicolaus lit another candle, threw away a heavily scratched sheet of paper, and laid down a new clean page to start a new stack of calculations.

"Do you think that if I give my inspiration to this man, my own father will try to stop me from doing it again? Is that what you came down here to tell me?"

Julian said, "I think no one will begrudge the little candle you lit for that man today. But if you give him anything more, you can expect your father to find out. And you can expect him to be *most* unhappy."

§ 6.

**Frauenburg, Warmia,
Kingdom of Poland, 1519.**

Frauenberg's Cathedral Hill was a cluster of fortifications in red brick and stern stature, surrounding a tall cathedral and a bishop's palace. It overlooked the Baltic Sea to the north and the timbre-frame town to the south. From the outside, the towers on the hill impressed a visitor more for their height than for their grandeur. In a dining hall that leaned against the inside of the fortifications, Copernicus treated some friends to a feast of cabbage soup, roast mutton, and ideas. The windows were small, so it felt like a cave no matter the time of day. Yet Nicolaus made his guests think of sunlight. He laid a diagram of the solar system on the table and placed coloured stones where the planets should go. His dozen dinner guests wondered at his diagram; some leaned forward to examine it closely, others looked to the ceiling as if they could see through it to the stars. One of them, Andreas Osiander, was a younger man with a square beard and a wooden cross hanging from a coarse twine round his neck. He touched the small lapis lazuli pebble on the diagram representing the Earth, then pulled his finger back as if the stone would scald him.

"So… when you say we are moving through space, in two different ways," Andreas began.

"The sun orbits the Earth, and the Earth spins on its axis," said Nicolaus, moving the blue pebble accordingly.

"What I'd like to ask is: *really*? Do you actually *believe* that?"

"In part, it is a mathematical shorthand, I admit. It makes the computations easier," Nicolaus replied. "But it's more than that. It makes the universe *elegant*." As he spoke, he placed a lit candle stub in the centre of his diagram, in the place of the sun. "Some people call the sun the lantern of the universe. Some say the sun is its mind. Some say, its ruler. Hermes Trismegistus calls the sun a visible god. So, what better place for the sun in this beautiful temple, than the place where it can light up the whole of creation at the same time? Here in the centre, as if seated on a royal throne, where it can govern the family of planets revolving around it."

Urania, wearing the gown, kirtle, and partlet of a noblewoman, the royal blue Arabian cloth shimmering in the candlelight, leaned on the door frame that led to the kitchen, watching and listening. When she caught Nicolaus' eye, she grinned. Nicolaus clasped his hands in prayer toward her, to thank her.

Bishop Tiedemann Giese, holding his bishop's skull cap on his knee, said "I think you should publish this."

"Oh no," said Nicolaus. "If I published it today, everyone will explode with laugher."

"That's what I did when you first told me about it," said Andreas. His companions laughed; they too had the same first impression.

"But I made some pamphlets for all of you," Nicolaus said, and he distributed the pamphlets from a leather binder. "It's a little commentary on the important points. I'm also working on a larger manuscript, with the full argument and all my tables of calculations. But it's not finished yet."

"How much more is there to do?" asked Tiedemann Giese.

"I need more measurements, to confirm things. My good friend, the Lady Urania," he waved to her, and she waved back, "supplied me with star charts and calculation tables by Al-Tusi and Al-Battani –"

"Mohammedeans!" Andreas exclaimed. "Muslims! They'll make you pay through the nose for whatever they give you. Ten times the real value, or more."

"He needs their numbers," Urania defended him, stepping closer to the table. "It matters not where the numbers come from; it matters only that they are accurate."

"I need those numbers to build the historical record; to see how far my theory will hold," Nicolaus added. "Lady Urania has been very helpful in acquiring them for me."

The bishop didn't like that answer but had no argument against it. "You have studied mathematics, then?" he asked her.

"And logic, rhetoric, history, natural philosophy –"

"You must have studied master Aristotle," the bishop tested her, "who teaches that all the elements must move to their natural places: earth and water must fall to the centre of the cosmos, air and fire must fly to the edges. So if the sun is the centre, what keeps the Earth from falling into it?"

"Aristotle was wrong," said the muse, pleased with herself.

Hearing everyone gasp with incredulity, Nicolaus tried to rescue the conversation. "Maybe – maybe earth-like things fall to the Earth, and sun-like things fall to the sun. I don't yet know. I still need to work these problems out."

"You have more difficult problems," said Andreas, who had been glancing through Nicolaus' pamphlet. Fingering a line on one of its pages, he said, "Here you say that the distance between the Earth and sun is only a sliver compared to the distance between the sun and the fixed stars. People will read that, and they'll ask: then how much more distant is God? Hmmm? Here you wrote that the centre of the Earth is not the centre of the universe – and they will ask, but is Man not the crown of God's creation anymore? I can't argue with your computations, Nicolaus. But it feels like you have torn up the good floorboards to build a bad raft and thrown us all into the sea."

Nicolaus contemplated his model of the solar system for a moment, then said, "Those are more reasons I am not yet ready to publish in full. But I shall say this much: that we find in this arrangement a beautiful harmony, such as cannot be discovered any other way. And with a universe so much larger than we imagined before, surely its Creator is larger, and all the more worthy of praise?"

While Nicolaus and his friends contemplated this, a messenger fell into the hall, breathless and panicked. "Doctor Copernicus! Doctor Copernicus!" he panted.

"I am he," said Nicolaus.

"Apologies, I have come a long way – I have a message from the Prince-Bishop of Warmia."

Urania recognized the messenger's voice. "Julian?" she whispered.

"Take your time, my good man," Nicolaus advised the exhausted runner.

"There has been… an emergency," said Julian. "A column of knights has seized some of the territory and all the roads to the south of this city. Your lord summons his principal men to arms." The messenger handed Nicolaus a letter.

"That's the Prince-Bishop's official seal," said Nicolaus.

"You are to command the garrison at the castle of Allenstein," Julian continued.

"This is a *military* commission?" Nicolaus asked, seeing the sealed letter in a new light. "Why me? I don't know anything about the art of war."

"May I?" asked Bishop Giese, with his hand open to take the letter. Nicolaus gave it. The bishop opened and read it. "Quite extraordinary," he said. Then he handed it back and said, "The Church sent the Teutonic Knights to bring the light of Christ to the nations of the Baltic Sea. The knights decided to bring it everywhere else along the way."

"Poland is already Christian," said Nicolaus.

"Yes, it is – hence our problem," said the bishop, folding his arms. "Christians fighting Christians over who loves Jesus properly. I do not like it. All the same, you had better go and defend your castle."

Nicolaus put his hand on his unfinished book and said, "I can't go. I need your library, to finish my work. I need the observatory we are building in the tower."

"The library will be here for many years to come," the cardinal said. "The people of Allenstein may not."

Julian said, "I have a horse for you, and a team of guardsmen, ready and waiting."

Nicolaus acquiesced. The bishop held out his hand, and Nicolaus kissed his ring. Then he followed Julian away. As they passed close to Urania, she saw his face.

"Julian?" she said. "What are you doing?"

Julian winked at her, and ushered Nicolaus out of the dining hall.

Urania followed them. Amid the rush of people and animals and noise in the courtyard, Nicolaus was met by a small team of men wearing leather armour, some carrying swords and some crossbows. Their tabards were red and sewn with the crest of Warmia: a holy lamb carrying a Christian flag, and its heart bleeding into a chalice.

Urania grabbed Julian by the shoulder. "Julian! Did my father put you up to this?" she demanded.

One of the armed men, seeing her hand on Julian's shoulder, grasped the hilt of his sword, ready to draw. She let Julian go.

"I told you the journey would be dangerous," Julian said to the soldiers. Some of them chuckled.

Nicolaus saw the scuffle, and said, "I know this woman; she's a friend."

Julian said, "Sir, we have no time to wait."

"The men are still loading the supply cart," Urania told him. "You want to leave sooner? Go help them. I need to talk to Nicolaus."

Julian grimaced at her but left to help the men load the cart.

"Don't go," Urania said to Nicolaus.

"The letter had the correct seal, and I know my lord's handwriting," said Nicolaus. "I must do my duty; I'm sorry."

"But if anything happens to you before you finish your book –"

Julian, helping to load the supply wagon yet close enough to hear the conversation, said, "He will be well protected." He winked at her.

Urania grasped the threat in his words which Nicolaus and the other men could not. She turned to Nicolaus and said, "Give it to me then. Let me keep it safe for you."

Nicolaus thought for a moment. He looked at the weapons the men were carrying, to protect him on the road. "It should be safe enough," he said.

"Please?" Urania implored him. She leaned closer to Nicolaus and pointed to Julian. "I know that man. He is not who he says he is," she warned.

"No? Then who is he?"

Urania paused to consider how to answer. She said, "His name is Julian Augustus. He was once a great leader of men, in war and in peace, a long time ago. The rest is not for me to tell you. Learn from him, but do not trust him completely. His loyalties may not be the same as yours."

Nicolaus contemplated this. Then he gave Urania his manuscript: a stack of loose-leaf handwritten papers, held in a folder and wrapped in a coarse twine.

"This is the only copy," he said.

Julian, who saw Nicolaus hand over the manuscript, shook his head and returned to loading the supply wagon. Then one of the guardsmen tapped his shoulder and said, "Time to go."

Nicolaus nodded. He took Urania's hands to say goodbye. "I don't know if mankind has had three days without war since Cain slew his own brother," he said, with some worry in his breath. "But until now, I've never had to fight in one."

"I once saw you snap your mouth at the pope," Urania said, smiling. "If you can do that, you can do anything. And I will keep your book where no harm can come to it," she promised.

Nicolaus held Urania's shoulders, to hold the moment in his memory. Then he followed Julian and the guardsmen.

Urania held the stack of his loose-leaf pages close to her heart as she watched Julian and his centurions taking her student away. The clop of horse hooves echoed from the red brick walls of the courtyard, and was swallowed under the noise of the relic merchants and chanting pilgrims.

§ 7.

It was not only the sudden danger Nicolaus was about to face, that I found so bewildering. It was the thought that Julian might have arranged it, to stop Nicolaus from finishing his book. Something he said to me the last time I saw him, something about a contest of wits between Prometheus and my father, made me wonder about him.

So I decided to visit the old titan himself, and get the story from the source. I was sure he would see me; I am his cousin, and we Olympians like to be close to our families.

In our world, by the way, we have some well-worn customs for travellers. Most of our sanctuaries have a hollow hedgerow, a cave, an attic trap door, or similar place where you could go in one side, and come out to a completely different sanctuary, dozens of leagues away. You have heard of 'Seven League Boots'? We call them our 'Seven League Doors'.

From Warmia to the forests of Germania, I passed through the secret forest glades tended by álfar and dvergar, where the canopy of the trees was almost heavy enough to block the sun. In the plateaus of the Alps, I stayed overnight in the gardens of nymphs and satyrs, far from the knowledge of the mortals below. I paid my hosts with the promise of hospitality returned, should they or their friends or family happen to be passing near my sanctuary, on mount Helicon. It is an elegant custom. It brings new stories, new people into your life. I know of many long friendships, and no small number of marriages, that began with the simple gift of hospitality on the road.

But on this occasion, I did not rest long between the doors. Prometheus has a villa in the Caucasus mountains, close to where my father once imprisoned him. I wanted to reach him before Nicolaus found himself neck-deep in war.

* * *

Urania found Prometheus seated on a terrace beside a simple clay-moulded villa with small windows and a dome roof. Beside him was a table with an extra chair and two chalices of wine. Evening settled upon the land below. The sun turned the whitewashed houses to orange and gold.

"*Kháìre*, Urania," he said, when she came close. He knew she was there without needing to turn around.

"*Kháìre*, Prometheus," she said, and she sat in the extra chair.

Urania's head was level with the titan's elbow even while he was sitting down. He wore a white tunic loose at the waist, white trousers, and dirty sandals. His face was creviced from deep thoughts, though someone might think it was from age. He took his chalice and gestured that she should take up hers.

"I know it is the custom to pour a libation to your father, at a symposium such as this," he said. "But for reasons I trust you understand, we do not honour him here."

Urania acknowledged it. "Tonight, I have my own reasons not to honour him. Let us honour Heracles, instead. The hero who set you free."

Prometheus smiled, and said, "Flattery, hmm? You're here because you *want* something."

"Only knowledge," she replied.

Prometheus nodded. He raised his chalice and said, "*Yiamas*, Heracles, beloved of Hera, greatest of the race of heroes."

Urania saluted Heracles with him; they poured some of the wine on the ground, then they drank.

"You might have seen that I have been mentoring someone," Urania began.

"Your mathematician, Doctor Copernicus."

"Did my father send him to the war in the north? To make sure he can't complete the work? To kill him, perhaps?"

"It's very possible," Prometheus replied.

"Why would he do that?" Urania said, her voice carried by frustration almost to a shout. "I taught philosophy to mortal men before they even had a word for it. What's different about this time? Why would he do this to me *now?*"

Prometheus leaned back in his seat. "This time, you found a student who *understands* you."

Urania considered this for a moment. "So Julian *is* working for my father," she concluded.

Prometheus said, "When Julian was Emperor of Rome, he tried to restore the old Olympian religion. He failed, as you know. But for his effort, your father rewarded him with immortality. Imagine the gratitude a gift like that can inspire. Imagine the *loyalty*."

Urania imagined it, and shuddered. Then she said, "When you taught the mortals how to make fire, you must have known my father would punish you for it. But you did it anyway. Because you loved them."

"That's what the stories say. And it is a good story," Prometheus answered. He sipped his wine and stroked his beard.

"Is it not the truth?"

Prometheus sighed, and said, "Zeus didn't punish me for giving them fire; they already had fire. And bronze working, and ship building, and civilization. No, he punished me for meddling with the sacrifices."

"What do you mean?"

"Many ages ago," Prometheus said, as he shifted his seat and remembered, "I went to the Olympian festival, and I found the place where the mortals were preparing their offerings of meat and wine for the gods. I hid the good meat in a rotted stomach-skin, and I covered a pile of old bones under a layer of fresh fat, so the priests would think they were giving their best to the gods, when in fact they were giving the worst. A simple deception, and the priests quickly saw straight through it. But that was what I wanted. I revealed a truth that Zeus wanted hidden from the mortals. From all the Olympians. Even from himself."

"What truth?"

The lumbering old titan took another sip of his wine, and said, "That it doesn't matter what you offer the gods. They are not paying attention; they are doing nothing for you. And you don't need them. *That lesson* was the fire that I gave them. A lesson I do believe most of them still haven't learned."

Urania shook her head. "No, that can't be right. They need us!"

"No they don't," Prometheus said. "And if they ever understand that, your father will do the same thing to them that he did to my people."

"What? He will round up all the philosophers and imprison them somewhere? Others will rise to take their place."

Prometheus rose, and faced the distance as he spoke. "You are too young to remember the Titanomachy," he said. "So imagine a war, with the whole world for a battlefield. Earthquakes and volcanoes for weapons. Entire cities crushed by storms of fire. Lions and wolves, as tall as trees at the shoulder, stalking the land, rooting out anyone in hiding. The bodies of the dead piled as high as the hills. The stench of them, carried on the wind for miles. And the survivors herded like farm animals into workhouses and mines, forced to build temples to honour their oppressors, and to pour out their own blood to make food for the gods. That's what your father will do to them."

Urania gripped her wine chalice close, as if she could use it to protect herself from that vision of the future. "He wouldn't do that, just because I taught some of them astronomy."

"He would, if he thought you were helping them grow strong enough to take his place," Prometheus told her. "So, you have a choice to make. Return to your sisters, to your home on Mount Helicon. Drink your wine, sing your songs, forget about your philosopher and his trivial human problems. Or... go to him. Help him and his kind to grow up. And see what happens when your father gives you his complete and undivided attention."

Urania looked down to the wine-cup in her hand, and her toes in her sandals, and an earwig that crawled near the leg of the table. The sun was now fully beneath the horizon, and on the opposite horizon the stars were taking their places for the night.

"Are those my only choices?" she asked.

Prometheus slunk himself lower in his chair and put his feet up on the terrace wall. "Yes," he said, with a firm finality.

Urania held her chalice close to her lips, but only contemplated it; she closed her eyes, and shook her head. She clunked her chalice down on the table, giving some nearby dogs a slight startle.

Seeing her dejection, Prometheus said, "You are still very young," and he sipped his wine.

§ 8.

Nicolaus pushed a wheelbarrow full of turnips through the streets of Allenstein, where the snow was higher than his ankles and still falling. He prayed a quick thanksgiving that God had not at the same time sent a northern wind, to chill the town colder. Teams of peasants, bundled in cloaks and hoods and soft leather boots, pulled wagons loaded with grain sacks, barrels of beer, and firewood, into the courtyard of the castle. The tracks of their cartwheels ploughed a narrow path through the snow. Someone slipped on an icy patch and fell, spilling the sack of apples he carried on his back. Those nearest to him dropped their loads and ran to his side, to gather him to his feet again and carry him to the courtyard gate.

"What happened?" asked Nicolaus, when they brought him near.

"He's sixty years old, sir," said one of the helpers. "He shouldn't be outside with this weather."

"Get him to the castle. Tell the kitchen to make him a hot meal," Nicolaus ordered, and the others took him there. Then Nicolaus took the man's sack of apples, to finish the job himself.

Julian, who was working nearby, saw Nicolaus' decision and moved to his side. "Why didn't you have him flogged?"

"Flogged!" Nicolaus sputtered. "Didn't you hear? He's sixty years old!"

"We need everyone working," Julian said. "A little *fear* will keep them working."

"There's an army of Teutonic Knights camped to the south. That should be fear enough," Nicolaus reminded him.

"Of course," Julian conceded.

Nicolaus took a few sticks of firewood from a cart and brought it to a brazier, where a few workers were taking a moment to warm themselves. "It's a *sacred* thing, to be the leader of a free people," he said. "I have to organize and command them, but I have to respect them, and provide for them."

"You also have to defend them," Julian said.

"I have called up every man in this city of fighting age," Nicolaus told him. "I've got scouts watching the roads, and ambush teams to keep the knights from getting too close. We're making the best use of what we have, to keep everyone safe."

"It's a good plan. But I can think of a better one," Julian said.

"Yes?"

"Surrender."

Nicolaus nearly dropped the sack of apples. "Surrender? That's not a plan!"

"Those knights out there," Julian explained, "are the descendants of the men who claimed this land for Christ, in the Northern Crusade. For two hundred years, they ruled it as their own kingdom, until the peasants betrayed them to join Poland."

"Poland treated them with kindness," Nicolaus grumbled. "The knights did not."

"Nevertheless, this is *their* kingdom. Or that's how they see it. They're here to take it back. Surrender, and no one will die."

"If I surrender, they will certainly kill *me*," Nicolaus said.

Julian suppressed a smile. "But no one else," he said. "Surely, there is no greater love than that of a man who lays down his life for his people? Isn't that the Christian thing to do?"

Nicolaus recognized the passage from scripture. "Do you truly believe that our only choices are between surrender and death?"

"What I believe doesn't matter. The *fact* is: they have a much larger army." Julian produced some paper from a satchel on his belt. "The latest scout report: four hundred foot soldiers, around twice as many cavalry, and heavy cannons. More arriving every day," he reported. "And they're all professionals, not like the shit-shovellers and nose-pickers you've rounded up here."

Nicolaus glared at him.

"These good and noble people," Julian corrected himself.

In his mind, Nicolaus compared this number to the strength of his own forces. "If we met a force like that in the field, they would rout us, that's true," he admitted. A moment later he brightened: "But here in the city, we can hold them out for weeks. Long enough for King Sigismund to send a relief force. Here, take this to the cold storage cellar," Nicolaus gave to Julian the wheelbarrow of turnips he was pushing. "I'm going to write the King a letter."

Julian folded his arms. "I'm not pushing a wheelbarrow, that's peasant work."

"Everyone's doing their part, Julian," Nicolaus chastised him. "If I can push a wheelbarrow, then so can you."

"I'm your military advisor," Julian said. "I can be much more useful to you in other ways. Negotiating on your behalf with the King, perhaps. You could let me take your letter to him."

Nicolaus decided Julian had a point. He nodded. "I'll call for you when I finish writing it. Until then," he gestured toward the wheelbarrow, "help with the turnips."

Julian smiled. He waited until Nicolaus was out of sight and earshot. Then he grabbed a peasant by the shoulder and said, "You – move these turnips!"

§ 9.

With Nicolaus' letter to King Sigismund of Poland in his belt satchel,

Julian took the road south from Allenstein. At one of the roadblocks, he asked the guards where the Teutonic Knights were camped, and which roads were safe. When he was out of the city and out of sight, he took the road that the guards told him not to take. As soon as he spotted the first squad of scouts, he sang an old Roman travelling song to himself, to be sure that the scouts would also spot him. They quickly did; they loaded their crossbows and marched toward him.

"*Sie! Halt!*" they shouted.

Julian stopped, and put his hands up. "Don't kill me, don't kill me!" he pleaded. "I'm only a courier, I have no weapons."

"Warmian spy, more like it," one of them accused.

"I didn't see you there – it's easy to miss you, with your white tabards, in all this snow," Julian said, as the knights bound his wrists behind his back with leather strips.

"Shut your klapper," a knight ordered him.

"I'm not a spy, I'm a courier!" Julian insisted, as they pushed him down the road toward their camp. "See- look in the pack on my belt. I have no weapons. Only letters. Letters!"

They searched his belt satchel and found the letter Nicolaus wrote to the King of Poland. The knight who found it handed it to another knight and said, "I can't read. Can you?"

"A little," the second knight answered. He looked at the letter for a moment, then said, "We need to take this to the group captain."

Julian smiled.

§ 10.

Urania slept that night on a wicker *chaise-longue* on the terrace. When she awoke, she found that someone had draped a blanket over her, and placed a straw hat on her face to shade her from the sunrise. She could hear Prometheus inside the villa, talking with someone whose voice sounded familiar. She sat up and found a decanter of water and a cup waiting for her on the table. She drank, and admired the view of the valley below, where the golden cornstalks and green grasses rippled in a gentle breeze. The terrace was high enough up the mountain that some of the sky birds and clouds passed below her. For a moment, she wondered why a man like Prometheus didn't choose somewhere more secret to live, as most Olympians did in this age. But she could not deny the view was glorious.

When Prometheus saw that she was awake, he joined her on the terrace, carrying a breakfast platter. Behind him followed a broad-shouldered, smiling woman. "*Kháìire*, Urania!" she shouted.

"Kynisca!" she recognized her and held out her hands. Kynisca took them in hers, and they squeezed their fingers together.

"The Old Man here said that you would arrive later today; I thought I'd come early to surprise you," said Kynisca. Her flesh was stained slightly reddish, like many who spent half a human lifetime in the open air. But her muscles moved under her skin with well-defined sharpness. Her hair was dark blonde, and bound in various braids and bandanas. Her traditional peplos was hitched up to her knees, so it would not impede running or wrestling. No one seeing her would doubt she led the life of an athlete; as such she made an acute contrast with Urania, whose hair was loose and flowing, whose dress was long, and whose hands were untouched by callouses or scars.

"I got here last night," Urania told her. "But I didn't tell him I was coming; I just showed up."

"You don't have to tell me these things," the old man said. "I can see them coming."

"Where are you living these days?" Urania asked Kynisca. "Are you still running the training camp near Sparta?"

"I am," Kynisca said. "And I brought one of my horses for you!" She led Urania around the villa, to a patch of grass enclosed by a fieldstone wall. There grazed two golden horses, one with its mane tied in a dozen braids. Kynisca whistled and called them: "Parmenides! Heraclitus! Come!" Both horses trotted close.

"They're brothers, and directly descended from the horse that won my Olympic laurels for me, back in the day," Kynisca said. "They can ride through the sky as if on solid ground, and faster than the wind. Pick one."

"Oh no – too generous – I couldn't" Urania gasped.

"Go on, pick one," Kynisca insisted. "The Old Man already paid me; it's his gift."

Prometheus, standing back from the two women, shrugged and grinned as though it was all whimsy.

Urania smiled, hugged her friend, and chose the horse with the braids in its mane. She petted him and fed him an apple from a nearby basket.

"That's Heraclitus," said Kynisca.

"Interesting choice," said Prometheus. "Now come, and breakfast with me."

They sat down around the table on the terrace and shared the breakfast dishes: pancakes with a choice of butter or honey or olive oil for dipping; grapes and figs on the side.

"I hear you took on a new student," said Kynisca.

Urania said, "I did. But a few days ago, he was called away to fight in a war."

Kynisca nodded. "You need me to protect him," she surmised.

"Well, ah – "

Prometheus said, "Yes she does."

"As this man is your student, so he is my brother," Kynisca declared. "I shall be glad to protect him. So, who is he? And *where* is he?"

"Well, he's an astronomer," said Urania. "And he's in Poland."

Kynisca whistled. "Never been there before. But it's been a long time since I've had a decent adventure. Nothing ever happens in Olympus anymore."

"It won't be an adventure; it will be a war," Urania said.

Prometheus said, "It's important that he *survives* this war."

"Why? What's so special about him?" asked Kynisca.

A moment later, with the breakfast table cleared, the three of them examined the diagrams and computations in Nicolaus' manuscript.

"It's beautiful work," said Kynisca. "Also, rather *familiar*. Reminds me of Aristarchus. But no one ever believed him; why will anyone believe this man Copernicus?"

"Because these computations are impeccable," said Urania. "Aristarchus could not have done this. He did not have the Hindu-Arabic numerals."

Prometheus said, "But it isn't finished. That's why its author has to survive."

"Well, that settles it," Kynisca declared. "We're leaving for Poland today."

Urania wasn't sure whether to be grateful or annoyed at her host for arranging this meeting. She furrowed her brow at him. "Why are you helping me?" she asked him.

"Why are you continuing to help your astronomer?" Prometheus returned the question. "Especially in the light of the warning I gave you."

Urania collected her thoughts before answering – she could sense that the old titan was testing her. "I can't bear to see people staring at the sky and... blinking," she said, choosing to answer honestly. "There are so many wonderful things out there. I don't want to be the only one who can see them."

"And if, because of you, their young eyes open?" Prometheus asked her. "If they learn the truth about who they are, and their rightful place in the world? And if your father comes to think they are a threat to him? And if he launches a war to stop them?"

Urania shifted in her seat, though it did not ease her. She said, "I don't want a revolution. I only want to know who my people are."

Prometheus smiled. "That, my dear Urania, is why I'm helping you."

Urania decided she passed the test.

Kynisca, who had been buckling a saddle on to Heraclitus, said, "Is there some history between you that I don't know about? Some secret you're keeping?"

"Nothing to worry about, Kynisca," Prometheus said, his voice deep and definitive. "There's a man whose life needs to be saved. That's all."

Kynisca stood up. "Then it's time to go save him."

§ 11.

From the saddle of her faerie horse racing through the clouds, Urania saw the torches and fire pits of the Teutonic Knights camp before she saw lights of the city. She guided her faerie horse around them. Most mortals, she felt sure, would not notice her while she was riding that high above them. Still, she did not want to chance that some among them might look up. The moon was full that night, though half-dimmed by passing clouds, so the snow covered fields glowed with a silvery light of their own, and the hedges and forest patches became black holes and chasms. But a cluster of yellow lights in one of them caught her attention. She waved to Kynisca, who was riding her own faerie horse, to signal that they should go on to the city ahead of her. Then she swung her horse closer to the edge of the forest where she saw the torches. She found a score of knights in full armour, clunking along a narrow path. Their squires in the rear pulled three small cannons on wooden carts. A fourth cart held the cannonballs and sacks of gunpowder. Each cannon was no longer than the length of her arm, but together they might be enough to batter down the city gate with enough direct hits. They put their torches out as they reached the edge of the woods and stepped on to the road. One of the knights appeared different from the rest. Nothing in his armour or his actions revealed it; Urania simply felt a tingle in the centre of her forehead when she looked at him.

"That's probably Julian," she told Kynisca. She urged her horse to sprint away, before Julian might spot her. Inside the city, she set down on the ground in a narrow lane near the castle, where no one was looking, then galloped to the castle. Seeing as she was still dressed in the kirtle and partlet of a noblewoman, the castle guards let her pass. She found

Nicolaus in his tower, sitting by a table covered in letters and maps, and surrounded by his captains.

"The city is under attack!" she shouted.

Bishop Giese stepped toward her. "I know you. You're the one who supplied Nicolaus with those Islamic books. If the city's under attack, how did you get in?"

"I saw a team of knights approaching the outer walls," Urania said. "At least twenty of them. And three cannons."

"So it's not the whole army?" Bishop Giese asked.

"Three cannons are bad enough," said Nicolaus. "How long until they get here?"

Urania pointed at a spot on a map of the city and surroundings. "They were here when I saw them. And that was only a moment ago."

As Nicolaus discussed this with his captains, the bishop realized something, and turned toward her. "That forest is more than two leagues from here. How did you see them 'only a moment' ago?"

"I've a horse that can run faster than the fastest bird in flight," Urania said.

"What breed? Arabian?"

Realizing she could not tell the bishop the truth, she said, "Spartan."

"Greek horses? Faster than Arabians? What – do they have wings?"

Before Urania could answer, two soldiers entered the room, breathless from running up the stairs. "Sir! We are ruined!"

"The knights are attacking?" Nicolaus asked.

"No – *czaronice* – witches! We saw one on the sky! On horses!"

Bishop Giese immediately pointed at Urania. "Arrest her!" he ordered.

The guards drew their swords, but their hands trembled. Most everyone else in the room backed a few steps away from her. Two men braver than most seized her by the arms, though she could feel the hesitation in their grip.

Nicolaus, however, said, "Let her go! She's a friend."

The bishop turned to him and with his angry glare demanded an explanation.

"She helped me with my work. She knows things; she has never steered me wrong."

"Witchcraft," someone in the room whispered.

"Mathematics!" Nicolaus shot back.

Urania said, "It doesn't matter anyway. What *does* matter is that before the sun rises the knights will smash down the city walls with their cannons."

"And how will they cross the moat?" sneered the bishop. "Walking on the water, just like our Lord?"

Urania shook off the men who held her arms and stepped toward the bishop. "They will send a team to kill your gatekeepers and lower the drawbridge. Then their cavalry will pour into the city, crush your defenders, burn this tower, and take everyone in this room as prisoners. You may have enough time to organize the defence. But you have to start now."

The bishop pursed his lips and said no more. Nicolaus and some of the other onlookers chuckled at the bishop's foolishness but suppressed it when the bishop glared at them.

"Send someone to tell all the scouts to report in," Nicolaus ordered. One of his captains obeyed and left the room.

"If they report that there's *no* raiders tonight," the bishop warned Urania, "then you will spend the rest of your very short life in an oubliette."

"And if there *is* a raid," Nicolaus told the bishop, "then maybe you could treat my friend with more respect?"

The bishop frowned. "I like you, Nicolaus. Don't put me to the test over a *woman*." He held out his closed hand, so that Nicolaus could kiss his ring. Nicolaus did, and the bishop left.

"You might want to find somewhere safe to hide, until the raid is over," Nicolaus recommended to Urania.

"I can scout for you," she offered. "My horse is faster than any other." She moved closer to Nicolaus so that her next words would be for him alone: "Julian has joined the raiders."

Nicolaus paused to control his surprise. "Now we know why Sigismund never sent his army," he muttered. "Julian was carrying my letter to him."

"I did warn you about him," Urania said, attempting to be sympathetic.

Nicolaus nodded. "So why is he here?"

"I don't know. But I will find out." Urania moved to leave.

As her feet crossed the threshold to the stairs, Nicolaus said, "And why are *you* here?"

Urania turned and said, "I wish that I could tell you." Then she dashed down the stairs.

One of the guards whispered the word *witchcraft* again.

Nicolaus glared him into silence, then turned back to the table with the maps.

§ 12.

Julian, now dressed in the armour and tabard of the Teutonic Knights, stood near the commander of the raiding party. A Warmian scout was lying on the snow beside him, twitching with blood loss and shock. Julian stilled him by plunging his sword into his heart. Then he tore the bottom off the same scout's cloak to clean the blood from the blade. Around him, the knights in the raiding team pulled the other bodies into a nearby copse of trees and covered the blood spots with fresh white snow.

"Good work, men," the commander told his team. "Now load the cannons. We won't be able to hide them, so we have to move them up to the gate and fire them in one swift action."

As the squires prepared the guns, Julian put his hand on one of them and whispered, "*Ave Iupiter. Praesta fortuna servavit.*"

"You speak Latin?" the commander marvelled.

"All my life," Julian smiled. He removed his Teutonic tabard and gave it to the commander. "Keep these clean for me."

"Where are you going?"

"The enemy will know something is wrong when this skirmish team doesn't return," Julian explained, as he removed one of the Warmian scout's cloaks and put it on himself. "So I'm going to tell the city's general to expect your attack. From a completely different direction, you understand. You'll possess half the city before they know you breached the walls. And in the confusion, I will murder their general. Then you can summon the cavalry to take the rest of the city. Give me one hour, then –"

The commander grabbed Julian's shoulder before he could leave. "I am the one who gives orders here. You played the spy for us when you gave us that letter. How do I know you weren't playing spy for them, the entire time?"

"Life is complicated. And I don't have time to talk about it," said Julian. With his fingers clasped like a bird's beak, he tapped the commander on the centre of his forehead. The commander immediately let go of Julian's shoulder and dropped his arm to his side. He stared into the distance, lost inside his mind.

"Remain hidden for one hour, then attack," Julian whispered into the commander's ear. Then he walked away.

The commander blinked, then turned around to speak to his soldiers: "We remain hidden for one hour. Then we attack."

§ 13.

Nicolaus stuck his head out a window of his tower and squinted at the distance. He could see his soldiers on the walls, some with arrows notched to their bows, others with their arms wrapped around their bodies to keep warm. Fewer than one in ten had any armour worth mentioning: most bundled themselves in heavy cloaks and padded tunics, and hoped for the best.

"Such a fragile design," said Julian, as he examined the beams and girders holding up the tower's conical roof and imagined them destroyed by his army. "Only one cannonball would be enough to bring it down."

Nicolaus spun around to see Julian standing by the door, wearing the livery of the Teutonic Knights, and poking at a ceiling beam with a dagger.

"Guards, guards!" Nicolaus shouted.

"They cannot hear you," Julian said. "Unless you can shout loud enough to pierce the veil."

"You killed my guards?"

Julian shrugged. "Not that it matters," he said. He gestured toward the side of the room where Nicolaus' quadrants and triquetrums were stored out of the way. "I was thinking about all these instruments of yours. It might be weeks, or months, before the King sends reinforcements. And in that time, your toys might come to a great deal of damage."

"You turned spy for the enemy," Nicolaus accused. "Urania told me. Were you always working for them?"

Julian dismissed the question with a laugh. "Urania told you that? How much do you really know about her?" Julian asked.

"Enough to trust her more than you," Nicolaus said.

Julian grinned. "Heh. Did she tell you that she is one of the nine muses, a daughter of Zeus, and that she's two thousand years old?" Seeing the surprise on Nicolaus' face, Julian said, "Oh, she did! And you believed her! Hey, would you believe me if I told you I was once the last pagan

Emperor of Rome?"

"No, I would not," Nicolaus answered, though his hesitation made Julian chuckle.

Then Julian picked up a burning candle from a table and pretended to be interested in the flame. "But let's talk about the war. How safe are your books? Surely those are harder to replace, if this tower were to catch fire."

"I sent then to Frauenburg," Nicolaus said. "They're completely safe."

"Where have you been, Nicolaus?" Julian laughed. "Your books are a heap of ashes – the knights burned the city to the ground!"

"With your help, I'm sure," said Nicolaus. He paced around the perimeter of the room, keeping as far from Julian as possible, searching the wall behind his back for anything that he could use as a weapon.

"But I never did find one particular book that interested me," Julian said.

"Urania has it," Nicolaus told him.

"But it's not finished, is it?" Julian guessed. "It would be a shame if you died in the battle to come. Then the book would never be complete."

Julian laughed, then threw the candle on the floor, and lunged at Nicolaus with his dagger.

At almost the same moment, a broad-shouldered woman bounded up the stairs and into the room. She saw Julian, and the knife in his hands.

"*Stamató!*" he shouted.

Julian saw the intruder, and his eyes widened when he recognized Kynisca, another Olympian. He swung his weapon arm down, aiming to stab Nicolaus in the back. But Kynisca reached him fast enough to deflect the swing. She wrestled the assassin to the floor and sat on him.

"Get off me, you dog-headed sack of rocks!" Julian ordered.

Nicolaus, who had caught the candle before it ignited the loose papers on the floor, pointed to Kynisca and said, "Who in God's name are you!"

Before Kynisca could answer, the thunderous crack of cannon fire drew everyone's attention to the nearest window.

"The raid's begun!" Kynisca exclaimed, as she pried the dagger out of Julian's hands. "You have to lead your men in the defence."

Julian stretched his neck to try and face Nicolaus. "They're coming from the north," he said. "Along the banks of the Lyna."

"From the south!" Kynisca countered. "And this *troglos* here was with them. I saw him."

"Can you keep him here?" Nicolaus asked Kynisca.

Julian struggled some more, but Kynisca held him down with ease.

"He's not going anywhere," Kynisca promised. "Go and defend your city."

"Thank you, friend," he said to Kynisca. He squeezed her shoulder, to show his thanks one more time. Then he dashed out of the room, into battle.

§ 14.

The morning sun rose over a scene of half-collapsed houses, some of them blackened by fires that escaped their hearths when the winds whipped them up. The bodies of horses and dogs and fighting-men lay around them. Cannonballs lay like eggs in a nest of smashed stones and bricks and wooden beams. Most of this mess lay near the southern gate, which was now a wide hole, open to the world outside. But the men who stood on guard there, clearing the paths of rubble and building new *cheval-de-frise*, wore the red of Warmia, and not the black and white of the Teutons.

Nicolaus walked along the top of the walls, surveying the damage to his city.

"We still need the Polish troops to relieve us," he said to Urania.

"I can carry your letter to the King this time," she offered. "And Kynisca has agreed to stay and be your bodyguard, until the war is over."

Two soldiers passed them, one leaning on the shoulder of another, unable to walk on his own. Nicolaus stopped to hug them. "You did very well last night. God be praised, for filling this town with brave men like you! There's hot food and a bed in the basilica, for every man who stood on this wall."

The soldiers thanked him and moved on.

"I think I might stay here, when the war is over," Nicolaus said. "When I was first appointed canon of Frauenburg Cathedral, I didn't want the post. It's too far from any libraries or universities. But I've grown to appreciate this remote corner of the earth. There are good people here. And interesting work to do."

"Please tell me you aren't giving up mathematics," Urania said.

"Oh no, never. In fact, I found a problem in this town which needs a mathematician to solve it. A glut of coins in the market made from diluted metals. Bad money, chasing out the good. There has to be a way to stop that. Maybe that's something we could do together."

Urania smiled. "Perhaps Kynisca could help you. She has a better head for practical questions than I do."

Nicolaus nodded. "Or, we could build an observatory. A quadrant the size of my tower. A library the size of the basilica! We could make this city into a new great centre of learning."

Urania realized what Nicolaus was really asking. "I think I should deliver your letter to the King, before I do anything else," she replied.

Nicolaus nodded. He handed her the letter.

They came to the stable where Urania had kept her fairy horse. She took the reins and walked with Nicolaus to the gate.

"Will I ever see you again?" Nicolaus asked.

From her saddlebag, Urania took out a large cloth-bound object, and handed it to Nicolaus. He unwrapped it, and found his unfinished manuscript on astronomy.

"You will," she promised. Then she mounted her horse and trotted away.

§ 15.

**Fromborg, Warmia,
1543.**

A frail and elderly Nicolaus lay in a plain wooden bed, in a room with smoke-stained plaster walls, a small fireplace in the corner, and one small window. Several friends sat around him: Bishop Tiedemann Giese, wearing a white stole and holding his prayer book for administering the sacraments; Andreas Osiander, his square beard was grey now, but the same wooden cross still hung on his breast.

"I showed your pamphlet to Herr Luther, when I met him in Marburg," said Andreas. "I dare say he didn't like it any better than Tiedemann's colleagues, in the Roman church."

"Truth be told, most of my brother bishops are ignoring it," said Bishop Giese.

"Herr Luther said – and I wrote it down here..." Andreas searched his pockets and found nothing, "something about turning the whole order of astronomy upside-down – well, it's not important. What matters is that he thought your work was worth commenting upon at all. I see that as a kind of praise."

Nicolaus smiled, and reached his frail hand to touch Andreas' arm, to thank him.

The bishop said, "It was wise of you to dedicate your book to the Holy Father. That will go some distance toward getting the acceptance that it deserves. I will promote it as best as I am able. Though I may be joining you in heaven rather soon."

Nicolaus reached out to touch the bishop's hand but could not quite reach. The bishop reached the rest of the way and warmed his friend's hand in both of his own. Then his face fell.

"His heartbeat is very faint," Tiedemann said to Andreas.

"Stay with us, my friend," Andreas urged him. "We have one more gift for you." He got up and opened the door.

Urania entered. She carried a cloth-bound book. Nicolaus saw her, and he pushed himself higher in the bed, to sit up. His friends pushed some extra pillows in place to help.

"*Khâìre*, Nicolaus," she said. "I promised we would meet again."

Nicolaus grinned brightly, and laughed to see her, though it caused him to cough and wince with pain.

Bishop Giese grew puzzled and curious. "Lady Urania. You seem unchanged from the last day I saw you. Decades ago. Still so young."

Andreas said, "If this be witchcraft –"

"My friends," Nicolaus addressed Andreas and Bishop Giese, "we are in the presence of an antediluvian."

Bishop Giese and Andreas turned to Urania, to awe at her youth, and decide whether to believe what Nicolaus said about her. Urania placed the book she was carrying into Nicolaus' hands, and helped him to open it.

"*De Revolutionibus Orbium Coelestium*," Nicolaus read the title. "*On the Revolutions of the Heavenly Spheres*."

Andreas and Bishop Giese relaxed when they saw the title of the book for themselves.

"I wrote a preface for you," said Andreas. "I had to say that your argument was only a mathematical convenience, not the true shape of things. I had to do it – else wise, it would be heretical; no one would read it."

"It *will* be read," Urania promised. "And more than that: it will be loved."

Nicolaus reached Urania's hand and said, "Thank you, my teacher and my friend. Thank you."

* * *

And so it was loved, for centuries to come. It was scorned and hated too. In some places it was banned. And for the crime of merely reading it, some men died. But for all that, it survived. I have lived a very long time; but I believe the name of Nicolaus Copernicus shall live longer still.

§ 16.

Julian passed the time in prison by teaching his cell mates to sing Roman drinking songs.

"So, you were once the King of Rome," said a ragged thief, as they finished the last song.

"I was," Julian said. "And I was a good king. I purged the bureaucracy of the boot-lickers and sycophants. I faced the Alamanni in battle – their army was three times bigger than mine – and I destroyed them."

"Yeah? And who were your soldiers? All the rats in the Roman sewers?" the thief laughed. Other nearby prisoners snickered.

"Fortune is a fickle mistress, I grant you," Julian smiled. "But I shall not share these bars with you for long. My lord *Iupiter*, king of the Olympians, will see to my escape."

"Sure. And my people will break me out of here too, any day now. I'm the king of the Ottomans!" the thief laughed again.

As he spoke, a shower of warm gold light fell down the ancient stone tunnel. The prisoners shifted in their beds to see where it was coming from. Then they held up their hands to protect their eyes from the glare.

"That would be him now," Julian smiled.

The lock on Julian's cell unlatched itself, and the door swung open, though no hand could be seen to do it. Julian stepped out of the cell, then turned to the thief and said, "Well? Aren't you coming?"

The thief squinted in the light, then scrambled to his feet, and followed him.

Brendan Myers

Book Two: Tycho

§ 17.

My sister Clio is better at telling stories than I am. But here, let me say a little more of who my people are, and where we came from.

We began a long time ago. Before the first priests and kings. Before the first cities. All humanity was in its childhood. We had glorious adventures. Life was beautiful and good.

Yet some of these first people were unsatisfied. They had questions. They wanted to know why they lived, why they died, what all their adventures were finally for. They looked deep into the waters, and the embers of old fires, the stars, their own dreams, searching for the essence of things, for ultimate knowledge of the mysteries of being. They became the first philosophers. The more they learned, greater they became in body and mind and spirit. In time, some of them became the beings whom the old stories call the gods.

Then the gods had children, and their children had children. And so, things continued, like the turning of the seasons.

Today, there are more than four hundred family dynasties, descendants of the gods, living all over the world. You, your family, your friends, anyone you know, might be a thousand generations descended from them.

For my part, I come from the first generation born after the Olympian victory over the Titans. When the world was still new, and the essence of things was still easy to find. That is why I can live so long. Why I can see the universe the way I do. Others among us can do things that you might call magical. Though to us it doesn't feel like magic. It feels like walking, breathing.

But I am still like you, in other ways. I need food and drink, and sleep, just as you do. I need art, and music, and friends, the same as you. I can be killed, the same as you. Though it may take more effort.

Well, there is more to this story. But that is enough for now.

Prometheus said my father was afraid humanity might unseat him, the same way he unseated the Titans. So I decided to go to him, to show him I had no such rebellion on my mind. All I wanted was for someone to see the cosmos as I do. If not my sisters, then why not a mortal man like Nicolaus? Why not anyone? Why not you?

What was so wrong about wanting that?

* * *

As Urania arrived at the foot of the temple complex on Mount Olympus, the rising sun turned the stone columns of the temples into glittering pure white light, and the earth below was a sea of mist, making other nearby mountain peaks seem like islands. Urania handed her faerie horse's bridle to the stable master, then she marched toward the largest of the temples. A closed gate barred her way. She turned to the stable master for an explanation.

"I'm sorry, my lady Muse, but the gate is closed to you now," he said, as he took down his hood.

"Julian!" she shrieked.

Julian laughed, enjoying the sight of her shock. "I'm glad to see you too, Urania."

"How did you –!"

"I am an Olympian. No mortal prison can hold me," Julian explained.

She looked into the temple complex. A few people saw her and pretended to be too busy to wave or say hello.

"Why is this gate closed?" Urania grunted.

"Our glorious king has given his divine command," Julian told her. "All the mythic sanctuaries of Greece are closed to you."

"Our 'glorious king' is my father," Urania reminded him. "He wouldn't bar *me* from Olympus."

Julian grinned as he spoke: "In fact He recommends that you throw yourself into the dung-heap world of the mortals and find an interesting way to die."

"I'm sure he does," Urania said. She pulled on the bars of the gate again, mostly to see if anyone would notice. When no one did, she turned to Julian again. "But he still owes me an explanation," she demanded.

Julian agreed with a nod. He strode to the edge of the plateau, inviting Urania to follow. With a wave of his hand, some of the clouds below cleared, and a view of the land presented itself. Water wheels turned; blacksmiths hammered their anvils; dyers examined their colours; merchants drove their horse wagon trains over the hills. Every daily struggle and simple pleasure of human life was open to Urania's view.

"The problem," Julian explained, "is that you don't fully understand the problem. These mortals – they're not ready to know the cosmos the way we do. They will *never* be ready. Not even a stone-cold, through-and-through genius like Copernicus. And he was the best of them."

Urania shook her head. "If that's true, then it doesn't matter what I do for them, and there's no point in punishing me for helping them. But if it's *not* true, wouldn't it make more sense to lock me away from the mortals? To stop me from working with them? There's a rumour, you know, that my father secretly *fears* them –"

"Do not pretend to know the thoughts of our God-king," Julian snapped at her.

"Well then, was there some other reason why he banished me?" Urania demanded. She folded her arms, and kept her face stone-cold against Julian's anger.

Julian adopted a businesslike tone. "At first, the great god Zeus *did* want to imprison you," he said. "But I persuaded him that you should see for yourself the fault in the soul of humanity; that you need to learn the painful futility of doing anything for them. Furthermore, I asked him to grant a condition for your return. A faint hope, as it were, in the form of a wager. You can thank me when you're ready."

"Let me hear it, first," said Urania.

Julian drew her attention back to the spread of the mortal world below. "Find a man who could prove me wrong. Find *one man* whose mind will not be broken by a direct and complete vision of the naked cosmos, in its glorious entirety. That's all you need to do to win, and to come back home. What do you say?"

"No interference from you? Or from my father?" she asked.

"If I'm right," Julian offered, "I won't *need* to interfere."

"And if *I'm* right," Urania countered, "I *will* find someone. And that person will be the greatest philosopher since Hypatia. And both you and my father will never interfere with my life again."

Julian grasped his testicles and said, "I swear by all that's holy."

Urania contained her disgust. "Swear on the name of my father."

Julian rolled his eyes, and said, "I swear by Zeus Panhellenius, the most high, the giver of the laws, the father of all. May my ass shit nothing but rocks if I break this solemn vow."

"And how do I know that he's listening?" Urania demanded to know.

A thunderclap sounded in the distance. The clouds over the highest temple in Olympus darkened.

Julian glanced upward and grinned. "There you go," he said. Then he sauntered toward the gate, and grinned at Urania as he opened it and stepped through.

§ 18.

"It's done, then?" Prometheus asked, interrupting Urania's wistfulness. She sat in a chair on the old titan's belvedere, facing east. Towards Greece.

"It is," she confirmed, without looking at him. "The book is published. People everywhere in Europe are reading it. But the rest of his life was too short to enjoy it."

"He is mortal, after all," Prometheus said. "But that is not why you are melancholic, no?"

"No."

Her host gestured that she should follow him inside the villa. A dinner of baked lamb and onions with wine was waiting for her there, as was Kynisca, who had already begun eating.

"He won't let me come home ever again, will he?" Urania asked him.

"He will honour his promise if you win his wager," Prometheus offered. "But he will not give you a fair chance. His agents will fix your students with accidents, diseases, turns of bad luck. I can already foresee that your next student will be abducted by his uncle, when he is only two years old –"

"Not now, please," Urania asked him. "I have to decide what to do. Where to live."

Prometheus smiled. "Live here, with me."

Urania looked down. "I don't want to be a burden."

"Not at all. My house is yours," Prometheus promised. He handed her one of the wine cups.

A heavy breath of trepidation filled her as she took the cup. "I suppose I have nowhere else to go," she said.

Prometheus grinned. "*Khàìre*, Urania, muse of the philosophers, the true benefactor of humankind," he toasted her, and drank deeply.

Urania drank only a sip.

* * *

As I laid out my bedroll and pillows that night, I felt a warm breeze come to me, infusing my clothes with the smell of sea salt from home. It felt like the same wind which blew when last I danced on Mount Helicon with my sisters. The same which witnessed me building my first armillary sphere. Showing it to my mother. She was so proud. The same which tousled my clothes and hair, as I played fox-and-rabbit in the olive grove with Amphimaros. Such a lovely young man; I didn't mind that he found me. The same as dropped the blossom-petals from the apple trees as I birthed our sons, Linos and Hymenaois. The same as comforted me on winter nights on the top of Mount Helicon, where I stayed up late counting the meteors, on the night that he died. The same as I might never feel again if I were never to return.

And so, the next day, I resolved that I would take my father's wager. Julian and his 'natural justice' be damned – I was going to bet my life that the king of the gods was wrong about humanity. Wrong about its potential. Wrong about its genius.

And I wanted to win.

§ 19.

Tostrup, Kingdom of Denmark, 1552.

At the family dinner table, Joergen Brahe dug into his plate of roast mutton and cabbage, and smacked his lips as he drank his wine.

His small nephew, however, ignored his food. A slate in a wooden frame lay on the table where his plate should have been, and a few sticks of chalk took the place of his cutlery. He had drawn stick figures of two smiling people on it. His food had been pushed to the side.

"I know you miss your parents," Joergen said. "They miss you too. But this is for the best."

The boy said nothing but drew another character into his picture.

"They have more children now than they have money to pay for," Joergen continued. "And by staying here, you are fulfilling a promise your father made to me before you were born. It's best for everyone that you stay with us."

The third character in the drawing took shape: a frowning child, inside a house. Joergen sighed to see it. A knowing look passed between him and his wife, Inger.

She moved to sit beside the boy. "I know you're feeling alone. It was the same for us when we were small, too. But we have a special guest coming to see you tonight, and we think you will love her."

"Is it another lawyer?" the boy asked.

A smile grew on one side of Joergen's face.

"No," said Inger. "The adoption is complete now; no more lawyers."

"It's your first private tutor," said Joergen. "She speaks at least ten languages – only God knows how she found the time – and she was recommended to me by the royal astrologer himself."

A servant entered the dining room and said, "Sir, the new tutor is here."

Dressed in the simple bodice and gown and nanny cap of muted colours but fine fabrics, Urania carried herself as though she owned the house. She acknowledged Joergen and Inger, but moved directly to the seat next to their nephew.

"*Khâìire!* You must be the young master Tycho Brahe. My name is Urania. I'm very glad to meet you."

§ 20.

Copenhagen, Kingdom of Denmark, 1560.

In a tavern near the university, Joergen glared at his nephew, nearly a man now, although he still preferred to doodle on his chalk slate rather than eat his dinner.

"It's horrible," said his nephew Tycho. "I'm one of the youngest boys on campus. Everyone looks down on me."

"One of the youngest *men*," his uncle corrected him. "You're thirteen now."

"Still the youngest."

Joergen wiped his mouth on the tablecloth. "What have they got you reading?" he asked.

"The usual. Augustine, Aquinas, the twelve tables of Roman law. You know."

"Well then. Aren't you glad we drilled you with Latin, when you were young?"

Tycho shrugged. "They're drilling me on it here, too."

"Latin is the language of all educated people," Joergen reminded him. "You can take it anywhere, from Dublin to Cairo, and you'll find work in the universities or the courts or the church, anywhere they might need a lawyer."

"Law is boring."

"Law is a respectable and well paid profession for when you're older, that's what it is," Joergen said. He swigged his beer to the bottom of the flagon, then waived at the waiter to bring more.

"What are you drawing there, anyway?" he asked.

Tycho held up his drawing and showed his uncle. "It's called the Golden Section. It's where the short line of each rectangle is the same as the long line of the next one. They spin around toward the centre like they're falling into a whirlpool, until they get so small you can't see them anymore, but they're still there. They go on like that forever."

Joergen examined his nephew's drawing. "Astonishing. I didn't do things like this until I was much older than you are now," he said.

"One of my professors said it was like seeing into the mind of God," said Tycho, admiring the diagram.

"Well? Is it?"

Tycho shrugged. "It's more interesting than law."

Their conversation was interrupted by a commotion outside the tavern. Looking up from his slate, Tycho saw through the diamond-paned window that the sky had darkened. The chatter in the restaurant quietened as other patrons noticed as well. Some moved closer to the nearest windows, others went outside. A voice from outside shouted, "Something's happening to the sun!"

Most of the tavern patrons ran outside, including Tycho's uncle. Tycho himself, however, saw that the sun motes passing through the leaves outside the window had taken on a crescent-like shape, as they fell on the table. He held out his hand, allowing the shape to fall on his fingers. Then he looked up and squinted his eyes at the source.

"It's not wise to look directly at the sun," said a woman's voice from behind him. Tycho turned to see a tall, olive skinned woman, whose eyes were silver and gold.

"Hello?" said Tycho. "Oh! Miss Urania!"

"*Khâire*, master Tycho," Urania greeted him.

"I thought that after I left for university that I would never see you again."

Urania grinned. "I'm in town to see the solar eclipse."

Tycho leaned to the window again. "Is that what's happening out there?"

"Don't look right at it," she warned him. "Here, let me show you a safer way." She closed the shutters and covered the crack between them with her hands but left a small space where a small point of light could stream through. The light fell on his slate, making a small but crisp image of the sun, no larger than a fingernail. But a round shape blackened it on one side.

"It *is* an eclipse!" said Tycho.

"It is," Urania confirmed.

"It's really pretty," Tycho smiled. He tried to draw its outline on his slate with his chalk, and grimaced when his attempt looked nothing like the image. "Need a really sharp quill and parchment for this. Wait – how did you know there would be an eclipse today?"

"Because it was predicted," she said. She took a book out of her satchel and showed Tycho a page with several long tables of numbers.

"Amazing!" Tycho said. But he frowned as he examined the numbers. "Hold on – looks like it was predicted for *yesterday*."

"But still predicted. So, where do you think the mistake happened?"

Tycho leaned back and grinned. "You're going to play the part of my tutor for my whole life, aren't you?"

Urania smiled back. "Some people do remain my students for that long."

"They're that bad, are they?" Tycho laughed, and Urania laughed with him. Then Tycho returned his mind to her question. As he thought about it, his gaze drifted to the golden section lines on his slate. He fiddled with the chalk in his fingers for a moment. "Maybe their chalk was too thick."

"What do you mean?"

Tycho pointed to his diagram of the Golden Section. "I could draw these rectangles a lot smaller – even as small as the sharp edge of a razor – but the chalk is too thick. Look, it makes these ugly fat lines that are no good for measuring anything. Maybe the people who made this prediction had the same kind of chalk. I suppose they did pretty good, they were off by only one day – actually, it's kind of amazing they predicted an eclipse at all, really. I wonder when's the next one?"

Urania grinned.

Joergen burst back into the restaurant. "Tycho! Come and see the – oh!" He stopped, as he saw Urania. "Sorry, where are my manners? Miss Urania, I didn't know you were here today."

"I have always been here," Urania smiled.

"Come and see what's happening to the sun! You can never know when something like this will happen – "

"In fact, you *can* know – look right here," said Tycho, as he pointed to Urania's book. His uncle, however, was dashing outside again, so he followed.

Urania danced along behind them.

When the door closed behind them and the room was empty, Julian emerged from the far end of the long table, where he had been taking his own dinner. He wandered to Tycho and Joergen's place at the table, traced his fingers along the parchment of Urania's book, then slammed it shut.

§ 21.

**Rostock, Meklenburg,
The Holy Roman Empire, 1566.**

The smoke-darkened stone walls of the mansion's feasting hall were draped with long curtains, in the heraldic colours of the two great houses who had joined their children in marriage only a few hours before. From Urania's vantage in the musician's gallery, the feasting tables were islands in a liquid melange of neck ruffs and feathered hats. A small armada of waiters flowed between the islands, each delivering a different pleasure: roast pheasant rubbed with imported pepper and nutmeg; wild boar stuffed with garlic and onion; candied pears with cloves. At one of them, Urania saw her protege, now a tall bearded man, enjoying the attention of a small circle of admirers. He waved to her and invited her to join them. Urania grinned, and descended the stairs to join the circle.

Passing through the kitchen on the way, her senses perked at the presence of Julian, gathering a jug of wine and some goblets on a tray. She rushed to block the door to the dining room ahead of him.

"Julian! You promised me you would *not* interfere with my students!" she accused him.

"Did I say those *exact* words?" was Julian's preening reply.

Urania realized he had not. She pulled him by his ruff to a more private area of the garden outside the mansion. A full moon bathed the land in bright silver, yet also drew the jagged shadows of leafless winter trees like scratches on the snow.

"Promise me you will not interfere. Right now," she demanded.

"I'm curious about your new charge, this Danish fellow – what's his name?" Julian said.

"Promise me!"

"Of course, I already know his name. I have watched you grooming him since he was a child. Very clever."

Urania paced around him like a sword fighter looking for an opening. "If you don't promise to leave my students alone, it won't be a fair gamble."

Julian stood straight and unmoving. "Nothing in life is a fair gamble, Urania. You're old enough to know that now."

"Do not split hairs with me, young man. You know fully well the meaning of my words," Urania growled at him. "And I am well older than you."

"I see we are close to shouting now," Julian grinned. "Which philosopher was it who said the first person to lose her temper also loses the argument?"

"I want you to promise me you will leave my students alone!" she demanded again, though not much quieter than before.

"Why should I do that? I don't gain anything if you win your way back to Olympus," said Julian. Adopting a more charming pose, he said, "If you think about it, by helping you to lose the wager I am doing you a service. Exile from Olympus is surely preferable to having your liver torn out every day by a giant vulture."

Urania saw an opening. "Is that what will happen to you if I win?"

Julian paused; Urania did not miss the flicker of worry that crossed his eyes. But he quickly covered it with a grin.

"Tell me, how did you get the King's astrologer to recommend you as Tycho's private tutor?" he asked. "Did you cast a horoscope for him that came true?"

Urania moved closer to him. "What is your stake in this, really? Is it that you failed to restore the worship of the gods, when you were Emperor of Rome; now you're afraid of failing my father a second time?"

"No, you must have given him one of your famous cosmic visions, like you did to Copernicus."

"Or is it that my father threatened to exile *you* if I succeed?"

Urania's question nailed Julian's feet to the ground. "You want a fair gamble? Then no more visions!" he shouted.

Urania staggered back, as if Julian's outburst had pushed her. Then she smiled. "That's it exactly, isn't it?" she said.

"If I'm not allowed to interfere, then neither are you," Julian told her.

"What I'm doing – showing the cosmos to my students – is *the whole point* of *your* wager," Urania reminded him.

"*His* wager," Julian corrected her, as he pointed at the sky. "I am only his instrument."

Urania paced around him again; the cold of the night air had seeped through her skirts and the sleeves of her coat. "Promise me you will stay out of my way. No rhetorical games, no hair splitting. I want your oath of honour."

"If I make a promise like that, The Man will only send someone else to frustrate you," Julian spat. He gave her a moment to grasp this fact, then said, "As it is, you have *me*. An Olympian like yourself. Someone willing to talk to you. To *reason* with you. If it hadn't been for me, there would be no gamble; your father would have exiled you forever."

Urania glowered at him, then grabbed his arm and pushed his hand between his legs. "Then promise me you will not *kill*."

Julian resisted, but found her grip surprisingly strong.

"Promise!" she shouted.

Julian relented. "I swear it," he said. "No one of your students will die by my hand." Then he smiled, like a boy who stole a box of sweets and got away with it.

Urania said, "You're planning something."

Julian only grinned wider. "Maybe," he said.

Urania let him go and pushed him away.

Julian picked up the wine jug from the snow where Urania had made him drop it. He drank, then threw it at a nearby stone fountain, where it smashed on the ledge.

Returning to the kitchen, he saw a man arguing with the servants. "What's wrong with you?" the man barked at another servant. "That roast mutton should have been served an hour ago. Do you want me to starve? And what happened to the wine?"

"We don't have enough people working today, so close to Christmas, some of us went home –" the servant complained.

"Send someone to go and bring them back. And tomorrow you can tell them to go home again and never return! They're all fired!"

Julian followed the man to the dining room and tugged the collar of his jerkin. "Excuse me sir – what's your name?"

"Manderup Parsberg," the man replied. "Lord of Hagesholm. And no one you should be touching like that."

"You seem like a spirited fellow," said Julian. He tapped his fingers on Manderup's forehead and said, "I need you to find a sword, then join me at Tycho Brahe's table."

Manderup blinked for a heartbeat, then strode away. To the first servant he passed, he said "You! Where is your master's sword? Bring it to me."

Julian grinned. When Manderup returned with a fencing rapier on his belt, the two pushed their way into the dining room and sat on a bench across from Tycho and his listeners.

"I would like to say I am well privileged to have seen two solar eclipses in my lifetime," said Tycho, just as they arrived. "But the truth of the matter is: I knew the second one was coming."

"How is that possible?" asked Manderup.

"Easier to show you than to explain it, cousin," said Tycho. He pushed his plate to the side, then dipped his finger in a wine goblet so he could draw a circle on the tablecloth. "Imagine this is the path of the sun, going around the Earth. We can divide this circle into triangles, like this..."

he cut the circle into four quarters, then joined the ends of the lines to make four triangles, "and the space left over can be divided into smaller triangles –"

"It looks like one of those *magic* circles, like the alchemists use to talk to the angels," said Manderup.

Julian chose that moment to enter the conversation. "But it's not. It's mathematics, it's philosophy. And it's a touch of the muse."

Tycho regarded Julian for a breath, to give his mind time to change its train of thought. "Sir, I believe we have not met," he said.

"Julian Augustus. Honoured to meet you," he introduced himself.

"Julian Augustus! A name like that sounds like it came from a history book," Tycho grinned.

"But, I'm sorry to say, it came from my parents," Julian grinned.

"What brings you here?" Tycho asked him. "Do you know the happy couple? Or perhaps the groom's father, professor Bachmeister?"

"Not at all. But I know *you*, master Brahe, by reputation. I hear you are an especially talented astrologer."

A teenage girl sitting beside Tycho said, "This is the man who correctly predicted the death of King Suleiman of the Ottomans."

Tycho grinned. "This is my sister, Sophie Brahe. Perhaps you already know her? She usually finds my clients for me."

"A vision of Aphrodite herself," said Julian, as he kissed Sophie's hand. She laughed.

Tycho grinned but wagged a warning finger. "I know we are at a wedding. But she is still too young."

"*Mea culpa*, my lady," said Julian. Turning back to Tycho he said, "But how did you predict the sultan's death? Did you conjure an angel with that magic circle there, and make him tell you?"

Tycho laughed and tapped his diagram. "The diagram *looks* like magic, I grant you. But this is cosmology. Philosophy." As he spoke, he divided his diagram into twelve segments. "The sun, moon, and five planets are like characters in a play. That's why they're named for the old Roman gods. The twelve houses are like guest houses where these characters might rest a while, as they make their way about the sky. The twelve signs of the zodiac are like the costumes they are wearing. And the lines that connect them – squares, trines, oppositions, conjunctions – they're the conversation they're having."

"Hmm... and this is philosophy, you say?" Manderup asked.

Tycho grinned. "And theology, too. Those who study the stars have God for a teacher," he answered.

Julian asked, "So, what conversation were the gods having on the day you cast the Sultan's chart, and saw his death?"

"A very animated one," Tycho grinned. "I was asked to interpret the lunar eclipse we all saw this year. It happened with the sun in the constellation of Leo, the sign of kings. And it was shortly after sunset that day, so the moon was still low in the east, clearly signifying a nation in the east. The moon, the symbol of the Islamic religion, darkened by an eclipse – it can only mean the end of the Ottoman empire. Or else it could mean the next best thing: the end of its warmongering king."

"Wonderful, wonderful!" Manderup applauded.

"Alas, as it happened, my calculations were off the mark by three days," Tycho said, with a shrug. "A good enough result for most purposes. But I want to do better. If we could read the stars more precisely – imagine what we could know! The rise and fall of empires. The birth of the world's next great artists, great conquerors, great prophets. The second coming of Christ himself! We could hold all of time and space in our hands. If only our philosophers are careful enough. And our equipment less thick and clumsy."

"Of course," Julian said, as he drank from Tycho's cup. "Yet surely your labour was eased by the fact that when you predicted the Sultan's death, he was already more than eighty years old?"

Manderup clunked his wine goblet on the table. Sophie lost her smile and turned to her brother for an explanation.

"So, his death could have been predicted by anyone," Julian drew the obvious conclusion.

Tycho said, "It's not unusual for healthy men to live a full century."

"Actually, yes, it is," said Manderup.

"Or..." said Julian, "were you assisted by the fact that while we were all enchanted by your lunar eclipse, the old sultan had already been dead for six weeks?"

Manderup rose to his feet. "What game are you playing, cousin?"

"No game," Tycho defended himself. "No one told us of his death until the middle of November."

"I have searched all of Denmark for a philosopher who is not also a liar," Manderup growled. "But you're all the same."

"Indeed, we are not," Tycho scowled back. "We take our work rather seriously – we study it our whole lives."

"Heh! I suppose it does take that long to fool *yourself* into believing it!"

"Weren't you listening to me just now? A planetary position chart is a microcosm of creation. It takes hours to make one –"

"Aye, hours to make them look complicated enough to hide the fact that *they don't mean anything.*"

Now Tycho rose to his height. "You dare call me a liar? If I had my sword, I would cut your tongue out, right here and now!"

Julian placidly unbuckled his sword from his belt and handed it to Tycho.

Tycho grasped it without hesitation and leapt over the table. "On your guard, you child!" he shouted.

A wave of shrieks and hollers rippled through the room; the sea of banquet guests parted to make way for the combatants. The minstrels in the gallery ended their tune on flat notes, as their music was drowned in the noise of the storm below.

Sophie tugged on Tycho's arm. "Sit down, brother. This is a wedding!"

But Manderup drew his own sword and raised it to Tycho's throat. "You're a fortune teller in fancy dress. A cutpurse who can count," Manderup taunted him. "By God's wounds, you are a thespian, pretending to be a philosopher – perhaps you are also pretending to be the famous Tycho Brahe –"

"You say philosophers are all the same? But no – it's the enemies of reason who are all the same," Tycho declared. "They always attack what they cannot understand."

"I understand you perfectly," Manderup declared. "You are a swindler, a dissembler, a highwayman holding us hostage with a quill –"

"And you, cousin, are a lotus-eating Thrasymachus who can't even spell his own name –"

Manderup shrieked and lashed out with the first sword-lunge of the bout. Tycho parried it easily and caught his blade in the quillons of his rapier. The musicians in the gallery stopped; the sea of ruffs and hats and wide-bottom dresses parted; some of women shrieked, some of the men cheered.

Manderup escaped Tycho's hold on his blade by pulling back, then lashing out again. He grabbed a dagger from someone else's belt, to wield with his left hand. Tycho, seeing the extra threat, backed away while parrying Manderup's thrusts; he pulled a curtain off the wall to wield like a net. He entangled Manderup's next thrust with it, and pulled it to cast him off balance. Manderup, however, pulled back, bringing Tycho within range of his slashing attacks.

Julian, smirking at the sight of the chaos, took a goblet of wine that someone else had set down near him, and drank deeply.

The master of the feast, professor Bachmeister, rushed to intervene between the two fighters. "No duelling! No duelling in my house on my son's wedding day!"

"I am only defending myself," Manderup told him.

"He is the aggressor!" Tycho countered. "He called me a liar!" With that he advanced again, thrusting at Manderup's hands, neck, and knees. Manderup blocked them with a swing of his sword, though by swinging instead of parrying he opened new opportunities for Tycho to snipe at his legs or chest.

"Look at the way he fights," Tycho announced to the now growing crowd. "He thinks a rapier is a broadsword – exactly what you can expect from a weekend nose-painter such as him."

"You seem to think a bolt of cloth is a shield –"

Manderup interrupted him with a flurry of slashes with his sword, which Tycho intercepted by whipping the curtain around the attacker's blade. This made it easy to grab the sword and pull it from him. The move also pulled Manderup slightly over balance, allowing Tycho to kick his ankles and send him tripping to the floor.

"No, that was you who thought it was a shield," Tycho mocked him. "It's actually a weapon."

Manderup jumped up. "Stop laughing!" he yelled at the crowd. "Stop laughing! That man has hoodwinked you all. How many of you have given him hard-earned money to read your fortunes in the stars? Can you not see that he's a charlatan?"

"I am no charlatan!" Tycho shouted back, and leapt to the attack again. Trusting the length of his rapier to keep his opponent at a safe distance, he poked at Manderup's extremities just enough to step him backwards and keep him on the defensive. The sea of dinner jackets and petticoats swirled around them, only a hand's breath away from danger. Professor Bachmeister threatened them both with a variety of holy curses for disturbing the peace of his son's wedding. Julian, however, stopped him with a tap on his forehead and a command: "Sit down and do not speak!"

The professor sat and did not speak.

Tycho had forced Manderup against a wall. He made no further move to attack, but neither would he let his captured opponent escape.

Brendan Myers

"Apologize, and I will let you go," Tycho told him.

"Apologize? For not believing in fake philosophy, fake mathematics?" Manderup taunted him.

"For calling me a liar!" Tycho's next thrusts struck close enough to prick small scores in Manderup's leather jerkin.

"You *are* a liar, Tycho! You and every Babel-talking money-grubbing stargazer in all Christendom –"

Tycho lunged again, sniping at Manderup's shoulders and chest, enough to bruise if not to draw blood. This time Manderup dropped his dagger and used his free hand to grab Tycho's blade near the fort, and pull Tycho off balance. Tycho lurched to the side, giving Manderup the chance to punch him in the belly with the pommel. Tycho wheezed and staggered back, which allowed Manderup to knock Tycho's sword away with a swift upward swing, and catch it in his own hand. He brought it down over Tycho's face and sliced the bridge of his nose clean away.

Tycho howled, and covered his face in his hands. Manderup, seeing the blood, lowered his guard and stepped back. "Oh, I – I only wanted to…" he stammered.

Julian pushed his way to the front of the circle. "Kill him, you coward!" he hissed at Manderup.

But before he could tap his champion on the forehead and seal the command, he felt a heavy hand drop on his shoulders and pull him out of the crowd. He struggled to see who was manhandling him, and saw Kynisca, with an ill-fitting dress, and a stern look on her face. "Haven't you killed enough people already?" she grunted at him.

At the same time, Urania grabbed Manderup from behind and pulled him into the crowd, away from the fight. Sophie reached for Tycho, placing herself between him and his attacker. When Manderup was fully swallowed by the sea of people, she offered a strip of cloth torn from a tablecloth to bandage Tycho's wound. The fight was over.

Kynisca, also emerging from the crowd, tapped Professor Bachmeister on the forehead and said, "You can get up now, and you can speak again."

The professor snapped out of his daze and rushed to his nephew's side. "Bring him to the forge. We need a hot iron to cauterize the wound," he ordered. Then he pointed to Manderup and said, "And you, sir: get out of my house!"

§ 22.

With one hand on the collar of his jerkin, and the other pressing one of his arms into the small of his back, Kynisca marched Julian out of the mansion and into the back garden again. She pushed the offender over the ledge of the patio. He landed in a patch of roses, bristling with thorns as the leaves and flowers had all fallen away for winter. But his pride was hurt more than his body; he rolled out to the grass and brushed off the snow.

"Don't even *try* a move like that again," Kynisca warned him.

"It wasn't *me* who cut off that boy's nose –" Julian countered.

"And don't pretend innocence either," Kynisca interrupted. "I know you pushed him to do it."

Julian stepped up to the patio again. "They're only mortals – there's nothing special about them. So why are you protecting them? What's in it for you?"

Kynisca only waved him away. "What's in it for me is the chance to push your ugly face into a rock. Now get out of here."

Julian wandered away, leaving a slightly meandering path in the snow. Kynisca watched him for a while, to make sure he left. As the music returned to the feasting hall and spread into the garden, she offered her hand to the first person to emerge from the hall to investigate the noise. It happened to be professor Bachmeister.

"Good work tonight. We should dance to celebrate," she said, and took him in her arms to waltz him in the snow, innocent of his effort to free himself from her grip.

Julian picked his way to the mansion's stable and collected his horse and cart. When he had driven it far enough outside of the town, the cart became a gleaming bronze chariot, and it took him into the sky.

He arrived at the gate of Mount Olympus some hours later and marched along its gold-bricked avenues to the Temple of Zeus. Inside, the acolytes bowed before him, and cleaned up his muddy footprints on the marble floor almost as fast as he made them. The statue of Zeus in the temple's altar depicted the god seated in royal glory, a lightning-topped sceptre in one hand and an orb with a winged Victory on the other, and a great eagle at his feet. The ivory and gold glowed in the ambient light of the translucent marble pillars and walls, the burning braziers, and the wafting smoke. By comparison, Julian was only as tall as the foundation on which the throne rested. He approached with reverence, keeping his eyes on the statue's face even as he handed off his hat and cloak to an acolyte. He touched the statue's foot, then turned to the acolytes behind him.

"I need to be alone with him," he said. The acolytes scurried away.

Julian calmed himself and placed a handful of small grey stones on to a brazier at the statue's feet. They struck up sparks and burned with green and blue and purple flames. He stepped back, to give the incense time to rise, and to recite the epithets of his god. "My lord Zeus, Agathos Deos, Limenoskopos, Stratius, Tropaeus, Soter –"

A gentle yet deep voice resonated in the temple: *Welcome, my general.*

"The matter of your daughter, the muse Urania, proceeds exactly as you have foreseen," Julian said. "With one complication. She no longer works alone."

She is sponsored by my old nemesis, the titan Prometheus, said the voice of the temple.

Julian made a tired smile. "That explains it then."

Why are you here, my general?

"Since Urania and her students are protected, I should like to ask you to grant me the means to remove that protection," Julian explained. "A team of warriors to command."

My young soldier, the voice chided him. *You have been with us on Olympus for centuries, yet you are still a man of your time.*

"My lord?"

You still assume that the sword is the only weapon you need.

"I am a general without an army. I need men. I need – something!"

You need patience! the voice thundered.

Julian bowed down and lowered his head. "Yes, my Lord," he said. He could hear the footsteps of his god walking behind him, but he resisted the wish to turn around and look.

The survival of Olympus is a spiritual war. Our weapons must be subtle, Zeus told him.

Julian struggled back to his feet. "Yes, my Lord. But what are those weapons?" he asked.

Then he waited, in hope that his master would answer. But the only answer he received was the sound of his master's departing footsteps across the marble floor.

§ 23.

Some days later, Tycho set up a polished metal mirror on his work bench, so he could see himself brush an ointment on the crater where the bridge of his nose had once been.

"Does it still hurt?" Sophie asked him.

"Not as much as the day it happened," Tycho said.

Urania moved to a chair next to him and said, "I've a present for you." She offered him a small cloth sack. He unwrapped it, and found a brass prosthetic nose.

Sophie laughed. "Oh, perfect!"

Tycho shook his head and sighed. "This isn't very funny," he said.

"Yes it is," Sophie said, still grinning. "Put it on, let's see if it fits!"

Tycho faced Urania and said, "Did she put you up to this?"

"No, this was my idea," Urania said. "I thought it might make you feel a bit more like yourself again."

"I'll look like one of those mercenaries coming home from the war, you mean," Tycho complained.

"You look like that already without it," Sophie chided him. "Honestly, Tycho, the way it is now, people can see all the way up into your brain."

"It's not that bad," Tycho protested, covering his nose with his hand. But Sophie was laughing again, and Urania was finding it hard not to join her.

"Think of this as a story you can tell your clients," said Urania. "A story that they'd never believe if not for the evidence –"

"That's staring them in the face!" Sophie cackled.

Now Urania's own laughter burst out full-throated. Tycho grimaced at them, polished it with spit and a rub on his sleeve, then put it on his face and consulted the mirror again.

"You're right," he said, "I don't look like a mercenary, I look like a clown!"

"Not at all," Urania said, and Sophie agreed, but they laughed louder anyway.

"But just think," said Sophie, "it is better to make your clients laugh, than to make them run away in terror."

Tycho, holding the brass patch in place with his fingers, decided that his resistance to Urania's gift was more absurd than the gift itself. He rolled his eyes and stretched his mouth, and joined the laughter.

They settled down only when Tycho asked, "How does it stay on?"

"With beeswax. Here, let me show you," said Urania. She took the nose and dribbled some liquid wax from a candle along its edges, and placed it on his face. Tycho winced as the hot wax touched him, then nudged it into a more comfortable position as the wax cooled and solidified.

"There. That's –"

"Better? Worse?"

"Well, it's… different."

Sophie snorted, and laughed again.

Then Tycho looked down to his shoes. "Urania, Sophie, why are you both so good to me?"

Sophie said, "Because you're my brother. Why do you ask?"

"Because I don't deserve it," Tycho said. "I nearly killed my own cousin!"

Urania smiled. She dipped her finger in the liquid wax of a candle, flinching slightly with the heat, and spread it on the edges of Tycho's new nose, to hold it more strongly. "I want you to win, Tycho. But our contest cannot be won by drawing swords. Our true enemy is not an ignorant man like Parsberg. It is ignorance itself. Such an enemy can only be fought with subtle weapons. Curiosity. Reason. Kindness."

"And brass noses," Sophie grinned.

Tycho laughed. "I would not call those things weapons, at all," he said.

Urania grinned. "That's right, they're not. You are catching on," she encouraged him.

Tycho smiled. He examined his reflection in the mirror again. "I think I'll grow a beard and moustache," he said. "Might make the nose look smaller."

"You still don't like it?" Urania asked.

"Oh no, I think it's fine," Tycho said. "But I don't want to draw *that* much attention to it. Sophie, what do you think?"

"Beard or no beard," Sophie laughed, "I think that if you can go about in public with a nose like that, then you can do absolutely anything!"

* * *

We stayed up late that night, drinking good wine, talking of all things in the sky and below the earth, and of all things that stagger in between. But after they retired to their beds I left them, and did not return for many years. I still felt that I did not belong. Much as I wanted the Brahe siblings for my friends, I had been Tycho's teacher – a figure of authority in his life. And what is more, he still could not see me for who I truly am.

Tycho would remain my student for the whole of his life. It goes that way between teachers and students, sometimes. Yet it also happens that teachers learn things from their students. His friendship, his gladness to see me, even when later in life he would reject one of my teachings – that was the lesson that he taught me.

§ 24.

Knudstrup, Kingdom of Denmark, November 11th, 1572.

Tycho was in his lab, polishing a glass alembic with spittle and rags, while Sophie lit candles and recorded the fruits of the day's research in the logbook. The sky outside the windows was Egyptian blue, and only the horizon still glowed turquoise; the first stars of the evening took their places on the celestial stage.

"A decent day's labour, today," said Tycho.

"I'm glad you agreed to study alchemy with me," Sophie observed. "It's easier for me to find new clients for you."

A knock on the door interrupted their pleasantries. Tycho rose, but it opened before he reached it. Urania stepped in, carrying a lamp.

"*Khàïre*, my friend," she said.

"Miss Urania!" Tycho exclaimed, and he rushed to kiss her cheeks. "What a delight to see you! How long has it been?"

"Since shortly after your cousin's wedding," Urania said, and she tapped her nose. Tycho laughed.

Sophie greeted their visitor by offering a chair by the table. "Welcome! Sit, join us!" she said.

"I can't stay, but I want you to come outside with me for a moment," said Urania. "I want to show you something."

"What is it?" asked Tycho.

"Come, both of you, come and see!" Urania urged. The Brahe siblings followed.

They left the lab and strode down the lane toward the outskirts of the village. No moon graced the sky, so the lane was dark, but for the small pools of light spilling from the windows of the houses.

"I read the book you sent me," said Tycho, making conversation on the way. "But I can't say that I liked it."

"No? Why not?"

"It seemed unbearably silly – the idea that the sun is the centre of all creation," Tycho said. "It's absurd on its face. But I quite appreciated Mr. Osiander's preface. If you *pretend* that Doctor Copernicus is right, you can do your calculations in less than half the usual time."

Urania sighed. "I'm glad it helped you in at least that small way. Sophie, what did you think of it?"

"Oh, I liked it," Sophie answered. "But I much prefer reading alchemists. The heart of philosophy isn't up there in the stars. It's down here on Earth. Have you read Paracelsus? He said 'the art of healing comes from nature, and not the physician. Therefore, the physician must start from nature, with an open mind.' To me, that feels like the heart of medicine – the heart of all all knowledge."

Urania smiled. "It's very close."

Tycho made a quiet laugh. "I must confess… at first I thought alchemy was too messy to be enlightening. But since then, I've come to appreciate it. It's only the fatheads of the world who want to turn lead into gold. The real philosophers want to turn flesh and body into soul."

"Well, we didn't do that today," Sophie said. "But I think we're ready to test your new salve for gangrene. If it isn't a cure, then it might ease the pain, and that's a spiritual thing, too."

"I never felt drawn to alchemy, myself," Urania said. "I'm sure that it's inspiring, but I've always felt that it's astronomy that brings us to the truth. From the light of sun and stars, to the light of the mind."

Tycho laughed. "When I was your pupil, you said that about astronomy almost every day," he said. Then he stopped walking.

"What is it?" asked Urania.

"Nothing," Tycho answered, as he walked on again. "It suddenly seemed to me that you look no older than when I first met you – but that was twenty years ago."

Sophie eyed Urania with curiosity for a moment.

Urania smiled. "The people in my family tend to age very gracefully."

Tycho laughed. Then he asked, "Now what was it you wanted to show us?"

They had arrived at the edge of a field, with a hedgerow blocking the light from the houses behind them. "Yes, I think it's dark enough here," Urania decided. She blew out the candle in her lamp, and set it down. The whole cosmos opened above them. The Milky Way made a path from the west horizon to the zenith and down to the east.

"Turn to the north-west, and then look up, about halfway to the zenith," Urania instructed. "Can you see the great queen?"

"Cassiopeia?" asked Brahe. "Of course; she is always in the sky. She's upside-down at this time of year."

"How many stars make up her throne?"

"Five, like always – wait, no! What's that, just to the right? Another star? A *new* star?"

Urania grinned. A new star had joined the constellation: steady, hypnotic, and glorious.

"So bright!" Sophie marvelled. "Brighter than Venus. Almost as bright as the moon!"

"It can't be a planet," said Tycho. "It's too far from the ecliptic."

"So beautiful!"

"No," said Tycho, suddenly frowning. "It's not a new star – It can't be. The firmament is eternal and unchanging. That's why we call it the firmament! Whatever that is, it must be closer to the Earth. At least inside the sphere of the moon. Perhaps closer."

Urania said, "Is it your reading of *nature* which makes you say so? Or the traditions of the ancients?"

This question made Tycho hold his breath for a moment. Then he dashed back toward the village.

"Where are you going?" Sophie shouted after him.

"I need my equipment!"

A short while later, Tycho had set up an impromptu observatory outside his front door, in the middle of the street. The largest instrument was his triquetrum, which consisted of a long straight sighting-rod attached by a hinge to the top of a pole. Tycho aligned the sighting rod with the star, measured its angle up from the horizon using the graduation lines on a third rod that attached to the pole near the bottom, and slid along the length of the sighting rod.

"It's 44 degrees from the horizon," said Tycho. "That makes its declination from the celestial equator..." he moved his triquetrum to another position and measured the difference from its previous position, "sixty-three degrees. Correction, sixty-four. Got it Sophie?"

Sophie, quill and paper in hand, said, "Got it."

Tycho moved the triquetrum again and made a new measurement for Sophie to record: "Right ascension: zero hours, twenty-six minutes," he said. "Correction: twenty-four. No, it's twenty-five. Damn this brick of an instrument, it's not big enough!"

At the same time, a dozen local townsfolk had been roused from their beds by Tycho's excited raving about the new star. They gathered around him, some marvelling at the star, others curious about Tycho's equipment. Urania beamed like a proud parent.

"Why isn't it big enough?" said one of the townsfolk.

"Because if it were longer, small angles could be extended out and measured more precisely," Tycho explained.

Next Tycho took up his cross staff: a long pole with graduated lines on its length, and a shorter arm with two sights on its ends that could slide up and down. He held one end of the long arm up to his eye, and then moved the shorter arm until he had matched the new star in one of the sights, and a reference star in another.

"What's that for?" asked one of the local women.

"I'm measuring the angular distance between the new star and several other bright stars nearby," he explained. "So that when I look at it again tomorrow, I can tell whether the new star has moved."

"Can't you tell just by looking?"

"Not if it moves too slowly."

Sophie added, "Even the planet Saturn moves too slow for us to measure it one day to the next."

"What does it *mean*?" asked the woman.

Without looking up from his equipment, Tycho said, "Seeing as it appeared in Cassiopeia, I should say that it portends events in the lives of queens. They will appear at first to bring love and harmony and new inspiration, because the moon is in Aquarius tonight. But the sun is in Scorpio, so these events will in fact bring struggle and tension, a freezing of the imagination, an irrational insistence upon dogmatism and tradition –" he stopped speaking, and stood straighter, to take in the sight of the star directly.

"What is it?" asked the woman, when Tycho's silence grew uncomfortable for her.

Tycho shook off the reverie. "I was thinking of something Miss Urania said, about the ancients," he said. Then he noticed Urania was missing.

"Where did she go? I didn't see her leave."

Urania had withdrawn to a perch partway up a nearby hill, where she could enjoy watching the Brahe siblings discover the star on their own. Smiling like a proud mother, she whispered as if her father could hear: "Closer to the truth, a small step every day."

As Tycho made more measurements with his cross staff, the woman with the questions played with the triquetrum, to figure out for herself how it worked. "How do you know that's what it means?" she asked.

Tycho smiled and said, "Well, I shall know more about this new star and its augury after I have measured its parallax. Then I'll know how far it is from the Earth, what part of the sky it came from, and where it's going. But for now, it can only mean that good things shall come to queenly maidens as yourself." He kissed the woman's hands, and she grinned.

"Tycho!" his sister playfully scolded him.

Tycho smiled and shrugged, to apologize to her. Then he asked the woman, "What's your name?"

"Kirsten Jørgensdatter, my lord," said the woman, as she curtseyed for him.

A man standing beside her, who wore a wooden cross on a coarse rope around his shoulders, said, "My daughter."

Tycho shook the man's hands and kissed his cheeks. "Mister Priest," he said. "You should be proud of your daughter's curiosity."

"Thank you, but curiosity is what caused Adam and Eve to fall. I would have preferred my child was curious about spinning and weaving, not reading and writing," said the priest.

"But, tonight is a good night for bending the old traditions," Tycho announced. "Sophie: if you would be so kind, bring out the rumtopf. And if anyone has cake, or butter and olive oil, or tables and benches, or anything festive, bring it here! Whatever else this star may mean, it has brought us all together, and we should celebrate the wonderfulness of the world!"

§ 25.

As the townsfolk scattered to their houses and returned with the makings of a feast, Tycho saw the silhouette of Urania watching from the edge of the town, then turning to slip away into the cricket-haunted darkness of a hollow hedgerow. He jogged to her, calling for her to come back.

"Not staying for the feast?" he asked when he reached her side.

"Not tonight," Urania said. She waved to a shadow that hovered by the tree line of a field. It moved closer, and resolved into the shape of her faerie horse, trotting toward them.

"Why not?" Tycho asked. "There will be plenty of food. And you're the one who showed us the new star. You should be the guest of honour."

"It seemed the right moment for me to step back," Urania replied. "To let you study it on your own."

"Why? Is the astrological portent something terrible? Or is it not really a star – is it a new kind of comet?"

Urania grinned, then mounted her horse. "There's something about it which will seem impossible to you. So, it's best if you discover it for yourself. And when you do, I shall return."

Tycho watched her trotting into the hedgerow for a while. Fireflies, like the stars, blinked in her wake. Then the first of the townsfolk returned to the street, Kirsten among them, bearing baskets of bread; her father carried a keg of wine. Tycho returned to them.

"My father saves this for special events," said Kirsten, as she offered a jug of rumtopf. "A new star in the sky counts, don't you think?" Then she whispered into his ear, "He doesn't know I took it!"

Tycho's puzzlement over Urania's departure gave way to a bright smile.

On the opposite side of the town, Julian sat on the clay tiled roof of a farmer's cottage. He smiled to see Tycho enjoying Kirsten's charms.

"My lord Zeus, if you can hear me –" he said, "I think I found one of your subtle weapons."

§ 26.

The following morning, Kirsten took the front pew of the local church to kneel and pray. The building had recently been dedicated to that rebellious new religious movement begun by brother Luther of Wittenberg. Consequently, all the building's artwork had been removed. White rectangles showed where framed pictures of the stations of the cross had once protected the wall from the incense. In the place of the high altar there now stood a single candle, resting on a pillar almost as tall as Kirsten herself.

"Praying to God for Mister Brahe's hand in marriage?" said Julian, sitting behind her.

Kirsten tried to ignore him by reciting the Lord's Prayer.

"He's a good catch," Julian continued. "Educated, vivacious, rich. I'm sure every maiden in town is praying to catch his eye. But last night, you caught it, didn't you?"

Kirsten recited her prayer slightly louder, and with a bent head and closed eyes.

"Oh, pardon me," Julian apologized. "He ploughed your furrow last night. And now you're praying for a healthy harvest."

"*Shhh!*" Kirsten hissed at him. "Adultery is a mortal sin! Don't tell my father."

"I rather suspect your father would *approve*, given that it was such an eligible gentleman who planted his seed in your field," Julian suggested.

"He will never want me again," Kirsten whispered back. "I'm a commoner. A child of a country vicar. If I married him, he would lose his title, and all his noble privileges. He will never build his observatory. He will never be the great man he wants to be."

"Yes, I know," Julian said, with a sardonic smile. Then he rose and stepped near to her. "Have you ever heard the old Roman motto: *amor vincit omnia*?"

"Love conquers all things," Kirsten translated it.

"You are the child of a minister," Julian praised her. He put his hand on her head and said, "Conquer him with your love, dear girl. Make him love you more than he loves his title. More than he loves the stars."

A slightly glazed look overtook Kirsten's eyes for a heartbeat, as Julian's command lodged in her mind. She turned around to ask, "Do you know him? Could you tell him that I –"

Julian was already gone; Kirsten was alone. She returned to her prayer, though a sob or two interrupted the rhythm.

§ 27.

Tycho's many pages of measurement numbers for the new star were posted on almost every wall in his laboratory. The table was cleared of its alchemy equipment, to make way for his abacus and compass, and for his elbows on the occasions that his numbers made no sense and he had to rest his head. Such was his posture when Kirsten entered the lab to bring him his evening's aperitif.

"It has not moved in six months!" Tycho complained.

"Not at all?" Kirsten asked.

"Not a single measurable fraction of an arc degree. And to tie a ribbon to it, now it's bright enough that you can see it during the *day*!" he howled, as he flung a window shutter open. The cheerful blue of the high noon sky was punctuated by the white point of the new star.

"It's not supposed to be possible. But there it is. Clear as a candle and steady as a rock," Tycho described it.

"It hasn't brought on the end of the world," Kirsten said.

"The astrological meaning is not what troubles me anymore," Tycho said. "It's the fact that it hasn't moved. I don't know what it means."

Sophie sat by an end of the table that she had protected from her brother's obsession. "I know. Your triquetrum isn't big enough. You say that all the time."

Kirsten smirked, "I think it's plenty big enough."

"Ha! Good thing your father didn't hear you say that!" Sophie laughed.

Tycho cracked a smile, but returned to his pensiveness. "Six months should be enough for the tools I already have. No, I must conclude that this star is not some kind of comet or a fiery meteor, but that it is a star, a new star, shining in the firmament itself – one that has never previously been seen before our time, in any age since the beginning of the world."

Kirsten said, "Why does that distress you?"

Tycho said, "Because that's supposed to be impossible!" It's called 'the firmament' because the stars hold firm!"

Sophie touched the wooden cross she wore around her neck. Then she said, "Who was the woman who took you out to the field, to see it? Maybe she knows what it means. Or, what to do."

Tycho brightened. "My old teacher! She might know, that's true. But there's no way to find her..." he regarded the star for a breath, lost in thought. Then he ordered: "Bring out the good pewter dishes, and the good Bohemian glassware. We're going to have a visitor tonight!"

Tycho and Sophie immediately moved to make preparations. Kirsten, however, gazed out the window at the star.

§ 28.

From the late afternoon and onward, Kirsten sat on a bench by the front door, to be the first to greet the visitor. At almost the exact moment of sunset, the visitor arrived.

"*Kháìre*," said Urania, dismounting from her horse.

Kirsten said, "What? I mean – you must be miss Urania."

"I am," Urania confirmed. "And you are?"

"Tycho's betrothed," Kirsten announced.

"How wonderful!" Urania exclaimed. She kissed Kirsten's cheeks. But Kirsten only froze in place and did not return the greeting. Urania gave her a puzzled look.

"I think it's not right for a man's tutor from his childhood to pay a social call," Kirsten told her.

"He is expecting me," Urania replied.

"I don't want you to see him!" Kirsten insisted, and she moved herself between Urania and the door. But she moved slowly and cradled her belly with her right hand.

"Oh my stars!" Urania gushed. Then she gave Kirsten her most loving smile. "You must be so happy."

Tycho appeared at the door, attracted by the voices. He gently took Kirsten's arms and made room for Urania to enter the house. "Welcome, miss Urania, welcome! Please come in!"

Kirsten's desperate face told him how she felt about Urania's presence. But Tycho ushered his favourite tutor inside anyway and led them both to the workshop. Sophie was already there, pouring four glasses of wine. Urania greeted her, but her attention fell on the mathematical tables pinned to the walls.

"You've discovered the problem with your new star," she said.

"I can't understand it," said Tycho. "The new star has to be – can only be – fixed to the firmament with all the others. But the firmament is the sphere of eternal perfection. Nothing is supposed to change there!"

"Why not?" Urania asked.

"Isn't it obvious? It's as if God is telling us that everything we read in Aristotle, Ptolemy, all the ancients, and the Holy Bible itself, is wrong. But those books are the foundation of all knowledge. Without them, we're lost."

"That's why I keep telling you to leave it alone, my love," said Kirsten. "The new star will drive you mad, if you let it."

Urania studied Kirsten's desperate and lonely face. "It appears your real problem is not the new star," she said.

Sophie said, "Thank you! We have been telling him that for days!"

"You're right, naturally," said Tycho. "My real problem is that if things can change in the firmament, it might mean that *everything* can change. That nothing in Creation is stable, nothing reliable, nothing eternal. But that cannot be possible!" He grasped Urania's hands and said, "You once had some pull with the royal astrologer. I need you to ask him for the funds to build a better observatory. I need a quadrant that's no less than twenty-five *alen* long –"

"Tycho, please!" Kirsten cried.

Tycho stopped talking, and closed his eyes. Urania let go of his hands, and motioned for him to go to his lover, which he did.

"I know, I know," Tycho said to Kirsten, "If I marry you, they will take all of that away from me."

Sophie said, "Thank you for talking *sense* into him!"

"The problem," said Urania, "is that I need him to study the new star, too. I need him to understand it. To see it like I do."

Urania moved to the window and contemplated the sky. The horizon glowed cyan, but the rest of the great dome of the firmament was navy blue and darkening with every breath. The constellations were taking their places, and the waxing crescent moon touched the horizon, ready to follow the sun on its apparent path below the Earth.

Urania said, "The King won't build you an observatory just because I asked him to do it."

"Then what should I do?" Tycho asked.

"Write a book about the new star," she said. "You've been studying it for six months; probably more intensely than anyone else in Europe. So, it's time to share what you've discovered. All your evidence, all your conclusions. All your doubts and fears, too. Let this book prove that the world needs your observatory, and that you are the man to build it."

"What about me?" said Kirsten.

"He won't write his book alone," Urania advised her. "Sophie will help. That way, he will have more time for you. Now, what sort of books do you have here in the house?"

"Not much in the way of classics," said Tycho, waving to the shelves opposite the windows. "Some theology, Sophie's books on alchemy, some old Danish law texts –"

"Danish law! Perfect!" Urania exclaimed.

Tycho said, "Whatever it is, I can help too!"

Urania smiled and said, "I believe you could. But tonight, the mother of your child needs you more than I do."

§ 29.

Copenhagen, Denmark, 1573.

Much to his surprise, Tycho found himself in the throne room of King Frederick II of Denmark. A small room made smaller still by the courtiers who crowded it. Elk antlers, wolf heads, and other hunting trophies hung between the windows. A servant lit the candles on an iron candelabra, then with pulley and rope he raised it to the ceiling, tying off the rope to a post on the wall.

"Master Tycho Ottesen Brahe of Knudstrup," the majordomo announced.

Tycho approached the carpeted platform where the King sat on his throne and presented His Majesty with a copy of his finished book.

"*De Stella Nova,*" he named it. "It includes all my calculations and proofs for the new star, all my astrological assessments, and the possible implications for theology and philosophy."

The King accepted the gift, skimmed the first page, then handed it to a courtier. "Our royal mathematician tells us it is a work of uncommon excellence," he said. "It has brought fame to you, and to Denmark."

Tycho kept his head low, as the presence of royalty required, though he still smiled. "It is the sum of my life's work so far, Your Majesty. Though it is also my earnest intention to produce better work in the future."

"Better? How is that possible? Are more new stars soon to appear in the heavens?"

Tycho hoped that his majesty did not see the slight smile that tugged at one side of his mouth, or the wink he flashed to Kirsten, who watched her man's presentation from the side.

"Your majesty, no one can predict the next *stella nova*. But when I have finished building my new observatory, I shall be able provide a better model of the cosmos and of our position in it, than anyone has ever produced before. So to provide better astrological forecasting for all the crowned heads of Christendom."

"Your new observatory?" asked the King.

"Yes, sire. I have been corresponding with several princes of Europe, one of whom is keen to provide me with land and financing for the construction of a new dedicated facility."

"Who?" the King demanded.

"Sire, the prince showing the greatest interest in my work is His Majesty Maximilian II, King of Germany, Emperor of the Holy Roman –"

"Damnation!" King Frederick burst out. "The Hapsburgs are not satisfied to own an empire here on Earth, now they want to own the sky as well? No! You shall remain in Denmark."

Tycho risked looking up and meeting his King in the eye. "Majesty? You intend for me not to build my observatory?"

"We intend for you to build it *here*. We intend for our realm to be known as a centre of knowledge, greater than all others," the King confirmed. "And for ourselves, to be known as her enlightened patron. Now go, build your cathedral of knowledge. My ministers will see to the details."

"Your most gracious majesty!" Tycho gushed. "I shall be forever thankful to you, forever indebted –"

"Nothing," the King replied, as he dismissed Tycho with a wave.

Brendan Myers

Tycho bowed, and left the throne room, grinning all the way.

§ 30.

The tavern was a forest of timbre pillars holding up the ceiling beams. Tin and copper oil lamps hanging from the pillars swung in rhythm with the two competing groups of musicians in opposite corners of the hall, both of them somewhat out of tune. They performed for a dense crowd of off-duty soldiers, wine-swilling merchants, and the sycophants who surrounded them. Between a table of longshoremen shouting that their dinner was taking too long, and another where several women caressed the cheeks of the youngest soldiers and picked their pockets, Tycho found a space where he and his party could celebrate the day.

"I can barely believe it, Tycho –" Sophie exclaimed. "You hoodwinked the King into giving you a private island for your observatory!"

"I hoodwinked the King!" Tycho shouted, his beer tankard raised high.

"Not so loud – you want him to find out?" Sophie warned.

"I can barely believe it myself," Tycho admitted, still flushed with pride. "It's going to be brilliant. I'll have a dozen assistants. And a library. And a print shop so I can publish my stuff my own way. And an alchemy lab for you, Sophie."

"Perfect!" Sophie grinned.

"For you, Miss Urania, who has always been with me," Tycho announced, "I shall call my new observatory, The Castle of Urania!"

"Oh, that's too much," said Urania, although she did grin to hear it.

"It's not nearly enough," Tycho said. Then he spun toward Kirsten, almost spilling his beer on the way. "And for you, my sweet daughter of a country vicar, who never thought she would set foot in Copenhagen, never mind the King's throne room: I'll put in a bedroom! With the biggest bed in the world –"

"You will not –" Kirsten chided him.

"I will," Tycho insisted. "Because we are going to live there. Together.

You and me. With our twenty assistants. And our twenty children –"

"How can you say that!" Kirsten burst out. "Can't you understand what you're doing to me? To watch you stand before the King, lie to him like you were haggling some jobber in the market, then run away to some island and leave me to feed your child without –"

"But that's not the thing at all," Tycho said. "The thing is: you're coming with me. You, Sophie, Urania, this whole tavern – tell her what you found in those law books, Sophie."

While Tycho drained his beer into his gullet, Sophie said "There is more than one kind of marriage in Danish law. In a church marriage, yes, my brother would have to give up his noble title and all his privileges to marry you. But there's another way. If for three years you hold the keys to his house, eat at his table, and sleep in his bed, then you will be his wife in common-law."

"That's the thing exactly!" Tycho exclaimed.

"Your children will not be considered noble-born," Sophie explained further, "and they will not inherit his titles. But they will be *legitimate*. And Tycho will not have to give anything up in order to marry you."

Having emptied his tankard, Tycho announced, "And the very best part of this, is *this* part of this. The three years begins today!" Then he plopped his keys on the table in front of Kirsten.

Kirsten touched the keys, as if she wasn't sure they were real. She drew them toward her, then clutched them close to her heart.

Tycho pulled her to her feet and announced to the whole tavern: "Hey, Denmark! I am Tycho Brahe, hoodwinker of kings, and I'm getting married!"

The tavern erupted in cheers for him. A line of men immediately formed to slap him on the back and shake his hand. Similarly, a circle of women surrounded Kirsten, hugging her and sharing stories of their own betrothals.

Urania was the only person nearby who was not celebrating. Instead, she was studying a diagram on a page in Tycho's book. It showed a model of the cosmos, with the Earth at the centre, the sun and moon orbiting the Earth, and all other planets orbiting the sun. Tycho saw her glum face, and sat next to her.

"Miss Urania, won't you have a drink with us?" he said.

"I already have one," she replied, and took a sip from a wine goblet.

"Then drink it, and put the cosmology away for one night," he said, and he closed the book with a slam.

"Why do you insist on keeping the Earth at the centre of your system?" she asked him. "I've been telling you for *decades* that it's the sun!"

"Because you're asking me to... to not believe my own eyes," Tycho burped. "I read your book by that old Polish priest. The numbers add up easier when you do it his way. But that's not enough. You have to see the truth of it in the world. Or else it's not good philosophy."

"I could show you," she offered, "if you think you're ready."

But Tycho was too busy drinking to care. "Why are we talking about this right now anyway? I'm going to get married in three years – I got some heavy drinking to do!"

He rejoined his friends, dancing to the music from one of the bands. The other band gave up and ordered a round of drinks.

Urania retreated to the relative solitude of the night outside. The gravel on the earthen street crunched under her feet, quietly at first, then seemingly louder as the raucous tavern receded behind her.

Sophie, however, saw her slip away. She jogged outside to find her.

"I won't be joining you at the observatory," said Urania, when Sophie had caught up.

"No? Is it that he doesn't accept Copernicus?" said Sophie, tapping the diagram with her fingers. "I heard you arguing about it with him. I don't accept it either; it's so obviously silly."

"It's the one lesson I have given him which he still does not understand, after all these years. But that's not the important reason."

"Why, then?"

Urania shook her head. "Because I don't belong among you. I'm not – I am not like you."

Sophie shifted closer and said, "Is it because you don't age?"

Urania turned her face away.

Sophie caught her arm. "You found the Philosopher's Stone," she insisted. "You know how to make the Elixir of Eternal Life. The true gold every alchemist is searching for. You found it."

"I was born a very long time ago, that much is true," Urania admitted. "But I don't know how to make the stone. I don't know anyone who does."

"Who are you, Miss Urania?" Sophie asked. "You seem to know everything about us, but we know nothing of you. Where are you from? How is it that you… you cannot age?"

"I want to tell you, truly I do," Urania apologized. "But you won't believe me. No one ever does."

"How can I decide not to believe you, if you don't tell me?" said Sophie.

Urania sighed, and said, "I am a first-generation descendant of the gods. The daughter of the titan Mnemosyne, and of Olympian Zeus."

Sophie shook her head. "No. The gods are only stories. Exaggerated histories. Pagan idols. They never existed as people."

"The gods did exist, Sophie," said Urania. "They were women and men, once. Stronger and wiser than most. Their souls in closer harmony with the immensities of the world. But women and men, all the same. And I inherited their legacy."

Sophie's furrowed brow and furtive eyes told Urania how she felt about that story. "Are there more people like you in the world?" she asked.

Urania sighed. She said, "Yes, but very few."

With a serious and determined voice, Sophie asked, "What about the gods of the Romans? The Egyptians? The Northmen? How do I find them? How do I *join* them?"

"You really believe me?" Urania marvelled.

"The evidence is in front of me – your youth," said Sophie. "And I have to know that there's more to life than joining a convent or getting married. I have to know there's a way *out* for me."

Urania understood. "Maybe you are ready to see the world the way we do. Take my hands," she offered.

Sophie nodded, and cautiously accepted Urania's hand.

They fell up beyond the rooftops and into the sky. The tavern dwindled to the size of a child's toy beneath them, followed by the surrounding houses, then the great castles and city walls. Sophie's knuckles whitened with the tightness of her grip on Urania's hands. The haze of the horizon spread outward, revealing all the towns within a day's ride of Copenhagen, then the lakes to the west, the coast of Sweden to the east, and the rest of Europe to the south. Sophie shrieked.

"Don't look down, look up!" Urania told her.

Sophie did, and the great sphere of the stars enclosed her on all sides. Tycho's new star lay directly above. It grew into a yellow-orange cloud, glowing with its own light. They flew by the wisps and knots of the cloud's extremities, each the size of a world.

She shrieked again, and buried her face in Urania's shoulder.

"Take me down, take me down!" Sophie cried, her eyes squeezed shut.

Urania said, "You're safe now."

Sophie opened her eyes and found herself in the middle of the lane again, enfolded by the din of laughter and music from the tavern, and the scuttling of stray dogs.

"What was that!" she cried. Before Urania could answer she staggered away and fled to the tavern.

Urania's shoulders sagged, and her gaze fell to the gravelled street. Her horse stepped out of a shadow and nuzzled her head under her arm.

§ 31.

"I have mentored him for more than twenty-five years," Urania grumbled. "And even now, he does not understand!"

"Patience," Prometheus counselled her. "Your instinct to mentor him from an early age was correct. And you still have plenty of time."

The old titan sat in his usual chair on the belvedere of his villa, overlooking the Carpathian valley. A decanter of wine lay within reach of his hand, and a cup sat near it for his guest. Urania, however, paced from one end of the railing to the other, pausing occasionally to shove a chair out of the way. Tycho's diagram of his Earth-centred, sun-orbiting system lay on the table.

"I showed the new star to his sister, Sophie Brahe – have you been watching? I was sure she wasn't ready, but she insisted. It terrified her, same as it did everyone else. It will terrify him too – after all this time, he is still not ready."

"Well then. Don't show it to him."

Urania stopped pacing. "You mean that?"

As Prometheus poured a new cup of wine, he said, "I wanted you to mentor the man, but not for *his* sake. He is not the one who will win your bargain for you. He will remain attached to his Tychonic System," he patted the diagram, "for his whole life."

"Then why did you want me to mentor him?"

"Because he will prepare the way for the one who *will*."

Urania sighed, and dropped into a chair. Prometheus pushed a cup of wine toward her, and she drank it.

"Master Brahe, together with his sister and their assistants, will produce measurement tables and predictions ten times more precise than any before him," Prometheus explained. "What is more: soon he will observe another new star. And a comet. And an eclipse. And in studying them he will further shatter the old wisdom. His work shall lay the keel of the ship that will fly you back to Olympus. But he will not be your pilot."

Urania breathed, to give herself time to accept what Prometheus was telling her. "Who, then, should I be looking for?"

Prometheus sipped his wine and said, "A man who knows how to cut the sails and turn the wheel. I believe you will find him in Italy."

Book Three: Giordano

§ 32.

Naples, Kingdom of Naples,
February 1576.

The way I met Giordano Bruno is more like the usual way I found my students, before Prometheus tried to find them for me. I would climb a rooftop or a hill, any place with a good all-around view of the night sky. I liked hills because the stars could be in front of me, as well as above. I would look at them for a while. Then the answer to any question would come to me. An hour, more or less, was usually enough. Sometimes I brought a small astrolabe with me, so I could measure any meteors or comets that might appear. But most of the time, I brought a skin of warm apple cider, or wine. And a blanket to sit on. I would pick out the north star, then any planets that were above the horizon, then let the starlight bathe me. Sometimes I did that with my eyes closed, by listening to them. You mortals once believed that the planets made music: you called it 'the music of the spheres.' But I knew it as a kind of moving web, as if each planet held one end of a harp string, and I held the other, and the note each string played would change as its planet swung close or swung away. Then I could touch the string and feel its vibration, the voice of each planet saying 'Kháìre, my love, here I am!'. Sometimes I would pluck the string and send a greetings of my own in return.

Waves of light, each a different colour, a different feeling, Each of them a different way of saying, 'here I am!'

Oh, but you were asking how I find my students.

I found Giordano when I was out walking at midnight, along a narrow country road. Listening to the planets, feeling for which direction in the sky their voices came from. And I felt a sound, or I heard a feeling, that I should go to Naples.

That's how it usually is, for me. I only need to look up to the stars for a while and clear my mind of the noise of the day. And the stars answer my questions.

Brendan Myers

Well, most of them.

* * *

Urania arrived in the biggest market square in Naples by mid-afternoon, as dark clouds mumbled with the possibility of rain. She bought a small basket of grapes and found a bench to sit and eat them. Nearby, a monk with the white robe and black tabard of a Dominican Brother haggled with another merchant over the price of a roll of blank parchment. Urania might have ignored the scene, but she heard the monk mention the name of Nicolaus Copernicus. She stepped closer, to hear more.

"You made no sense!" howled the merchant. "How can you stand in the pulpit, right next to the holy altar itself, and tell us that everything we know is wrong?"

"Truth does not change because it is, or is not, believed by a majority of people," the monk replied. He had a gaunt face and a heavy moustache, and his brown hair was thick but uneven, in the manner of those who didn't much care what they looked like.

"It's in the Bible, too," the merchant added. "Joshua commanded the sun to stand still, not the Earth to stop spinning."

"Wouldn't it have looked the same to him, in any case?" said the monk.

Urania grinned, as she remembered saying something similar to Copernicus, decades ago.

The merchant chortled for a moment, then tapped the arm of another nearby merchant. "See, this is the man who was preaching last week that the sun in the sky is God, and that the Earth revolves around it."

The second merchant, seeing the monk, stepped forward. "I've got a mind to tell your Father Superior not to let you preach anymore. The sun in the sky is God – ha! Next thing you're going to say is that the clouds are angels!"

The monk held his breath to keep his temper, then said, "When I say the sun is God, all I mean is that Divinity reveals Herself in all things, and everything has Divinity latent within itself. She enfolds and imparts herself even to the smallest beings –"

"So, not only is the sun a god, but so are the rats and the fleas?" the first merchant argued.

The second merchant swatted the monk with a roll of leather. "Get out of here, you pagan!"

"But I need to buy your parchment –"

"Your money is no good to me. Get on!"

As the merchants and some of their customers pelted him with apple cores, the monk fled the market square. The two proud merchants congratulated each other, kissed each other's cheeks, and enjoyed some praise from those who witnessed the scene.

The monk traipsed away along Naples' narrow downtown streets, his pace steady, his head down, apparently oblivious to Urania following him. He entered the cloister of a monastery. Urania stopped when she was no more than a few strides past the gate. There were a dozen monks inside, all with the same white robes and black habits; and she had lost sight of her quarry just long enough to suppose that any of them could be the man she had been following. But before long, she saw one of them strike up an argument with two others. She recognized him as the man from the market, and she heard someone call him by name: brother Giordano.

Returning to the market, Urania found the merchant who had refused to sell the parchment to the monk.

"What is the price of your parchment today?" she asked him.

"For you, my lady? Ten ducats a roll," he said. "How many would you like?"

Urania handed the man a small leather purse. "How many do you have? I'll take all of them."

§ 33.

That night, Urania returned to the garden in the monastery cloister. Heavy clouds drifted over most of the sky, so the garden was sometimes washed in white by the moon, sometimes submerged in darkness. When most of the candles in the brothers' windows had gone out, Urania laid a roll of parchment at the threshold of the one cell whose window still glowed with gold. Then she knocked on the door.

Giordano found the parchment. He examined it for a moment, then called out: "Hello?"

"Khâiire, brother Giordano," Urania greeted him. She stood in the centre of the garden, where the moonlight spilled upon her from an opened cloud; all other things in the world lay quiet and dark about her. In that light her gown and her flesh seemed as flawless as a marble statue, yet luminous with divinity. She stretched out her arm, inviting Giordano to join her.

Giordano dropped the roll on his bed and went to her.

"Did you leave me that roll of parchment, just there?" he asked.

"I did," she confirmed. "I saw you in the market today, talking about the sun, and the divinity that dwells in all things," she explained, as she invited Giordano to sit next to her. "There are powers in this world who *notice* people who say such things."

"Powers like the Holy Inquisition?" Giordano offered.

"Powers like those who can directly *see* what you are only beginning to imagine," she explained.

Giordano considered her for a heartbeat. "At this precise moment, I'm imagining who sent you."

Urania smiled. "No one," she said.

Giordano shook his head. "It was the parchment-seller, wasn't it? He decided to take my money, after all. *Bene*."

Urania remained patient with him. "I am here because I knew you would be awake at this time of night. Your mind is always active, isn't it? Your imagination always at work? Or, perhaps you were reading books that your brothers discourage your from touching – books by Averroes, Erasmus, Copernicus –"

"So, you brought the parchment so I could make secret copies for you," Giordano concluded.

"The parchment is for *your* book, Giordano," Urania explained. "The one you will write, very soon."

This made Giordano smile. "So, you are a messenger from a secret patron! That explains why you came to me at this time of night. Please tell your master that I accept. But I want complete academic freedom. I want to write the truth, whether your master likes it or not."

"I am here on my own behalf," Urania said. "I want to speak to you as one philosopher to another."

"You're a woman," Giordano laughed. "And judging by your clothes, you are not under holy orders. Only two other possibilities remain: you are the servant of some patron of the arts who doesn't wish to be known. Or you are lying to me."

Urania pursed her lips; the muscles in her arms and legs tightened. Yet she knew that as a mortal man of his time, he could not see her any other way. She flashed her hands toward the sky, and the clouds vanished as though she had brushed away some fallen leaves. The garden flooded with moonlight. A glow emitted from her flesh, and stars emerged in her hair.

"I am the muse Urania, daughter of Mnemosyne, and of Olympian Zeus!" she announced, as she floated into the air above him. The glow from her skin brightened, and an aura of yellow and blue star-drops surrounded her. "I am the glory of the stars, and the wonder in the eyes that see them! All who seek the highest realms of knowledge come to me!"

Giordano took a few steps backwards and grasped a pillar of the cloister's covered arcade on the outer edge of the garden.

Then Urania softened her light and returned to earth. "You're doubting whether I am real," she reassured him. "That's good. It's part of what I like about you. Come, touch my hand, if you need to. See that I am flesh, and not illusion."

Giordano's widened eyes were fixed on Urania now. He stood still, taking in the revelation. When he found his voice again, he said, "I always thought that the gods were only allegories," he stuttered.

"In fact, we are your ancestors," she informed him.

"All those stories about the great artists, the great poets, seeking the inspiration of the muses – Homer, and Hesiod, invoking them at the start of their epic histories – those stories are true?"

"Some of them," Urania said. "I knew Plato, and his student Aristotle, when they were only boys. I knew Al-Khwarizmi, and Ibn al-Haytham, as they raised up the House of Wisdom. I knew Nicolaus Copernicus, and with my help he saw more of the cosmos than any man before him. And now I am here for you."

"But if you are real, and the gods are real, what then of Jesus? Is he not our Saviour?" Giordano asked.

Urania paused, then said, "I have never met him, so I have to say I don't know."

Giordano stepped closer and opened his hands. "And what of the *one* God – the creator of heaven and earth?"

Urania's eyes drifted skyward, as the many answers to that question crowded her mind. When she found the best answer, she smiled. She said, "Perhaps if I show you how to see the world the way I do, then you can decide for yourself."

Giordano nodded.

"Take my hands, and look up," Urania asked him.

He obeyed, and Urania grinned. Together they fell into the sky: past the rooftops of the monastery, past the high towers of the basilica, past the crest of Mount Vesuvius, to the south of the city. They rose to the atmosphere, high enough to see all of Italy in one glance.

Giordano breathed heavier and tightened his grip on her hands. Then something inside him decided he was not in danger. He relaxed. He let go of one of her hands, so he could turn around, and see more of what was revealed around him. Then he began to laugh.

Urania's eyes widened, and her mouth fell open. "You're – you're not afraid!" she marvelled.

"This is glorious!" Giordano exclaimed.

They swooped higher; close enough to the moon to see its mountains and craters, not so different from those on earth, though its beauty was stark with shades of grey. Then they fell onward, until the Earth and moon were only blue and white stars. Urania reached out with her finger and picked out other stars for Giordano to love: red Mars, with its two asteroids for moons; bright Jupiter, with its bands of brown and grey clouds, and its four elder children; golden Saturn, with its glittering rings; beyond Saturn, the unnamed giant worlds of green and blue; and the many millions of comets and ice-worlds that lay beyond the orbits of the outermost planets, which sometimes swooped closer to the sun and let down their streaming hair.

"All you see here is of only one world – there are so many more!" Urania grinned, then gestured to the Milky Way.

Giordano looked. The stars appeared to throb and pulse, as though each of them was a raindrop on an endless lake. He could see how some were closer than others, some larger than others, some brighter and dimmer. Millions more stars than he had ever imagined existed were now his to love, and to wonder upon. And to his great delight, planets swung around most of them. A dim red star carried seven planets swinging fast and close. A bright yellow-white star held several planets rich and green with life, and with fleets of metal ships shuttling between them.

"The stars are suns," Giordano whispered. Then he shouted it: "The universe is infinite, and all the stars are suns!"

He laughed with enlightenment, and Urania laughed with him.

§ 34.

"I found him!" Urania sang, as she danced up the steps to Prometheus's villa.

Prometheus grinned to see her happy. But at the same time, he sighed.

"Fillippo Giordano Bruno of Nola, in the Kingdom of Naples," she named him. "He saw the galaxy and didn't look away – he looked straight at it. He actually *laughed*! He's the first person to do that since Diotima of Mantinea."

"How wonderful!" Prometheus praised her.

"He *is*," Urania gushed. "We stayed up talking until dawn. I think I found the man who can win the bargain for me. In fact, I think I'm in *love*."

"Very good, Urania," Prometheus said, though his gaze was on the distance.

"What is it?" she asked.

Prometheus said, "Nothing. Only, strange that you found this man in Naples. I thought you would find him in Padua." Then his demeanour brightened. "But come, sit with me, and tell me what you want to do next."

She followed him to the belvedere. "I'll invite him to give a lecture at the Secret Academy," she offered. "The professors can question him. They can decide whether he meets the conditions of the bargain."

"I will arrange it," Prometheus promised. "Though I expect it will take time. The professors are spread around the world – in Baghdad, Timbuktu, Beijing, Hochelaga –"

"That's as well; I need time to prepare him."

"And you still need to *protect* him," Prometheus reminded her. "If anything should happen to him before the Academy can convene –"

"Kynisca will always be nearby," Urania assured him.

"It's a threat from the other mortals that concerns me," Prometheus warned. "They are stubborn, quick to alarm, and slow to change. You and Kynisca can stop another Olympian from interfering. But you cannot stop the mortals from panicking. Which they *will* do, if your new champion tries to enlighten them."

"I suppose some of them might not understand," Urania acknowledged.

"Not at first. But given time, and a rational explanation –"

"Has reason ever persuaded anyone to change their mind about anything?" Prometheus thundered. Before she could answer, he added: "We are not doing this for them. We are doing this for *us*. Have you already forgotten that you are banished from Olympus? Banished from your home?"

Urania remembered.

"That's better," Prometheus said. He poured some more wine for her. She took the cup but did not drink.

Prometheus acknowledged her hesitation with a kind smile. "You believe that I have other reasons for taking care of you, or that I might demand something in return," he surmised. "You're quite correct. So let me tell you. I'm helping you because I want your father to see that he failed. I want you to flourish as a scholar and a muse, entirely *despite* his designs. And I shall help you, in whatever ways you want or need. The sight of you, happy and self-contained, and returned to your rightful place among the Olympians, shall be payment enough for me."

Urania studied his face, to decide whether she believed this was his real reason.

Prometheus raised his wine to her.

Urania decided that the polite thing to do was to raise hers in return, and to drink.

* * *

The Secret Academy. It's a wonderful name, isn't it?

Some say it began with the Druids, who gathered every year in the centre of Gaul to share knowledge. Some say it began at the Great Library of Alexandria, some say at the Baghdad House of Wisdom. I think it started in all three places, and somehow they came together as one. I asked them to judge the bargain because they are the most learned people in my world. Descendants of the gods of wisdom, from all the great pantheons. Even the oldest of us respect their advice. If they decide against my father, and if he rejects their decision... well, he would have more problems than I do.

Oh, and the Academy is not our only institution. We also have a warrior's guild, an artist's guild, a bank, a post office. We even a parliament. Not that the more high-and-mighty among us give it much attention. But we have one.

And we also have Summoners, whose job is to search the world for the brightest and best of humanity – anyone with a drop of the old gods in them – and invite them to join us.

§ 35.

The following Sunday, Giordano stood in the basilica's pulpit again, leaning on a Bible as though it might fly off the podium. The congregation, some clutching their rosaries and scapulars, waited for Giordano to speak. Someone coughed, and the sound echoed around the vault.

The two merchants from the market wore self-righteous smiles on their faces. One of them whispered to the other: "Heresy last week; silence this week."

The other replied, "Next week he'll be speaking in tongues!"

Someone nearby shushed them, and they settled back into their seats.

Giordano closed the Bible in front of him with a thump that startled the pigeons in the choir loft. The whispers in the congregation grew again. Giordano stopped them by standing straighter and looking up.

"The ancient philosophers, Democritus and Epicurus," he said, "maintained that everything throughout the world undergoes renewal and restoration. They understood these matters more truly than those who would maintain belief that the cosmos is immutable. We recognize a more noble image: an infinite universe. Thus is the excellence of God magnified, and the greatness of his kingdom made manifest; he is glorified not in one, but in countless suns; not in a single earth, a single world, but in a thousand-thousand worlds, I say in an infinity of worlds!"

The glory of his vision raised his hands to heaven. The grumbles and complaints from the congregation pulled them down again. He could see his father superior shaking his head and gesturing that he should take his seat. He gave the blessing to the congregation, then retreated.

Julian listened to the entire sermon with arms folded and face scowling.

§ 36.

That afternoon, in the monastery garden, Giordano winced with each new item that his Dominican brothers ransacked from his cell. Blankets, handfuls of straw from the mattress, a stone wash basin on a wooden stand, and finally a small stack of books, flew from the cell door and into the cloister's covered arcade. Some items moved Giordano to lurch forward to rescue it. But the judgmental gaze of the priest who supervised the whole affair kept the annoyed monk at a distance.

"Is this what you call *talking* about my sermon?" Giordano protested.

"I should be in Rome today," said Father Bellarmine: a man with a stout and creviced face, as though he had smiled once when he was young, and he didn't like it. "I was drawn here by the story of a man who has memorized all the scriptures, all the works of sacred doctrine, and the books of all the ancient philosophers. A master of *ars reminiscendi*, the perfection of memory. Well, then, I had to meet this man! But who did I find at the pulpit today? An incomprehensible howler, screeching about astrology and infinity and only-God-knows what else!"

"You have no authority to invade my cell like this!" Giordano protested.

"Your superior was most accommodating to me," the priest continued, "when he learned that I am a professor at the New Roman College, and specially qualified for identifying dangerous ideas."

One of the books in Giordano's cell startled the brother who found it; he handed it to the priest.

"*Praise of Folly*, by Erasmus of Rotterdam," the priest read the title page. "You know this man's books are forbidden."

"That one shouldn't be," Giordano protested. "It is a Christian book by a Christian writer about the need for Christian virtue in the leaders of Christendom."

"It has been poisoned by the heresies in his other works," Bellarmine declared, and he tossed the book back in the pile of Giordano's other suspicious possessions.

Giordano shook his head. "A man who is strong enough in his faith can read anything he wants and never feel the pull of temptation. 'To the pure, all things are pure. But to disbelievers and the corrupt, noting is pure'." Giordano quoted to him.

Bellarmine felt the sting of the subtle insult. "Mind yourself, brother; pride is the most insidious of the vices," he said.

The frustrated monk was about to reply when the brothers found several sheets of parchment bearing diagrams that he had drawn. Most were circles containing geometric shapes, allegorical symbols, and various correspondences. The brothers treated them with great delicacy, as if they might catch fire.

"What is this? It looks like hermetic sorcery," the priest demanded.

Giordano snatched one of the diagrams away and pointed to a label he had assigned it. "It is a device for the practice of *ars reminiscendi*," he said. "It has nothing to do with magic. See how the letters in each corner represent the four categorical syllogisms?"

"This may be harmless on its own," said father Bellarmine, "but it may be a stepping stone to darker matters."

"Darker matters!" Giordano complained. "What could possibly be darker than the heart of a man who sees darkness everywhere? Know any such men, yourself?"

Bellarmine calmed himself before replying. "No one doubts your intelligence or your faith, my brother. But your sermons over the last few weeks have sown confusion in too many people's minds. We have to find the roots of it, before it grows too deep to pull out. Before it does harm to anyone else. I am doing you a *charity* here. No need for acrimony."

"The root of all my sermons is philosophy – *reason*," Giordano defended himself. "We worship an infinite God; it follows by logic that His creation should likewise be infinite."

"We also worship a God who inspired His children to write the Holy Scripture," the priest shot back, "where it is made abundantly clear that the Earth is set firmly in its place and cannot be shaken."

"That psalm proclaims the permanence of God's *laws* upon the earth, not of the physical Earth itself," Giordano argued. "And as our Jewish friends tell us, the psalms are works of praise; they have no *legal* significance –"

"You're hair-splitting," Bellarmine replied.

"And *you* are forgetting that I, too, am a doctor of theology," Giordano reminded him. "I know how to interpret Scripture."

"There is only one man on Earth who interprets Scripture, and he sits on the throne of St. Peter," Bellarmine snapped back.

"That man is our Holy Father, indeed," Giordano said. "But he is still only a man."

"He is the Vicar of Christ," Bellarmine said. "He stands in relation to us in the *place* of Christ."

Giordano winced as the brothers tossed more books out of his cell and into the garden. "Have you ever asked yourself, who is Christ? Yes? Who was Jesus? Is he the living Son of God, one-third of the Holy Trinity? Or is he a *creation* of God, born at a certain moment in history, and therefore not eternal? And therefore only a man?"

The monks who were searching Giordano's cell stopped to hear how Father Bellarmine would reply.

"There is a name for that line of questioning, brother Giordano. The Arianist Heresy," Bellarmine told him.

"I know," Giordano admitted. "But we have been wrong for centuries about the shape and size of the universe. Is it not conceivable that we have also been wrong about the nature and identity of our Lord?"

"Is it not conceivable that *you* are wrong?" Bellarmine asked. "The authority of Scripture and our doctrines, the tradition of the ancient philosophers, and the evidence of the senses, all weigh against you."

"So they appear," Giordano agreed. "But remember your Saint Augustine, who said God gave us two great books: the holy scriptures, and the world of nature. If they appear to disagree, it is because we have understood one of them wrongly."

Bellarmine smirked on one side of his face. "Which one do you think we are reading wrong?"

"Both of them," Giordano grinned. "And it's high time we asked ourselves how to read them right."

Bellarmine decided to ask no further questions. He grasped Giordano's shoulders and said, "Brother, I am your friend and I shall never want to silence those who ask the deepest questions. But some kinds of answers can lead you astray."

Giordano nodded. "I struggle with things; I feel no shame admitting that. Nonetheless, you and I are both students of divine reason. We should feel bound to *her*, who teaches God's wisdom. And to no others."

Bellarmine smiled, and released his hands. "As the prodigal son found his way back to the father, I do believe there is time for you to find your way back to the light." He gave Giordano his blessing and followed the other monks out of the cloister.

Giordano sat on a garden bench near the pile of his belongings. He picked up one of his *ars reminiscendi* diagrams and shook his head.

Julian, who had witnessed the argument, followed Bellarmine out of the cloister. "Father Bellarmine! Sir!"

The young priest turned around and cocked an eyebrow.

"I saw you talking to our brother Giordano, and – sorry, it is perhaps not my place to say –"

Bellarmine said, "Come, speak. If it is true, it is no sin to say it."

Julian tapped him on the forehead, and said, "You need to bring him to trial for heresy."

Bellarmine regarded Giordano for a moment, then said, "I think you're right."

§ 37.

"They took the parchment you gave me," Giordano complained. "And all my books. And they won't let me in the library anymore."

He sat on the stone floor of the cloister arcade, near the door to his cell, his knees drawn up. His hands clutched the crumpled parchment that summoned him to Rome to stand trial for heresy.

"They have not seen what you have seen," Urania consoled him. "They don't know what you know."

"Then show them," Giordano told her. "As you showed me. Then there can be no doubt. And this ridiculous charge of heresy can be forgotten." He crumpled the court summons into a ball and threw it away.

"Most people are not yet ready to see," Urania said. "Even Nicolaus pulled away in alarm."

"But he *understood* you," Giordano countered.

"More than others," Urania agreed, "but not as much as you."

Giordano rose to his feet. "This monastery is a prison. As much for my brothers as it is for me. I have to get out of here."

Urania smiled and said, "It has been arranged."

She waved toward the monastery's garden gate. A great bashing noise rattled the flowers and ornamental grasses of the garden. The gate fell down, like a drawbridge with a broken chain. Fragments splintered from its hinges as it clattered on the flagstones.

Kynisca crossed this new threshold, grinning from one side to the other. "Anyone looking for an escort to Geneva?" she said.

§ 38.

**Republic of Geneva,
1580.**

Giordano's hair was fully grown out, and he had traded his Dominican robe and tabard for the plain black frock and white collar of a Calvinist. But the three dour-faced men who pressed their gazes on him from the town hall platform did not care that he dressed like one of them.

The eldest of the three said, "Giordano Bruno, of Nola. Your elders and your peers in the Calvinist Republic of Geneva have found sufficient evidence to try you for heresy."

"You are frightened of God!" Giordano roared at them, as though it were a sudden realization. "You teach that God is infinite in substance and in being. But you fear the full implications of your faith. An infinite God cannot be separate from any part of His creation. He cannot be in one place and not another. He cannot be *for* one man and against another. He sees every lie you tell. Every crime you try to hide!"

"We can have the trial *right now* if you want it," the Calvinist elder threatened, as his followers called out for that very opportunity.

"I am finished with you!" Giordano announced. He ripped off his white collar and stepped on it as he marched out of the hall.

Urania and Kynisca met him in the square outside. Kynisca said to him, "How do you feel about France?"

§ 39.

**Paris, Kingdom of France,
1583.**

"It's not a question of your talent as a mathematician, Giordano," said the wizened professor, sitting in his cluttered office. "It's that we cannot have you teaching our students that a pagan Egyptian idol is the One True God."

Giordano had shaved his head. He painted a dark outline around his eyes, and dark lines from one eye down his cheek: the tears of Horus. He wore a hand-carved *ankh*, a cross with a loop for its top arm, on a string around his neck. He glared across the table, not understanding why the professor could be so obstinate.

A short while later, he joined his friends at the steps of the university hall, hugging his books and parchment rolls.

Urania said, "England?"

§ 40.

Oxford, Kingdom of England, 1584.

Giordano's audience in the Oxford University lecture hall argued, shouted, hollered, spat, threw crumpled papers, waved fists, stamped on hats, threatened criminal charges of blasphemy, threatened violence – anything but listen to him. Giordano, for his part, descended from the stage to argue, shout, holler, spit, throw papers, stamp on hats, threaten philosophical ignominy, threaten to ignore – anything but speak.

Julian, standing near the door, folded his arms and grinned.

§ 41.

"Is the Academy ready to convene?" Urania asked Prometheus.

The old titan sipped his wine and said, "No."

"No? It's been eight years since we asked them!" Urania complained.

"The time is not yet right."

"That's absurd!" Urania flustered. "What are they waiting for? Did you speak to the dean? What did she say?"

"I did not speak to the dean," he declared. He shifted in his chair to face her. "I looked into Giordano's future. He is not the man to win Zeus' bargain for us. He is soon to come to a most unhappy end."

"What did you see?"

"A betrayal, a prison cell, and fire," Prometheus related with a frown. "I'm sorry, Urania. Truly. I'm the one who told you to look for your next student in Italy. So I am partly to blame for this. But the man you need is someone else."

"Haven't you been watching?" Urania rounded on him. "Brother Giordano has come closer to the truth than anyone else I have trained in almost a thousand years."

"I trust your choice of students," Prometheus assured her. "Yet I also feel morally obliged to share with you my gifts of prophesy, my foresight of the future. Your victory would surely come easier if you made use of it."

"You have helped me this far, cousin, and I am grateful," Urania conceded. "But –"

"But nothing!" Prometheus interrupted. "If you want to enter Olympus again, my advice will get you there faster. Without me, you might be living rough with the mortals for another thousand years."

Urania's vision as an Olympian was sharp enough to see all the way from Prometheus' villa in the Caucasus to the mountains of Greece, over a thousand leagues away. Its grey and white slopes were topped by a golden city on the summit, where every house was a temple, glittering with marble, painted relief sculptures, and precious metals. Satyrs and nymphs danced in circles in the gardens. Audiences in the amphitheatres rewarded poets and singers with laurel wreathes and standing ovations. Philosophers gathered in the agora to share bread and wine and to examine beautiful ideas together. And fleets of gilded triremes came and went from the aerie, sailing on the clouds to every nation on earth and back again.

"The man you want is in Padua," Prometheus reminded her. "I see him as clearly as I see you now."

Urania sloughed away, towards the plot where her fairy horse, Heraclitus, grazed on mountain grass, waiting for her.

"You know," said Kynisca, who sat on a nearby fieldstone wall, "if we take Giordano to Padua, then Prometheus can be right about Padua, and at the same time you can be right about Giordano."

Urania laughed, but shook her head. "He won't be fooled by that. Giordano can stay in England. It is a Protestant country; the Inquisition will not reach him there."

"If you say so," Kynisca conceded. "Do you still need me to protect him?"

"Unless you'd like to come with *me*, instead."

Kynisca grinned. "You know, I think I would!"

§ 42.

La Rochelle, Province of Aunis, Kingdom of France, 1584.

Catherine de Parthenay liked to handle the Secret Academy's official correspondence while sitting at a small table in her garden, under a bower of ivy that shaded her from the sun. But instead of an inkwell and blotter, today her table held a copy of a manuscript by Giordano Bruno.

"*The Ash Wednesday Supper*," she read the title.

"It's not finished yet," said Urania, "and he doesn't know I took this copy."

"His penmanship is atrocious," Catherine scorned. "But his ideas are… quite imaginative. That's your influence, I'm sure."

"I only *showed* him the stars. The *meaning* he ascribes to them here, is his own."

"Would he have come this far without your help?"

Urania answered the question with a sly smile. Then she said, "I'd like for you to summon the Secret Academy for him. I want them to decide if this is enough to win the bargain with Julian."

Catherine winced. "What you're asking is not as easy as you may want it to be. There are more than a thousand professors, they live all around the earth, and they travel all the time. It can take months for my letters to reach them."

Kynisca, who had been strolling through the garden, stepped forward and said, "I can find them."

"And when my letters *do* find them," Catherine continued, "the professors may decide that they do not want to discuss your bargain. The Academy investigates metanatural philosophy. It does not investigate spats between the gods." And before Urania could object to the word 'spat', Catherine added: "That is how they will interpret your bargain. They will say that judging it is beneath them."

Urania nodded. Her gaze drifted to the garden, and the people working on the flower beds: the simple trowels in which they dug a bed for a seed, the love with which they planted it and patted the soil over it. She said, "This bargain with my father is about something more than whether I can go home. It's about whether anyone can change their thinking, and so change their nature. It is about whether they can lift themselves from their hatreds, their fears, and so realize how beautiful and good they can be. Or whether they will always hate and fear each other, always struggle to the death for transient glories. I'm not asking the Academy to examine one man. I'm asking them to examine the future of all humanity."

Catherine leaned back in her wickerwork chair, to breathe the fresh perfume from the garden's peppermint and basil beds, and to contemplate what to do. "A touch pretentious, don't you think?" she said of Urania's appeal. "But ever since the war made me a widow, I have wondered the same thing."

Catherine's remark about her widowhood made Urania wonder, for the first time, if her friend's severe black dress and conservative neck-ruff might be a sign that she was still in mourning. Urania let the tension out of her shoulders. "There are so few in these modern days who truly know themselves."

Catherine smiled. "I shall have to find a more esoteric way to phrase your request. The members of the Academy love a complicated problem more than they love an important one. After then, we shall see how many of them agree to attend your conference."

"Thank you," said Urania, as she rose to kiss Catherine's cheeks.

Kynisca saw that as the signal to gather the horses. Urania followed her, but she paused.

"What is it?" asked Kynisca.

"Nothing," Urania replied, as she shook the reverie off. "It seemed for a moment that if I had not been exiled, I would not have met you. Or

Catherine. Or any of the others – and you have all been such good and beautiful people."

Kynisca grinned. "What was it that Cicero said about exile? That it's just like an extended retreat to the countryside?"

Urania smiled. "Yes, he did."

They walked arm in arm together to the stables.

§ 43.

Julian had no trouble moving through the narrow streets of Oxford's university district, beneath the sputtering light of rain-stressed torches. He paused near the entrance to a tavern to tap someone on the forehead and command him to hand over his bottle of wine; the man did so, and when Julian was gone, he wondered why he did it.

He found a table with no candles, far from the fireplace. A white-bearded, uncomfortably seated, and slightly frightened elderly man sat there. His linen tunic, silk sash, and fur kaftan formed perhaps the only outfit in the tavern not torn anywhere nor stained with wine. Julian took a chair from another table and sat by him.

"*Avé*, Plotinus! Thank you for coming. I bought you some good Sangiovese, this time," Julian told his friend, as he handed over the bottle.

Plotinus sniffed it, then tasted it. "More water than wine, in whatever this is," he grumbled. "Now why have you summoned me to this noise-blasted prison for the soul?"

"Because you are one of the leading voices in the Secret Academy. You got the Dean's letter, calling for a conference?"

"I did," Plotinus confirmed. "She is proposing that a mortal man named Giordano Bruno of Nola should be Awakened to the Hidden World, and then admitted into the Academy."

"He's a vagabond and a charlatan," Julian said. "To examine him will only waste the Academy's time."

"But I am intrigued by him," Plotinus said. "And I trust the dean's judgment. If she says this man has discovered part of the Hidden World on his own, then I think I would like to meet him."

"That is not quite how it happened," said Julian.

"Oh no?"

§ 44.

"I showed him the truth about our place in the cosmos," said Urania. "And he did not pull away from it. In fact he loved it!"

"Did you show him *all* of it?" asked Moses Maimonides. His beard matched the white of his scarf and the embroidery on his skullcap. In one hand he held a steaming bowl of almond pudding; in the other, a spoon. Whenever he tried to taste it, someone spoke, and he held his spoon back, to be polite.

"As much as I myself am able to see," Urania replied.

"Rabbi," said Kynisca, "You have always supported the policy of inviting the best of humanity to join the Hidden Houses."

Maimonides smiled. "I have often enjoyed the assistance of a certain irascible daughter of a king of Sparta. Though she normally recommends athletes. Fighters. Today she recommends some kind of weird philosopher. *Oy gevalt.*"

Urania perked an eyebrow at Kynisca. "You two already know each other?"

Kynisca grinned. "Two thousand years is plenty of time to make new friends."

Maimonides covered his mouth, lest his laughter cause some of his pudding to spill out.

Urania said, "Brother Giordano belongs in our academy. His fellow mortals don't understand him – he needs a community of philosophical seekers like himself. That community is *us.*"

"Why do you suppose his fellow mortals are no longer enough for him?" the old teacher asked. Then he held up a finger to stop them answering, so that he could taste his pudding.

§ 45.

"Because he's insane!" said Julian.

"You can accuse anyone of being mad just for thinking differently than you do," said Hypatia of Alexandria. With her maroon peplos fastened at the shoulders by gold brooches, her gold himation, and her thick brown hair bundled in silver cords, she turned almost every head in the busy market square.

"Prometheus has endorsed too many mortals to join the Secret Academy," Julian said. "First he wanted Plotinus. Then he wanted all those Mohammedeans. Then he wanted Abelard and Heloise, a husband-and-wife together. Too many mortals raised up to our world! One of them is Dean of the Academy now. I'm telling you, it's madness! It has to stop!"

"All of his choices have been wise and good people," the scholar said. "And you, yourself, were raised to the Hidden Houses the same way. What makes you more worthy than any of them?"

"That was a different situation," Julian insisted. "Prometheus recommended all these people because he wants to control the Academy. Think of how many members must owe him their loyalty. His latest possession is that upstart French busybody, Catherine de Parthenay, who – let me remind you again – is now the academic dean."

§ 46.

"And she has been our best dean in three centuries," said Urania. "She opened the Academy to poets and playwrights. She keeps the Academy's mail moving even while France is fighting a civil war against the Huguenots. And she's a Huguenot herself!"

"And she agrees this man Bruno should join us?" said the bald and tan-skinned man seated on a carpet on the floor of his tent.

"She agrees that he should be examined. Given a chance," Urania said.

"Then the decision to include him can fall to a jury, and you can be on it."

"Tell her that I, Imhotep of Egypt, shall give him that chance."

§ 47.

"So where is he?" asked Catherine.

She stood in a room containing a table and a chair, some writing materials, a loaf of brown bread so stale it was as hard as a rock, and a bed covered in dirty clothes.

"This is the room he's renting. Maybe he's gone to town for dinner?" Urania guessed.

Catherine knocked the bread on the table, making a harsh noise. "I would say he has not been here for days."

They went downstairs and found the landlord in the kitchen. "Last I saw him," said the landlord, "he said he hated the English weather, and that he was going back to Italy. Said there was a job there waiting for him."

"Did he say where in Italy he was going?" Catherine asked him.

But Urania answered. "I know where he's going. Padua." She crossed her arms.

"The very place," the landlord confirmed. "And good luck to him, as far as I'm concerned. He was a bloody loon, he was. Kept everyone awake with his ranting, every night!"

§ 48.

Padua, Republic of Venice, 1591.

Giordano was sitting on a table on the street side-patio of a tavern, surrounded by a cluster of big-eyed students from Padua's university. Torches on wall sconces and candles in empty wine bottles engoldened the brick and stone shop fronts and cobbles. Ivy climbed the corners, their leaves turned as if they too wished to hear the philosopher speaking. A full midnight moon peeked around the side of a church tower.

"The genius of Copernicus, and yes I do believe it was genius, moved him to discover not one, but *three* enlightening thoughts," he told the students. "The first was the discovery that the sun is the centre of things. The second is that the universe is fantastically larger than anyone knew. And the third, was what followed by logic from those two discoveries."

"And what followed?" asked a student.

"That the great Aristotle, whom your professors love so much they call him *The* philosopher, was wrong."

A quiet stir troubled the students. "But Aristotle is the foundation of all philosophy!" another student complained. A third said, "No, it's Plato!"

"Both of them together," Giordano said. "And that is why rejecting them requires courage. Copernicus looked upon the cosmos, not with the reflected light of the moon, but with the full brightness of the daytime sun."

From down the cobbled street, Urania and Catherine spotted Giordano and his small audience.

Urania wanted to jog toward him. "There, I see him! Now let's take him to –"

But Catherine touched her arm. "No, wait – let him finish. I want to see what this man is like, before we invite him into our world."

Giordano acknowledged their arrival with a smile, and a gesture to invite them to join the circle.

"Copernicus travelled far. Now we, today, must go further. We must ask… what else in the old scholastic and peripatetic – very pathetic! – philosophy must be wrong? Perhaps the Earth and moon are not made of only four elements. Perhaps the sun and stars are not made of ether. Perhaps –"

A panicked student leapt to his feet. "Perhaps Man is not made in the image of God?"

The exclamation brought forth a round of troubled muttering from the students.

Giordano smiled. "That, my friend, is an excellent question. And to find an answer, we must do as Copernicus did, and try to see the world as if it was new. As if God created it only this morning. As if we knew nothing else about it besides what our senses can tell us, what we can measure, and what our intelligence can deduce from them both. Let me ask you, if I may: when Genesis and the Kabbalah say that man is made in God's image, what do we mean by God?"

"God is that than which nothing greater can be conceived," said the student, quoting from a book he held in his hands.

"And so, He may well be," Giordano nodded. "Now, could such a God be present in a man, but not, let us say, in the birds? In the fish? The flowers? The wind?"

The student sat down.

"There, my friend, you are learning!" Giordano praised him. Then he stood and said, "Everyone, look to the person sitting next to you. Go on, look at the face of your neighbour. The neighbour whom God commanded you to love. Look on these two women who have joined us," he gestured toward Catherine and Urania, "and the serving-girl who brought us our wine, and to anyone else here in this street, whatever his country, whatever his language, whatever his religion. Are you looking? Good. Now, think in your mind: that is what God looks like."

The students laughed to ease their embarrassment, at first. Some looked back to Giordano, with a smirking mouth or a puzzled brow. Giordano only urged them to look on a neighbour again. Soon, some of the students found their hearts beating a touch faster, their breaths held for a moment in their breasts, their voices whispering on their own accord: "Oh? Oh!"

"Now look to the world," Giordano continued. "See the water in the canal. See the houses. The trees. The clouds. The stars. There, all around us – that is what God looks like!"

Some of the students reached out to kiss each other's cheeks. Some stood up to wander around, or to spin in a circle, their arms stretched wide. Some laughed again, but this time with pleasure, as if seeing their familiar world for the first time, and finding it good. Catherine de Parthenay, though her gaze remained on Giordano, took Urania's hand. Urania squeezed it and wrapped her arm around her friend's waist. Giordano, pleased that his message had found a hearing, clasped his hands over his heart.

Only one person remained in his seat, paying no mind to anyone else. His gaze was on Giordano, and his hands stroked his beard. Though still younger than Giordano by almost twenty years, he was at least ten years older than most other students.

"So, is it God, then, who causes objects to fall to the ground, and not the elements of earth and water?" he asked. "And is it God who causes air and fire to rise, and the stars to turn round in the heavens? If it is the nature of earth and water to fall to the centre of the cosmos, why then do they not fall into the sun?"

Some of the students nodded or whispered in agreement. The man's name was mentioned: "There's the Wrangler!" Other quiet voices laid odds on who would win the debate that was sure to follow, or who would be the first to say, "I don't know."

The muse, sensing the students' change in mood, said, "This fellow thinks he can play gadfly to my Socrates."

"There's more at stake here than you might think," Catherine explained. "Depending on how this goes, there might be a formal challenge later. With judges, and published results, and a lot of money for the winner."

"When did philosophers start caring for money more than for the truth?" Urania balked.

"Philosophers still need to eat," Catherine reminded the muse, and fixed her attention on the two prizefighters in the ring.

Giordano, comfortable in his intellectual power and the admiration of his audience, chuckled as if to pretend the challenger's question was child's play. "Those were Aristotle's beliefs. But he was the stupidest of all philosophers. He perverted the opinions of the ancients and opposed the truth."

The challenger shrugged. "Nonetheless, his opinions were our best explanation for all motion through space, until Copernicus pulled the Earth out from under us."

"Copernicus was only the beginning of our return to the truth," said Giordano.

"Oh, do not misunderstand me; I quite *agree*," the man told him. "The Ptolemaic system was far too complicated for its own good. I'm delighted that old Copernicus put it to bed. But surely, by throwing out old Aristotle, we create more problems than we solve? Should we suppose that the planets turn on their crystal spheres because they are pushed by the breath of angels? What would be the *evidence* of that?"

Giordano said, "I acknowledge that in the new philosophy, there are heavy questions to answer," he said. "How could it be otherwise? If there were no heavy questions, it would not be interesting! Here is one possibility. In an infinite universe with no centre, there would be no point in saying, as Aristotle said, that the elements seek their natural places. Instead, it may be that the elements seek only to join into larger wholes. An atom of earth, mixed into something like this feather..." he plucked a feather from his hat, and held it high, "wants to join with the nearest largest whole, one that is likewise composed mostly of its own kind of element. For that is where it can best be preserved." Then he dropped the feather and watched it fall to the table.

"An interesting idea," said the wrangler. "But is a single drop of a feather enough to *prove* that you are correct?"

Giordano perked a brow. "Please explain, sir."

"Suppose... instead of dropping one feather, beside it I also dropped a stone. And beside the stone, a cannon ball. And beside that, the cannon itself! Suppose I dropped them at the same moment from the top of that tower in Pisa, you know the one I mean. The tower that cannot stand straight. Would those bodies fall toward each other, before they fell to the ground? Surely they must do, if a stone and a cannonball contain atoms of earth that want to form a larger unity. Or would the heavier things fall faster – having more earth within them, perhaps their will is the stronger?"

Giordano picked up his feather and studied it close to his eyes.

The wrangler said, "I am not saying you are wrong, *amici*. It remains entirely possible that you are right. I am suggesting only this: that there must be some way to put your idea to the test of experience. There must be a way to *experiment*. Do you know of such a way?"

Giordano held his thoughts on the feather for a breath longer, then admitted, "I do not."

The small audience gasped to hear it. Whispers of "I knew it!" and "Damnation!" and "Every time!" were heard. Money changed hands.

"It is not shameful to admit you do not know something!" Giordano chastised the students who snickered. "The very wisest of the philosophers claimed only to know that he knew nothing at all."

"Yes, and look what happened to him!" someone said, and the snickering continued.

"But come, brother Giordano," said the wrangler. "I have enjoyed our conversation very much. Let us call for a bottle of grappa, that we can empty down our throats together while we talk some more."

Catherine leaned into Urania's ear and said, "I want to meet him."

"Brother Giordano?" said Urania.

"No. The other fellow. The one they call The Wrangler." She stepped forward to introduce herself to him.

Urania dropped herself in a chair by a nearby empty table. She pulled off her gloves, and massaged her face, her elbows on the table. When she picked her head up again, she found Kynisca sitting beside her, offering her best sympathetic face.

"You're the reason I found him in Padua," Urania accused.

"I had to do it," Kynisca explained. "Prometheus told me that man over there is the one who –"

"I don't want to hear about Prometheus right now!" Urania barked at her. Then spoke slowly, choosing her words with care. "I have spent the last seven years convincing the most influential members of the Secret Academy to examine Giordano. Giordano – who will be taken by the Inquisition if he ever returns to Italy. You know that! And now, here we are, in Italy. I can't have my closest friend working against me."

"I *am* your friend, Urania," Kynisca reassured her. "But Prometheus will stop reading the future for us if we don't sometimes do what he asks."

"I'm almost ready for him to stop reading *my* future," said Urania. "I suppose he asked you to protect the wrangler, over there."

"His name is Galileo Galilei," said Kynisca, nodding to him. "Both he and Giordano are in the running for a new post at Padua's university. The Old Man asked me to protect whichever of them is chosen."

Urania looked over to the table where Giordano, Galileo, and Catherine were talking. Their hands flew as fast as their words, and the bottle of grappa they shared was already half empty.

"When will they decide who gets the post?" Urania asked.

Catherine said, "When one of them wins enough public challenges like the one we just saw. They're probably setting terms for a formal challenge, right now."

Aghast, Urania said, "They choose professors the same way they choose animals for pit fighting?"

"These days," Catherine explained, "you don't have to be wise to be a philosopher. You have to be famous."

Urania shook her head. "I do not belong among these people," she mumbled.

Kynisca put a reassuring hand on her friend's shoulder.

Then Urania stood up. "The Wrangler can have the post in Padua if he wants it," she announced. "Giordano will soon be one of us. Then we can all go live some place that isn't completely out of its mind."

§ 49.

The professors shifted on their benches, causing their joints to pop and the old floorboards to creak. The tassels and streamers of their academic bonnets and gowns gave the room's brown wooden tables and grey-white plaster a splash of colour. Giordano, seated on the stage, tried not to move as he spoke, so as not to be interrupted by the squeaking of his chair.

"How is it possible," said one of the professors, "that the universe can be infinite?"

"How is it possible that the universe can be *finite*?" Giordano answered with a grin.

"Do you claim that you can demonstrate this infinity?"

"Do *you* claim that you can demonstrate this *finitude*?"

The professor leaned away, glanced at a colleague and rolled his eyes. "To the point, if you please," he said, turning back to Giordano. "You are keeping us too long in suspense."

Giordano nodded, understanding what the nature of the occasion required of him. "If the world is finite and if nothing lies beyond, then I ask you: Where is the world? Where is the universe? Aristotle says, it is in itself. What does that mean? What will be his conclusion concerning that which is beyond the world? If you say there is nothing, then the heaven and the world will not be anywhere."

"The world will then be nowhere? Everything will be nowhere?" said the professor.

"The world is something which is past finding out," Giordano grinned. "If you say that beyond the world there is a divine intellect, so that God becomes the position in space of all things, then you would need to explain how God, who is incorporeal and without dimension, can be the very position in space occupied by a dimensional body. If you say that where there is nothing there can be no question of what lies beyond, I should reply that these are mere words and excuses. Divinity does not fill a geometric space. If the world is a cube, instead of a sphere, it would still be wrong to say God is the outer surface of that cube. That kind of talk is not compatible with the dignity of divine and universal nature."

The professor, on hearing this flood of argumentation, glanced at one of his neighbours and perked an eyebrow; the neighbour shook his head. Another professor coughed and caused his bench to squeak.

Galileo, seated on the stage next to Giordano, grinned and reclined in his chair, and put his feet up on the table. The university post, he was sure, was now as good as his.

In the last row of benches at the back of the hall, Catherine de Parthenay folded her arms.

Beside her, Julian leaned close and whispered, "Didn't I tell you – this is what he's like. If you let him into the Academy, his analytic nonsense will infuse into everything. We will be lost."

Catherine made no sign of having heard him, but her stern expression showed that she was thinking his way. He smiled.

§ 50.

Later that same afternoon, Giordano took his dinner at the same tavern with the outdoor tables where, some nights before, the local students had eaten up his every word. Those same students now surrounded Galileo, several tables away, drinking his thoughts, savouring his meanings.

Giordano finished his bread, soup, and wine, left some coins on the table for the tavern keeper, and walked away. He pulled his hood over his head so that no one would see his tears. And when he rounded a corner, out of sight of the tavern, he pounded his head on a wall.

§ 51.

"I've heard both of them lecture at the university now, and I have to tell you," said Catherine de Parthenay, "I think the university chose the right man."

"Galileo is more clever than wise," Urania judged him.

They sat in the front row of the same lecture hall where, a few hours earlier, first Giordano and then Galileo faced the professors. The hall was empty now, and the last sunbeams of evening streamed in through the upper windows.

"Now this man Giordano – he has a mind as active and energetic a storm at sea," said Catherine. "But what good is that if he cannot make himself understood? If he can't come to harbour once in a while?"

"*Our* philosophers will understand him," Urania promised.

"I am not certain of that anymore," Catherine said. "He speaks of so many immensities – God, time, space, infinity – of a universe with no centre and no edge, of stars that have their own planets, and planets that have their own people. It all seems so fanciful, so extravagant – even impossible."

Urania perked her brow. "Why impossible?"

"Because there is only this one sun, this one earth, this one universe," Catherine said. "And yes, it is greater than any mortal can know. But it remains one, as we see it with our eyes, and contained in the sphere of the stars."

Urania said, "But when you were Awakened, when you were made one of us... did you not see –"

"Oh, yes, my friend, yes!" Catherine brightened. "I saw that my soul is a wondrous thing, ancient beyond measure, and full of unquenchable light. I saw the geometry of reason, the algebra of redemption, the vectors of God's divine love!"

"That same geometry is what Brother Giordano has seen, and yet he is no Olympian. That is why we must –"

"But he goes too far, Urania," Catherine said. "He speaks of things that cannot be."

Catherine was smiling, as a mother might do to a small child. Urania felt her kindness as a chainmail blanket: safe, but too heavy to easily remove.

"Catherine," she said, "May I take your hand for a moment? I would like to show you something."

"Please do; what is it?" said Catherine, as she offered her hands.

They touched hands: and the walls and ceiling of the lecture hall dissolved into mist, and the mist dissolved into air. They ascended into the sky, over the rooftops of Padua, glowing in the half-light of evening.

"Urania, where are you taking me!" Catherine shrieked.

"The same place I took Giordano."

The horizon of the Earth spread out beneath them, and then shrank down and wrapped into a sphere, blue and white and green to the west, dark to the east. It shrank away until it was no larger than Catherine's hand at the end of her arm. Then the moon shot over their heads, half-lit with an almost perfect whiteness, half blacker than the midnight sky, and close enough to almost touch its mountain tops. Then it, too, shrank to the size of a fist, as Urania turned toward the stars beyond. Stars, more stars, and ever more stars, and vast reaches of black nothingness between them.

Catherine screamed.

Urania said, "All right. You're safe now."

They were back in the lecture hall, a little darker now as the evening advanced. Catherine leaned on the table behind her, to feel its solidity.

Urania said, "Had you never seen that before? Did you not know?"

Catherine whispered, "No... no..."

Urania bowed her head. "I'm sorry Catherine. I thought that all of us knew."

"What happened when you took Giordano into the sky like that?" Catherine said, almost sobbing.

"He *loved* what he saw," said Urania. "He wanted to see more."

Catherine breathed deeply for a while. She moved to stand in front of the chair that Giordano had used when the university professors examined him. Then she said, "A mortal man who can see joy in a place where a descendant of the angels finds loneliness and terror. Urania, this man must join our world."

In the corridor just outside the lecture hall, Julian pursed his lips, shook his head, and marched out of the building.

§ 52.

The following day, Urania knocked on the door of a boarding house, narrow but tall, and ornamented with flower boxes on every window. The landlady answered.

"We are looking to see Giordano Bruno, the philosopher; is this the right house?" Urania asked.

"It is. Or, it *was*," the landlady said.

"It was? How do you mean?"

"Strange little man came to the house this afternoon. White robe, purple thing hanging off one shoulder, said he was from Rome. Delivered a letter, offering your man Giordano a job. Packed his bag and left, right away. Left half his clothes behind. Left the letter behind, too."

"Can I see it?"

"You can *have* it," the landlady said, as she took it from a pocket and dropped it in Urania's fingers. "Tell him if he wants his clothes, he will have to pay to have them sent, or else I'm keeping them."

"Did Giordano say where he was going?"

"It's in the letter," said the landlady. "Now if it's all the same, I have work to do. God be with you." She closed the door.

Urania read the letter. "So, he is gone to Venice," she said. Then she remembered what the landlady said about the messenger. Her head snapped to attention.

"Julian did this!"

§ 53.

**Venice,
1592.**

*My faerie horse can fly much faster than a mortal horse could gallop overland.
Nonetheless, I goaded my poor friend Heraclitus to fly faster than ever before. I
had to find Julian before he could touch my beloved Giordano.*

*In most other great cities of Europe, the high and mighty built castles like bunkers,
and hid themselves deep inside. Here in Venice, they built palaces. Each seemed
to float on the surface of the lagoon, and each competed to be more extravagant
than the rest. In Giordano's time, this was known as a place where you could buy
and sell almost anything. Spices from India. Silk from China. A dozen warships
and cannons. A dozen slaves, too: this city could be as cruel in the shadows as
any other of its time. But the lagoon that opened the city to trade also kept it safe.
Safe enough for more people to make art, and music. To read poetry and
philosophy. To enjoy life, and to enjoy it in the open air. Even the stonemasons
and fishermen were better dressed here than some of the nobles I met in Rome.
Every canal bustled with them, pushing their hand-rowed boats from the markets
to the workshops and the taverns and back, boasting like schoolboys all the while.*

*The letter that brought me here came from a man named Giovanni Mocenigo,
whose family owned a palazzo near the centre of the city. I stabled Heraclitus at
an inn by the Grand Canal for the price of one gold florin, and hired a gondolier
to take me through the smaller channels to the palazzo. For his price, he asked for
a kiss on the lips. I gave him a bath in the canal.*

It's what Kynisca would have done.

*I found the palazzo surrounded by people. At first, I thought there had been a
murder. But as I drew nearer, the atmosphere of tavern banter and boat bells
gave way to a faint lilting of women's voices, like a whispering in my hair, or a
tingling in my fingers. It resolved into clear words as I reached the palazzo gate:
a choir of women and girls, somewhere inside. The people gathered by the gate
were an audience, assembled only to listen. They turned their faces to the sky, as
though that were the true source of the music. Some of them held hands, some
leaned their heads on another's shoulder.*

*A guardsman let me through the crowd and into the palazzo without delay. He
might have believed that I was a member of the choir. We immortals have that
impression on people, sometimes. I did not dissuade him of it; such is how I gained*

entry into this mortal paradise.

I followed the voices. Along the way I passed an open door to a small sitting room, where Giordano and a nobleman, probably signore Mocenigo, engaged each other in a tense discussion. I decided he was safe enough there for the moment, and I followed the music again. The voices led me to a large chamber on the second floor, where a choirmaster conducted a dozen women, most of them soprano voices, singing an operatic adagio. I stayed by the door. It felt wrong to simply walk in and sit down: it would be too much like disturbing a sacred revelation. For their music was complex in its arrangement yet elegant in its performance, ethereal yet earthy, mournful yet enriching. It felt to me that it belonged to a world that did not know the sting of human hamartia, nor the bane of Original Sin – as though it did not belong to the mortal world at all. And so, I thought I knew whose music it was.

* * *

"Polly, is that you?" asked Urania. "Polymnia?"

Urania stepped out from her hiding place. The choirmaster heard her footsteps and voice, and held up a finger to make Urania wait until the piece was finished. As the last notes faded into the frescoes and ornamented columns of the vault above, the choirmaster clasped her singers' hands to thank them for a job well done. Only then did she turn to see who the intruder was.

Urania jolted back: the choirmaster was not her sister, but another woman: fifty years old, a round and pleasant face, a dress that was stylish but not rich, and a heavy bun to control her brown and grey hair. "Who are you?" she asked Urania, equally startled.

"I'm sorry, I thought you were someone else," said Urania, and she moved to leave.

"Stay if you like," the choirmaster welcomed her. "What did you think of the piece?"

Urania shook her head. She felt like a mouse again, but accepted the invitation to remain. "I thought it was familiar – composed by someone I know."

"I'm Tarquinia Molza," said the choirmaster, extending a hand. "And now, it is composed by someone you know."

Urania grinned. "I'm Urania," she introduced herself.

"Like the muse! Is that your family name or your Christian name?"

"It's my only name, really," said Urania.

One of the singers interrupted to say, "Excuse me madam – we should continue the rehearsal."

"Yes, Laura, quite right," said Tarquinia. To Urania she said, "Can you read a music sheet? Want to join us?"

Urania shook her head, more from embarrassment than lack of skill.

The concerto practiced their madrigals next: a more up-tempo and light-hearted genre of music which allowed the performers to show their vocal range and control. But even while the women rehearsed their cheerful and comic pieces, Urania's face grew long, and silent tears fell.

That evening, with the rehearsal finished, Tarquinia invited Urania to join her and some of the other singers for dinner in the palazzo. Urania gratefully accepted. They gathered around a long table in the palazzo's dining room, attended by serving-men in red and yellow striped uniforms and feathered hats. The women gossiped and joked with each other, but Urania ate silently. Tarquinia, seeing her melancholy, moved to sit beside her.

"You want to talk about it?" Tarquinia asked.

"Talk about what?"

Tarquinia poured her a cup of wine and said, "You have an invisible black cloud hanging over your head. It rained on your eyes even as we sang happy songs for you. So, where did it come from? Why is it following you?"

"I am a long way from home," said Urania. "And some of the music you sang today sounded like home."

"How far?"

"Mount Helicon, Greece," said Urania.

"Oh, that's further from home than *I've* ever been," said Tarquinia, putting an arm around Urania and hugging her. "Are all your people back there?"

"Most of them."

"*We* could be your people," said Tarquinia. "Can you sing?"

Urania smirked, and shook her head. "I used to sing with my sisters all the time – there were nine of us. We had a lot of range as a group, but I wasn't very good. Truth be told, I was the worst. I can't carry a tune in a bucket."

"Oh, ha ha! I don't believe that," Tarquinia laughed. "If you think you can't sing, it's because someone in your life told you to stop. Today, I'm telling you to sing again. Welcome to the *Concerto Della Donne*."

The women surrounded Urania, patting her shoulders, hugging her, kissing her cheek, and thanking her for joining them. Urania smiled at all of them and wiped some raindrops from her eyes.

"I need to ask about the song you were performing when I came in," said Urania, when the group had taken their seats again. "How do you come by the inspiration?"

"I had been reading about the new philosophy," said Tarquinia. "About how the sun is the centre of things, and all the planets turn round it, always in motion. So, I went out at night to look at them. I want to imagine it – to see it in my mind's eye."

"You know about astronomy?" Urania brightened.

"Astronomy, philosophy, poetry, Latin and Greek and Hebrew, everything an educated gentleman learns at school," her companions enjoyed her use of the word *gentleman*, "and whenever I can, I pass it on to the choir here, too."

"So you study all things in the sky –" Urania started.

"And below the earth," Tarquinia finished.

"Like Socrates."

"At his trial, no less!"

Urania studied Tarquinia for a few heartbeats. "If the Earth moves round the sun," she tested her, "why do we not see the parallax of the stars?"

Tarquinia grinned. "So, *you* know about astronomy too! Interesting. Well, it can only mean that the stars are so much further away from us than anyone ever knew. And how much further away they must be from each other – and how *lonely* they must be! So I stayed out that night almost to dawn, thinking about that. And in the morning, I could hear the music in my mind. It's a calling: to the stars, to whoever can hear us, maybe to God, if he's out there. To tell them that we are here and that we love them. So maybe they will be less lonely."

Urania closed her eyes and said, "It was perfect." The other singers thanked her in their many voices, and expressed how much they, too, loved the piece. Urania smiled, and felt a new raindrop in her eye.

The woman whom Tarquinia had identified as Laura asked, "Do you think Copernicus is right?"

"Yes I do," Urania answered, without hesitation.

"Why?" said Laura.

Tarquinia said, "That's Laura Peverara. And I'll tell you this about her: she didn't need *me* to teach her letters!"

"What can I say – my family is rich, they could afford my education," said Laura. Then to Urania: "But please. Why the sun? Is it simpler to have everything go round the sun? Or is there another reason?"

"The best way to explain it," said Urania, "would be to show it. So, would you like to…" then she hesitated. The expectant looks on the faces of her new friends made her feel like she had a choice to make. She gave herself a few heartbeats to make her decision.

"Would we like to what?" asked Laura.

Urania said, "To reason about it together, like philosophers. Let's pretend it's the Golden Age of old *Hellas*, and we are discovering the world for the first time. Shall we?"

The girls agreed with smiles and encouraging words. "How do we begin?" asked Laura.

"We begin by asking good questions," said Urania. "When we look at the world with the natural eye, it does *appear* that the Earth is unmoving, and that all things revolve around it. But the philosopher's eye looks closer. It looks for the subtle things. It asks why things are the way they are. It tries to take nothing for granted in the search for answers. It follows the logic to the conclusion, no matter what the conclusion might be."

"So, it's the sun, because appearances are always deceiving?" asked Laura.

"Not that they always deceive; but the philosopher's eye wants to do more than look at things. It also wants to understand things. So it asks questions. Why do the planets have retrograde motion? Why do they appear to speed up at some times of the year, then slow down?"

"The old philosophy says that there are equant points and epiwheels and crystal spheres, all turning around each other," said Laura.

"All very possible. But what have scholars done whenever the theory didn't quite work? Like, when they tried to predict something, but the prediction turned out to be wrong?"

"They added another epiwheel," said Tarquinia.

"Yes," Urania grinned. "And what happens when we see something entirely unexpected, like those new stars we all saw in the sky?"

The concerto offered a variety of answers. "They panic," said one. "They pretend it isn't real," said another. Laura said, "They say it's a sign of… something. Something bad."

Urania asked, "What could they have done instead?"

This question caused the concerto to look down to their shoes, or to each other, or the ceiling – anywhere but on Urania.

"Here's another way to put the question," she said. "Is there a belief that they hold so deep in their hearts they do not even know it's there, but they will do anything to protect? A belief that goes together with the idea that the Earth, and not the sun, is the centre of all things? Perhaps a belief about who we are, what we are here on earth to do? A belief that is so intimate, that it hurts to doubt it?"

Laura was the first to catch on. "So that's why everybody hates Copernicus!" she laughed.

"Yes, it is," Urania agreed. "But that is exactly the belief we have to question and examine. To find out whether or not it is really true. And if it turns out not to be true, then we have to imagine a better one. And put that idea to the test as well! Remember the motto of the oracle. '*Gnothi Seaton*'. To study philosophy is not only to study the world. It is also to study yourself."

Tarquinia said, "You sound like you know your way around a library. Perhaps you could help me educate the girls? There isn't much money in it, but you can tour with us, and you can room and board with us in Ferrara. And we will teach you to sing."

"I will be glad of it," Urania agreed.

"So, what will be our first lesson?" asked one of the younger girls. "History?" asked another. "Can you teach me to speak Spanish?" asked a third. And a fourth: "Is your name really Urania? Like one of the Muses?"

"Yes, it is," Urania answered her, and she smiled.

* * *

You might be wondering why I didn't show the cosmos to my new friends. Why I decided to talk about it instead.

I was thinking of Sophie Brahe, and Catherine de Parthenay. If I showed the cosmos to my new friends in the Concerto, would they be as terrified as most everyone else? Would it drain away their beautiful spirits, leave them too full of melancholia to sing? Tarquinia seemed to grasp some of the truth, on her own. Or the terrifying part of it. And yet she turned it into art! It seems she did not need me to help her.

Or, it seemed that my help could do her harm. That thought, more than any other, began to trouble me that day.

And to this present day, it still does, sometimes.

§ 54.

Urania slept in the palazzo's guest quarters, along with Tarquinia and half of the Concerto. She was the last to awaken; and when she did, the man leaning on the door frame watching her sleep reminded her why she came to the palazzo in the first place.

"Julian!" she shrieked. She pulled her nightgown and blankets up to her neck.

"You're so predictable," he crooned.

"Where's Giordano!"

"He *was* here, only yesterday," said Julian. "You missed him."

"Missed?"

Julian swaggered into the room and toyed with the clothes that some of the Concerto women had left on their beds or in their travel trunks. "While you were enamoured of the Concerto Della Puella," he said, "the good master of this house, one Signore Giovanni Mocenigo, had Giordano in the library. He wanted Giordano to teach him the art of *reminiscendi*. But you know what Giordano is like. The good master wasn't learning fast enough. And Signore Mocenigo, for his part, didn't like Giordano using the occasion to preach his doctrine of infinity. It's heresy, you know. So, while you were enraptured by the performance of a new work of choral music which I might have stolen from Polymnia–"

"You stole my sister's music!" Urania howled.

"Signore Mocenigo denounced him to the Holy Inquisition. He was arrested in the idle hours of the morning." Julian finished, and be bowed as if he expected an audience to applaud him.

Urania threw a candelabra at him. "You bastard! You horrible, conniving, thieving –"

"Yes, I know," Julian said, deflecting her verbal arrows with ease. "But the best part is why I knew that it would work. Because you love beauty so much, you had to go to hear the music. You could not stop yourself. It was the same when you heard Copernicus talking about calendar reform. You heard him from all the way across the Ionian Sea. You had to find out who he was. Had to help him make his next advance. Your love of beauty is your *hamartia*, your heroic flaw."

Urania found more candelabras to throw at him, as well as wine cups, flower pots, and shoes. "The professors of the Secret Academy will break him out of jail," she shouted.

"No they won't," Julian contradicted her. "By now most of them have decided Giordano is too much trouble. They're going back to their homes."

"I'll find a way to free him – I'll break him out myself!"

Julian laughed. "You, and that Spartan horse-shagger? She's in Padua, protecting some straw-bearded sprout named Galileo. She doesn't take orders from you; she follows Prometheus."

Instead of hurling it at him, Urania dropped the last candelabra on the floor.

"*Gnothi seaton*, Urania," he concluded. "You do not know yourself as well as you think."

He left the bedroom. Urania slammed the door behind him, then moved back to her bed and sat on the floor.

§ 55.

**Rome,
1600.**

Robert Bellarmine, standing in front of the court prosecutor's table, pursed his lips and breathed, to give himself time to find his patience.

"After seven years in our custody," he said, "with privileged visits from some of the most respected theologians in the Dominican order, and every chance to save your soul made available to you –"

"I neither *need* nor *wish* to recant; I have nothing to recant; I *have* no views to recant; I do not know what I *should* recant!" Giordano insisted.

Bellarmine sagged his shoulders and shook his head. Then he looked to the judge of the court, opened his hands, and sighed.

The judge rose to his feet, and the court rose with him. He unfurled a document and read aloud: "We hereby publish, announce, pronounce, sentence, and declare: the aforesaid Brother Giordano Bruno to be an impenitent and pertinacious heretic, and therefore to have incurred all the ecclesiastical censures and pains prescribed by Holy Canon law upon such confessed heretics. We command that he must be delivered to the Secular Court, that he may be punished. Furthermore, we condemn, we reprobate, and we prohibit all his books and writings as heretical and erroneous, and we command that all of them be publicly burned in the square of Saint Peter, and that they shall be placed upon the Index of Forbidden Books. As we have commanded, so shall it be done."

Giordano acknowledged his fate with a stony face and relaxed shoulders, although beneath his Dominican habit one of his legs was shaking.

"It may be that you fear to punish me more than I fear your punishment," he said.

The judge waved at the guardsmen, and the guardsmen took Giordano away.

* * *

They killed him.

They took him to the Campo de Fiori, a town square in the middle of Rome, his mouth stopped in an iron gag. Hundreds of people came to watch. No, they came to celebrate! Like they had captured some kind of wild animal, some creature that had burned their crops and eaten their children. Something their leaders gave them permission to hate.

I wanted him to see me, so that he could know there was at least one face who looked on him with kindness… one face who saw him as a man, in that froth of death-frenzied screamers and the smug-smiling priests who encouraged it. But he never looked my way. How could he know I was there? How could he know which way to look?

Brendan Myers

They built an altar of logs in the square, tied him to a post on its summit, and sacrificed him in a fire.

It struck me some days later, that the priest called Bellarmine was the only one who looked away.

But the question that stole my sleep for years to come, was whether Giordano died that way because of me. If I had not shown him the immensity, if I had not revealed it to his very eyes, might he have never insisted upon its reality, against the tide of his entire society, even to his last morning on earth?

Book Four: Johannes

§ 56.

Island of Hven, in the Straight of Øresund, Kingdom of Denmark, 1597.

"Uraniborg Observatory. Beautiful, isn't it?" Tycho asked Urania.

Urania admired the building he was showing her: a four-story stepped tower, with perfectly symmetrical gables and porches, and much of the interior space open to the world through the arches and belvederes. Sky-blue tenements with starry ornaments gave it a sense of correspondence to the firmament above. It was set within a garden, enclosed in a diamond-shaped wall, with gatehouses at the corners.

"Beautiful," Urania agreed.

"Not just an observatory: it's like a city, contained in one building," Tycho said. "There's an alchemy lab, paper making workshop, printer, bookbinder, wine press, and bakery. And lodgings for all my assistants and students. Around fifty people, all in all. And a stable for my elk! Everything I ever wanted. Here it is."

"You've done so well for yourself, Tycho. I'm proud of you," Urania said, and she patted his shoulder. Then she said: "Wait – your elk?"

"I have a pet elk," Tycho said, gesturing toward a stable. An elk, its proud antlers rising taller than the roof-beam of the stable, glanced their way.

"Isn't that dangerous? They're not like horses. You can't tame them," Urania said, worried.

"Potentially, very dangerous," Tycho explained. "That's why I feed him the dregs from the wine press. It keeps him as good as tame. Most of the time."

"You have a *drunk* elk?" Urania gasped.

The elk, as if ashamed to be seen, lay down on the ground and fell asleep.

"I have the greatest philosophical and astronomical institution in all Christendom," Tycho boasted, gesturing to the observatory building. "A self-contained community dedicated to knowledge. Almost a model of the very heavens we are here to study. And I'm glad you got to see it," Tycho said. Then after a slow breath and a wistful smile, he waved to a group of nearby workmen: "All right, men: take it down."

The workmen took up their wheelbarrows, hammers, and rope for pulleys, and made their way into the observatory.

"What are they doing?" Urania cringed.

"They're taking the furniture and workshops away," Tycho sighed. "You remember how the King said this island would be mine for as long as he lived? Well, just last year he had the appalling bad manners to die. And the new King – God love him because I never will – he doesn't much care about the progress of knowledge. Or, better yet, he wants the benefit of the most advanced and modern centre of knowledge production in all the world, but he refuses to pay for it. So, we're leaving."

"Leaving!" Urania exclaimed. Then to herself she muttered, "Julian is behind this, I know it."

"Who?"

"Someone who has caused me this kind of trouble before," she said. They walked around the observatory gardens for a while, both with heads held down, their minds elsewhere.

"Where do you plan to go?" she asked.

"Anywhere, really," Tycho sighed, as he walked away from the tower. "My field of study is always overhead, after all. I need to find someone with sense enough to put money in my pocket. Once I have that, it doesn't matter where I work."

"Are your students coming with you?"

"Yes, around twenty of them. And my wife and children too, thank you for asking."

They left the walls of the observatory tower and made for Tycho's house, a short walk away. After what Urania hoped was an acceptable pause, she said "Do you have a student who stands out more than the others? Someone who you think could someday... surpass you?"

"They're all good kids. They'll go on to fine careers in business, or government, or whatever. They'll serve with distinction for some ungrateful bishop or some war-mongering king. And history will forget about them. Why are you asking about them? I just lost my home!"

"I looked at your stars," she told him. "I have a strong feeling that you will soon have such a student, if you don't already. And that you will find him in the centre of the empire."

"The centre of the empire? Does that mean the *geographic* centre? Or, what city does the Emperor live in now? I hope it's somewhere nearby, maybe Hamburg, or –"

"Also, I'm coming with you," she added. "I'm at a loss for a home now, myself."

Tycho stopped walking. "You, miss Urania? I could never have imagined you saying such a thing. When I was your student, I thought you lived somewhere in the sky."

Urania felt her hand move to her heart, of its own accord.

Then Tycho picked up his feet again. "But of course, you should come with us. I'll not have my favourite teacher thrown to penury. Plenty of work for both of us in the centre of that empire, I'm sure. Plenty of good food and drink, too. So: on to the next adventure, yes?"

§ 57.

City of Prague, Lands of the Bohemian Crown, Holy Roman Empire, 1601.

I'm glad that Tycho wanted to go to Prague.

Two centuries before, I had helped two students of mine, Mikuláš and Jan, to build an astronomical clock here, on the side of a lovely stone tower in the old town square. I often return to it. Not to think of astronomy – I do that all the time anyway – but to think of humanity, and the human point of view.

Have you seen the clock? In person I mean – not in photographs. I adore it. We painted it with nested curves to represent earth, sky, and horizon, then divided the twenty-four hours of the day. Inside that face we built a second ring, divided into the twelve zodiac signs. At last, we built two arms, one for the sun, another for the moon. Looking at it, you know exactly where you are in the cosmic wash of time, and so you know what will happen next. Where once things rose up and passed away according to their own strange laws, now those laws were codified and understood. They became our laws. We had conquered the mystery of time.

From the human point of view.

Stone, like the stone of the tower, says the opposite: some things can be frozen in place, made to defy the passing-away of things. Made to last forever. Everything in this old town square is made of stone. The cathedral, the palace, the cobbles that cover the changing earth: hard, hard stone. Yet somehow the people of this city made all this hardness seem joyful. Ornaments, mosaics, frescoes, and statues, everywhere you turned. With stones, they made their wish for the beautiful life into something you could touch. Wood, or clay, or even glass, can do that too, but there's something different about stone. Stone perseveres. Stone endures. Another conquest of time.

Again, a human point of view.

But I am here in Prague because my good boy Tycho was looking for a job. And if he was not to be the one to win my gamble for the soul of humanity, then perhaps he will point me to someone who will.

* * *

Urania waited beneath the astronomical clock on the south side of the city hall, in the old town square, in the night, in the rain.

Some of the taverns sheltered their outdoor seating under a turtle shell of canvass awnings. Groups of locals in threes and fives raced by, aiming to reach one of these shells before getting too wet. Urania sipped her hot apple cider; the landlord seemed happy to feed her as much as she wanted, seeing as her money was good, and so few others were about.

As another group ran by, she noticed a man standing almost directly beneath the clock, studying it with fascination, as drenched with rain as though he had fallen in the river. Urania felt cold on his behalf. He leaned on a long walking stick, to which a pair of old shoes had been tied near the top: the sign of a Protestant seeker.

"He comes by here every day, sometimes twice a day, that one does," said the tavern keeper, as he brought Urania another cup of hot cider. "Sometimes he takes notes."

"Do you know him?" Urania asked.

"Can't say that I do, except that whenever he comes to eat in my establishment, he's always a few crowns short."

The man might have sensed that he was being talked about; he slushed toward them, head down and walking stick tapping the ground ahead of his steps.

The landlord saw him and moved to stand between him and the awning. "You're not welcome here anymore – I keep telling you!"

The man grasped his walking stick a little more tightly. "I have enough money today –"

"We're also closed!" the tavern keeper shouted at him, and marched back to his kitchen.

Urania stood up. "*Kháìre, mein Herr*. What's your name?"

"Johannes," he said. He did not meet her eye when he spoke, which Urania found unusual. Instead, he offered his ear to whoever was speaking to him; his head tilted to one side, and down. "Do I know you?" he asked.

"I'm Urania. And yes, you do," she said. She handed him her cup of cider and said, "Drink this – you must be freezing."

Johannes drank. "Thank you. Now I don't suppose you could help me find my way home? I'm not asking for anything else, mind. Here, I'll give you three crowns right now –"

"I am not a woman of negotiable affections, sir!" Urania said, and she took back her cider.

"That is not what I'm asking. I am a married man, but my wife is in Austria right now. I need to borrow your eyes. Mine are not much good after dark. You can leave me at my doorstep, I shall ask of you no more than that."

Urania understood. She left some money on the table for the tavern keeper, took up her rain cloak and then took Johannes's arm. "Is it far to go?" she asked.

"Just the other side of the bridge," he said.

They walked together through streets whose tall houses buttressing against each other made the city feel like a deep and narrow ravine. The rain was not heavy, but it was persistent, and Urania wished she wore boots today instead of Mediterranean sandals.

"I was told you visit the clock every day," said Urania.

"Most days," Johannes confirmed. "I want to figure out how it works."

"Surely you have been inside, and seen the mechanism?"

"Of the clock, yes. But the mechanism of the *cosmos* – not so clear at all, you know?" he said. He paused as his imagination saw something in the clock which intrigued him. "Tonight, we must endure the rain to witness this marvel. On some other day, we might face heavy winds, or ice. Or the indifference of ignorant men. But this clock ticks on, regardless. Like the planets, turning on wheels greater than these, taking no notice of us. I once had this beautiful idea, that the six planets orbit the sun in the same way the six Platonic solids would do if they were nested inside each other, and turned on each other like the gears of that clock. But then I realized that would not explain their retrograde motion – oh but never mind, I don't suppose you know what I'm talking about anyway."

"I know about astronomy," Urania assured him. "I helped Tycho Brahe create his book about the new star."

"You did?" Johannes exclaimed. "How so? As a book binder? A typesetter?"

"As his tutor," Urania grinned.

Johannes raised his eyes to her face for the first time and examined her as he might do to a sculpture. He said, "I cannot see you entirely clearly – I had a touch of the pox when I was a child… but you appear far too young to have been Herr Brache's tutor."

"I live on nectar and ambrosia," Urania grinned. "They keep me in good standing with the gods."

Johannes laughed. "How astonishing to have found a woman-scholar of classics, here in Prague, as if by random chance! Perhaps the Lord brings people together when they need each other. So, you must know about the new madness taking hold of the world? The philosophy of Copernicus?"

"I do," said Urania.

"I found a way to fix it. Would you like to see it?" he asked.

Urania smirked at the familiarity of the question. "Show me," she said.

Johannes pointed to a building ahead of them. "That there wall, is the apse of the Church of the Assumption of The Virgin Mary And Of St Charles The Great. Completed around the time I was born. Most churches of this kind would have an apse in a half-circle. But do you see the shape we have there?"

"It's an oval," said Urania.

"It is. And that is what got me to think. As the planets speed up and slow down, could it be because they do not orbit in perfect circles? Could it be rather that they orbit in a shape like the apse of this church – a conic section, an oval, an ellipse?"

Urania smiled.

Johannes admired the church as he spoke, and the raindrops that fell about them, illuminated in gold for a heartbeat as the light from the candles and lamps in nearby windows reflected in them. "I know what the Bible says about this. The Earth was set in its place, and all that. But I feel as if God himself brought me to this street, so that I would see the clock, and this church, and in those things the design of His creation."

Urania's smile brightened to an ear-to-ear grin. She reached for Johannes's hands. "Would you like to –" she said, then stopped herself. The faces of other friends she had known, especially Tarquinia Molza, swam into her view for a moment.

"Yes, what is it?" Johannes asked.

Urania said, "Would you like to meet master Brahe?"

§ 58.

"Elliptical orbits?" said Tycho.

"It's the solution we've all been banging our heads together to find," said Johannes. They were in a walnut-panelled study in the Emperor's castle, where a row of narrow windows on one wall overlooked the Vltava River and the many pointed towers of the great imperial city. Johannes had taken a large sheet of paper on a table, stuck it in two places with long pins, and wrapped a loop of string around them. Then he used a charcoal stick as a third pin, to tighten the string into a triangle shape. As he moved the charcoal stick around the paper, keeping the string tight, he drew an ellipse. "Imagine the sun is one of those pins. The distance between the planet and the sun increases in exact proportion to how the distance between the planet and the other pin decreases," he said. "The total length of the two lines always stays the same. So there's no circles. But still: there is symmetry, elegance, perfection."

"What does the other pin represent? A black sun?" Tycho chortled at him.

"No, it's only a mathematical point, like the equant points in old Ptolemy's system," Kepler explained.

"But as everyone knows, *circles* are the only mathematically perfect shape," Tycho said.

"What is a circle," said Johannes, "but an ellipse in which the two focal points are in the exact same position?"

Tycho stroked his beard. "Interesting. Go on," he said.

"I also found a way to account for the relative velocities," said Johannes. "The planets hasten their flight as they approach the sun; they slow again as they fly away. It is as if the sun gives them some kind of vigorousness. Some kind of – I don't have the word... *gravitas*? Never mind. Now, suppose you could count the time as the planet moved. Choose a place where the planet is close to the sun, and moving quickly, like here. Now we draw a line from the planet to the sun... " he drew the line, "and then wait for whatever length of time you like as the planet goes by, then draw another line. See we have a triangle, with one side being the curvature of the orbit. Now we do that again when the planet is far from the sun and moving slower. Two lines, after the planet has moved for the same unit of time as before. Now we have two triangles. And this is the beautiful part: the area of these two triangles will be exactly the same. Any two triangles like this, anywhere along the orbit, will always have the same area. Every time."

"You have measurements for this?" Tycho asked. "Daily observations? Evidence?"

Johannes hesitated, then said, "I have some small difficulty using the optical equipment. My eyes –"

"Your eyes are good enough to draw this diagram, they're good enough to use an astrolabe," Tycho chided him. He handed Johannes a cross staff and said, "Take this to the window and tell me the angular distance between the two highest church towers you can see."

Johannes took the cross staff to the window and faced his back to Tycho. But Tycho moved to lean on the windowsill, where Johannes could not hide that he was fumbling.

"Just another moment... I almost have it," Kepler mumbled.

Tycho lost patience and took the instrument away. "Enough! I need an assistant who can actually measure things, and who won't complain about it. I gave you a chance because Miss Urania recommended you. But I won't hire you if you cannot do the work!"

Johannes glared at Tycho for a heartbeat. Then he rolled up the paper, ripping holes in it where his pins had stuck through, and marched out of the room.

Urania had been waiting for him in the hall. "Did he accept you?" she asked.

"The man is a fathead," Johannes spat. "Wouldn't look at my proofs unless I had ephemeris tables as long as this castle is tall."

He kept marching down the hall. Urania said, "Stay here, let me talk to him."

"What would be the point?"

"He listens to me," Urania said. Johannes rolled his eyes, but he found a bench in the hall and sat down.

Urania entered Tycho's study. "I take it you didn't like him?" she asked.

Tycho was recreating Johannes' elliptical orbit diagram with a new sheet of paper. "In fact, I think he is a genius," Tycho said. "He solved the most intractable problem of the new philosophy, merely by *thinking* about it. Like he had the whole of the cosmos contained in his head. As above, so below. Genius."

Urania didn't expect that. "So, then, you will hire him as your assistant?"

"Never," Tycho swore. "For all his genius, he cannot do something as elementary as handle a cross staff. Even my wife knows how to do that."

"Why is it surprising that a woman can use a cross staff?" Urania grunted.

Tycho remembered who he was talking to. "Sorry," he mumbled.

Urania said, "Johannes has the imagination, and he has already proven himself with his laws of planetary motion. You are the only one who has ephemeris tables accurate enough and complete enough for him to go any further."

"They're not complete yet," Tycho said.

"With your measurements and his brain attacking them, they will be."

Tycho glared at her for a breath, then said, "Is he waiting outside?"

"Yes," she said.

Tycho gestured that she should let him in, Urania opened the door and Johannes entered, hat in his hands, head down.

"Well?" said Tycho.

"When I was six years old," said Johannes, "I saw a comet in the sky. I had never seen anything so strange and wonderful before."

"You were six – of course you didn't," Tycho snapped.

Johannes bit his lip, then continued. "Years later, as a student of mathematics, I learned that you yourself had measured the parallax of that self-same comet, and you found that it travelled through the orbits of the planets. Through the crystal spheres! From which you therefore deduced that there are no crystal spheres. *That* is the kind of work I want to do, as a philosopher and as a man. To dispel the false, so that we may find the way to the real and the true."

Tycho regarded Johannes through narrowed eyes and under a furrowed brow.

When Johannnes could not wait for a reply any longer he said, "Sir, I can see I am not needed. I apologize for wasting your time." He turned to leave.

"Hold," said Tycho, and Johannes turned back.

"I am now fifty-three years old," said Tycho. "It is a difficult age at which to let go of an old life and to start another one afresh. The Emperor has commissioned me to produce a new star atlas and new ephemeris tables. With the observations I have made so far, and your young and nimble mind, perhaps we can –"

"Yes! Thank you, yes!" Johannes burst forth. He shook Tycho's hands so vigorously that Tycho had to adjust the setting of his prosthetic nose. "This will be glorious. We shall have to name them The Tychonian Tables! They shall be –"

"Named for the Emperor. The Rudolphine Tables," Tycho reminded him.

"Of course," Johannes corrected himself. "And they will be the new last word in all natural philosophy. I shall write to my family and have them join me here at once. It's an honour to work with you, sir, an honour of the highest order!"

He hugged Urania, who pressed her arms to her sides to try and preserve some personal space. Then he floated out of the room, singing a song.

Tycho shook his head. "This boy Johannes Kepler had better do what he's told," he said.

Urania said, "I hope he will do much more."

§ 59.

A crowd gathered in the courtyard of Prague Castle. Its great outer doors opened, and a parade of jesters, minstrels, jugglers, clowns, torchbearers, and other costumed characters fell out, to the delight of the imperial family and their guests at the tables. A herald at the head of the parade, costumed all in gold including a helmet that bore a pair of dove's wings, blew a long trumpet and announced, "Behold, mortals! I, Mercury, the herald of the gods, announce the arrival of the spirits of the arts, the Nine Muses! Here to bestow their blessings upon our glorious Emperor, upon the good people of Bohemia, and our Holy Roman Empire!"

The audience of aristocrats and courtiers burst into applause. Some rose to their feet and welcomed the parade with a toast of their wine cups. A group of men pulling a wagon entered the courtyard next, following close behind the revellers at the head of the parade. The wagon they pulled was the throne of an actress, masked and costumed as a muse, and carrying a writing tablet.

"Behold: Calliope, the muse of epic poetry!" said Mercury, and the actress showered the guests with flower petals. They cheered for her, and the parade musicians played a chorus for her.

Although Tycho was likewise on his feet and applauding, Kirsten, at his side, remained at her seat, wearing a frown.

"This is paganism, through and through," she grumbled.

A man beside them said, "This sort of spectacle is quite common all over Italy now. Even in Rome."

"You have seen such a thing there?" Tycho asked him.

"Many times. Some are better than others, naturally; it depends on who is paying for it. Oh, I'm Julian Augustus. Advisor to His Holiness the Pope in matters of military strategy and the arts of war," he introduced himself.

"Tycho Brahe, imperial astronomer," Tycho return the introduction. "And my wife Kirsten Jørgansdatter."

"Honoured to meet you both," Julian said.

Another wagon entered the courtyard, and Mercury introduced the goddess seated upon it: "Erato, the muse of love poetry!" The actress carried a lyre, wore a mask with bright red lips, and was otherwise entirely naked.

Addressing Kirsten, Julian said, "You appear troubled by the pageantries."

"My father was a Lutheran priest," she replied. "I was raised *properly*."

"We all went to Mass this morning," said Julian. "We said the prayers, and paid our respects to God. So now we are free to live the good life."

"You cannot appease God with rituals," said Kirsten. "The path to salvation is through faith, and work, and doing penance for your sins."

"Come now, madam, this is all a show anyway. There's no harm in it. The Great Father created the muses to bring happiness to the world. To remind us that life is good. So eat, drink, sing, celebrate yourselves! Here, your good man husband will show you how." Julian touched Tycho's forehead and said, "You will stay here at the feast until it is over, and you will eat every kind of food and drink that anyone puts in front of you."

Tycho made no obvious response to Julian's command. But he snatched a few grapes from a passing waiter who carried a bowl of mixed fruit and pushed them into his mouth.

"Enjoy the party!" said Julian, and he bowed and walked away.

Kirsten grabbed his hands before he could take more food from a nearby table, and said, "What – you'll do what a stranger tells you, but you won't take advice from me? Your wife?"

Tycho shrugged. "But he's right. Life *is* meant to be enjoyed, isn't it? Come my love, have some grapes."

Kirsten sat down and ate a single grape.

Julian, meanwhile, caught up with the waiter, tapped him on the forehead, and said, "Make sure that man," he pointed to Tycho, "never runs out of food. All night."

§ 60.

When the feast was over, Tycho had to lean on Kirsten's shoulder to walk home.

"I told you that you were eating too much," she chided him.

"But how could I say no? This was a feast for the Emperor – if I had refused his generosity, he would have been insulted! It is not wise to insult an emperor – ooh!"

He bent to one knee and winced. He squeezed his groin, attempting to control the pain. When he felt ready to walk again, he could only limp. He loosened his belt. It didn't help.

"What are you doing?" said Kirsten.

Tycho stumbled again. Through a tight-squeezed face he said, "I can't walk. I can't walk!"

Julian saw Tycho's pain and Kirsten's struggle to carry him.

"Hell of a night, wasn't it?" said Julian, as he sauntered near. "Come, let me help you."

"Very kind of you, sir," said Tycho.

"It's my Christian duty to help," said Julian, "and my pleasure."

Tycho reached out with a faltering arm, and Julian took it. Leaning on both Julian and Kirsten, he lurched over the cobblestone streets, down the hill from the castle, and to the guest house where he and Kirsten rented their rooms. At its threshold, he touched Kirsten's forehead and told her, "Go find a doctor. I'll take care of him from here."

Kirsten gave her husband a quick kiss and left to find a doctor.

When she was gone, Julian smiled. "Now, let's get you upstairs."

* * *

Your history books probably say that Tycho died when he drank too much one night which caused his bladder to burst. I always suspected that Julian poisoned him. But I could never prove it. And Tycho never needed much encouragement to eat and drink more than his fill. Such a big-hearted man, he lived a big-hearted life.

But I had almost no time to mourn him. I feared that Julian's attention would fall upon the other great mathematical genius in this city, and Tycho's collaborator. Johannes Kepler.

§ 61.

Tycho's funeral took place in the Cathedral of Our Lady Before Tyn, an imposing yet iconic landmark that stood across Prague's old town square from the astronomical clock. Urania remained by his coffin after most of the mourners had left.

"I barely knew him, and we did not get along," said Johannes. "Yet here I am, grieving like he was my best friend."

"The last time I spoke to him," Urania said to Johannes, "he agreed to leave you his papers. So long as you use them to finish the Rudolphine Tables."

Johannes acknowledged it with a nod. "I'm to take over the project, then?"

"If you want it."

Johannes only shrugged in reply. A monk swept the floor with a straw broom. Another cleaned the wax drippings from a candelabra with a small knife.

"It's important work," Urania said. "It will be the standard, for generations to come."

"Generations of astrologers and fortune tellers and false prophets. Fatheads and peddlers of nonsense, all of them," Johannes scorned.

"Natural philosophers will use it, too," Urania said. "Seekers of truth. Women and men, just like you."

A cat scurried down the cathedral's transepts, chasing a mouse.

Johannes said, "I should like very much to continue Herr Brache's work. But I should like to do it in my own way. Not like those dull and empty astrologers who say the planets are carried by currents in a sea of ether. I want to investigate the *physical* causes. I want to show that the machine of the universe is not similar to a divine animated being, but similar to a clock."

"A clock?" said Urania.

"The one in the town square, where I first met you," Johannes asked. "It's elegant, functional, beautiful, a thing to marvel and wonder about. But it is *not miraculous*. It is a work of human hands, human thought. If it seems mysterious to some, that is only because they have not looked at it closely enough. In truth, nothing about it is mysterious, everything about it can be fully understood. My aim in astronomy is the same: a complete and perfect understanding of everything. If the Emperor considers that aim to be heresy, then I cannot work for him."

The cat wandered back into view, with a dead mouse hanging in its jaws.

"Then do you not believe in the soul?" asked the muse. "or in beauty? *Aletheia*? *Logos*? *Agathon*?"

"I believe in God," said Johannes. "But my god is not a silly old man with a beard who lives in a cloud. My god is God, creator of heaven and earth. The best way to love Him is to *know* Him, and the best way to know Him is to study his works, penetrating all mysteries with the power of reason that God himself bestowed upon us. The only heresy is to throw His gifts away. The gift of reason. The gift of this beautiful world."

Three monks gathered nearby and pried up some flagstones from the floor. They mentioned that Tycho would be buried there, and that a memorial stone had been commissioned to mark the spot.

Urania opened and closed and opened her hands, each time leaning to offer them to Johannes, then hesitating, and drawing them back.

"Something wrong?" Johannes asked her.

"No," she replied. Then she stood. "Come outside, I want to show you something."

Johannes puzzled at her for a moment, then accepted her invitation. They stepped out of the cathedral, to the centre of the old town square.

"What is it?" Johannes asked.

Urania took his hands. The city of Prague fell away beneath them, then Bohemia, then all of Europe, and the stars opened before them. The planets swung round their courses. Johannes held his breath, awed by the sight.

"I was right – elliptical orbits – I was right!" he cried.

Urania grinned. "Yes, you were!"

Then Johannes looked to Urania. He saw her one golden eye and one silver, and the speckles of stars in her midnight hair. "You're a nephilim! A succubus!"

"I am your friend, Johannes," she countered. "I am here to help you."

But Johannes did not want to hear. He closed his eyes and recited a prayer of protection: "*Pater noster, qui es in caelis, sanctificetur nomen tuum-*"

Urania released his hands, and Johannes found himself in the town square again. Fewer than a dozen people wandered about, on their way to a tavern, or on their home from one. None appeared to have noticed that anything happened.

"What was that?" he asked.

"It was the clockwork of the cosmos," said Urania. "Exactly as you wanted to see. Don't be afraid. You can look again, if you wish."

"Get away from me, *diabolus*," Johannes grunted, and staggered back. "I don't want to see you ever again!"

He spun around and dashed back into the cathedral, leaving her standing alone.

Urania studied the cobblestones of the square for a while. Then she wandered away, toward the clock. The same tavern keeper across from it waved to her as he cleaned the tables. Seated at one of them, Urania saw Kynisca, with a bottle of wine and two goblets to share it. Urania flew to her side and hugged her.

"Urania! There you are!" Kynisca sang.

"So good to see you," Urania said. She dropped herself into a seat at the table, and drank some wine straight from the bottle.

"You're having a good day today," Kynisca quipped.

"The best," Urania replied. She contemplated the town clock for a moment, then asked, "When was the last time you went to Olympus?"

"Oh, I visit once every two or three years, usually," Kynisca replied. "But I don't stay long. I see a few friends from my days as a competitor at the games. We sing the old songs, do a bit of *pankration*, dance around the fire like we used to do. Then I go back home."

"Does anyone ask about me?"

"Oh yes! I saw some of your sisters, the last time I was there. Polly found out you are singing again; she's very proud of you. Clio has a copy of every book you've inspired someone to write. And Thalia –"

"I can easily guess what *she* would say!" Urania grinned, and Kynisca laughed with her. Then Urania said, "I wish they would come down here and visit me. Not even my own mother has come down here to see me," said the unhappy philosopher, and she drank from the bottle again, ignoring the goblet Kynisca had poured for her.

"I think some of them are afraid to be seen with you, in case they lose favour with the inner circle," Kynisca said.

"But you're not afraid," Urania observed.

"Olympus was never the centre of my life," Kynisca explained. "Back at home, I have my training camp and my horses, my family and my friends. A simple life. It's all I need."

"You don't want to explore the world?" Urania asked. "Or create things? Maybe start a school for horse trainers? You'd be good at it."

Kynisca said, "I'm tired of horses now. I've been thinking about breeding rabbits." Then, seeing Urania's disbelieving look, she broke into laughter.

"You really had me there," Urania said, enjoying her gullibility.

"Too easy," Kynisca grinned. "But seriously. It's been good to follow you and your philosophers around. Stopping assassins, breaking up bar fights, or starting them – I haven't had this much fun in ages."

Urania smiled. But soon after, she closed her eyes and said, "I'm going to be banished from Olympus forever, aren't I?"

Kynisca gave her friend a kind smile, but said nothing, refusing to be the one to deliver the bad news. Then she nodded toward the Prague town clock and said, "But you know, up there on Olympus, they still use sundials."

Urania smiled again, then she laughed.

Kynisca ordered another bottle of wine.

Brendan Myers

Book Five: Galileo

§ 62.

Near Padua, Lands of the Serene Republic of Venice, 1603.

That day in Prague, I buried one of my students, and lost another to his fears, all in the same hour. And what was worse: losing them might have had nothing to do with Julian. And if that was true, then Julian might have been right. He might not have to lift a finger to win our bargain. And if that was true... and if I kept trying to win it anyway.

Do you remember how Prometheus warned me, that if I carried on working with Copernicus, my father would torture me, imprison me, or in some way destroy me, every day, for eternity? By banishing me to live among the mortals, then holding out a bauble that I could chase but never catch, he did none of those things. And yet he did all of them.

Sisyphus and Cassandra had it easy.

But I was still determined to win. The stars showed me my next student was in Italy – the same country where Prometheus told me to look. Much as I didn't want to admit the old man might have been right, I had nowhere else to go. So Kynisca and I went back to Padua. Galileo was still a professor of mathematics there. We found him visiting some friends of his, in a cottage outside of town.

But Julian got there ahead of us.

* * *

"I've nothing to say to you!" shouted Urania.

"Like it or not," said Julian, as he followed her up the narrow country lane, "we have things to talk about." He took a wild plum off one of the trees in the lane's hedgerow.

"Giordano Bruno is dead," Urania seethed. "Catherine de Parthenay, forced back to France. Tycho Brahe is dead. Johannes Kepler is half blind –"

"None of those are my fault," Julian grinned. He bit the plum, decided it was too sour, and tossed it back into the hedgerow. "Well, maybe Kepler's eyes."

"You are the one who lured Giordano to Venice where he was arrested. You *had* to have known that they would kill him – that's what you wanted, wasn't it? Either that, or you really are as stupid as your toga makes you look."

Julian touched the purple sash of his imperial Roman toga, which he wore under a cloak. "This is the colour of royalty. Men once bowed and scattered before me when I wore it. And look at you – dressed like one of *them*. Have you forgotten who you are?"

Urania fingered the collar of her giornea, a sleeveless outer garment popular among Florentine women. Though its pattern was plain, and her bodice, chemise, and skirt were similarly plain, they were made of silk and brocade, which gave a noticeable shimmer to their colours in the dim light of the moon.

"Have *you* forgotten that your empire does not exist anymore?" she told him.

"Then let us return to the present. You're on your way to see Master Galilei, are you not?" Julian gestured to a cottage at the end of the lane.

"What about him," Urania monotoned.

"I believe the old man wanted you to meet him. He certainly caught my attention. His spirit *screams* with your kind of questions. Strange that you seemed reluctant to introduce yourself, until tonight."

"I'm choosing my own students," she told him. "I'm not letting him or anyone else choose them for me."

"But you are still attracted to his soul," Julian crooned. "It is your *hamartia*. Deny it if you will, but your nature will always betray you. And this is the perfect time of night for doing that thing you do."

"Get to the point, Julian," Urania muttered.

Julian grinned, nodded toward Galileo's cottage, and continued. "I *dare* you to show Galileo everything, right now," he said. "Same as you did to Giordano. No preparation this time. No warning, no hesitation. Show him the cosmos as you did Nicolaus, and Catherine, and what's-her-name Tycho's sister –"

"How did you know about her?"

Julian ignored the question, "and show him tonight. You will see that even the smartest man of his age, the best mortal brain on earth, cannot grasp his true place in the cosmos. If he *can*, well, you will have won the original bargain, and Father Zeus will have to open the gates of Olympus to you again."

Urania stood still, and regarded Julian, waiting with folded arms and glowering eyes for him to get out of her path.

"You're thinking about it," Julian crooned.

"No," Urania decided.

"Yes, you are. I can tell."

"I mean, no – I won't have him for my student," Urania clarified. "Like I told you, I choose my own students now." She spun around, and walked down the path from which she came, away from the cottage.

Julian followed her. "In that cottage where master Galilei is staying the night," he explained, "there is an ingenious system of vents and air ducts that connect to a cave. They open it during the day, to keep the house cool. And they close it at night, so that the fumes from all the dead things down there don't make them sick while they're sleeping. But since you have decided that master Galilei is not one of your people, then it should not matter to you that someone forgot to close the vent today, and that the air in the cottage is slowly poisoning everyone inside."

Urania ran to the cottage, flung open the shutters on one of the windows, and sniffed the air. It was cold, and carried the trace of carrion, feces, and the dankness of stagnant water. She suppressed an urge to retch. Then she dashed for the door, but Julian stepped in front of her before she could open it.

"You're going to let him die if I don't take him as my student?" Urania accused him.

"Not your student, not your concern," he replied.

Urania dashed around the cottage to find another way in, but found none; there was only one door, and all the windows were too high off the ground, or too small. She came around to the front again, where Julian leaned on the door frame, his ankles crossed, his fingers playing with a ring of keys.

"Why the rush, Julian?" Urania asked. "Why do you want to settle this tonight?"

"Just imagine," he said, "you could be back home again, with your sisters, as soon as tomorrow morning, if you can bring Professor Galilei to the light."

"And if he does not see what I show him?"

"Then you admit, before the throne of your father and in the presence of the highest gods, that I am right about humanity. And you give up your foolish quest. No more searching for others. After all, if a straight-up genius like him cannot win it for you, then obviously no one can. There will be no *point* in going on."

"You still haven't told me why the rush," Urania reminded him. "Why now? What's changed?"

"Nothing," Julian said, with one brow perked. "I'm just tired of this. Aren't you?"

"I'm tired of your interference," she growled at him.

"But you told me master Galilei is not your student. So, speaking precisely, I am not interfering."

Urania folded her arms. "If I choose him, then I want time to evaluate him, and one night won't be enough."

"Do you want to drag this game on forever?" Julian countered. "We could repeat this pleasant conversation every time another student of yours proves me right. Until we both die of boredom. Or we could finish it, tonight, and then get on with our lives."

"What kind of life do you think I'm living?" Urania shot back. "I have no home anymore!"

"But just imagine, you could be home again tomorrow," he tempted her again.

A new voice entered the conversation. "She can test him in her own time. Otherwise, it won't be a fair gamble."

Julian looked for the source of the voice. It came from Catherine de Parthenay, who had been watching from inside a nearby stable. She stepped into the moonlight and let herself be known to him. Julian bridled his surprise and smiled for her. "I sensed another Olympian nearby. I should have known it would be you."

"Furthermore," Catherine continued, "you will observe from a distance, and not interfere."

Julian put on an offended face. "I've never directly interfered in her student's lives," he pleaded.

"Directly, *or indirectly*, you will not interfere," Catherine repeated. "And we will be watching you. If you want Galileo to be her last student, then we want you off the board. If bishop takes knight, then rook takes bishop."

Julian said, "Or, knight takes queen, checkmate in three." He nodded toward the cottage door and breathed a deep satisfied breath. "I love the night air. So good for the constitution."

Catherine waved toward a nearby copse of trees. The sound of horse clopping and wagon wheels emerged from it. The silhouette of Kynisca, leading her horse by the reins, soon appeared; and as she approached the cottage Julian saw the horse was pulling a wagon which carried the sleeping Galileo on a bed of straw.

"While Urania kept you distracted," said Catherine, "Kynisca and I got here in time to rescue master Galilei. Though not soon enough for two of his friends."

Julian wanted to crush her with his glare. The muscles in his cheeks flexed as he ground his teeth.

"Knight takes knight," Catherine said to him. "Your move."

"All right," Julian said. "I'll give you what you want. No interference from me. But I am watching."

Urania said, "So are we."

Julian grunted something incoherent and marched away.

Kynisca joined Catherine and Urania, and squeezed their hands and laughed like schoolgirls awake past their bedtimes. But they ducked their heads lest Julian hear them.

"Catherine – brilliant timing!" Urania praised her.

"The look on his face when he saw me!" Catherine marvelled.

"When he saw Galileo, too!" Kynisca added.

"We should take him some place where he can recover," said Urania. She and Kynisca moved to take Galileo away, but Catherine did not move to follow.

"I can't be seen to help you again," Catherine said. "If anyone in the Academy thinks that we are working together like this –"

"I know," said Urania. "And you're right."

"Don't be in a rush to test him. Choose your time and place, don't let anyone else choose it for you. And if you need a home away from home, my salon in La Rochelle is yours."

Urania kissed her cheeks, and then hiked over the meadow with Kynisca, and Galileo still asleep in the cart.

§ 63.

Julian placed the offering of incense into the brazier of glowing coals at the foot of the statue of Zeus, then stepped back and sat on the marble floor.

"I had to do it," he said. "I know you asked me to use subtler weapons. And I understand that: we don't want the other great pantheons to notice what we're doing. But I had to do it."

A distant but firm round of thunder supplied Zeus' answer.

"It wasn't *me* who killed Tycho Brahe," Julian pleaded. "I only turned one of his own vices against him. It was the same for that Italian fanatic: I only arranged to have him arrested for the heresies he proclaimed on his own. Of course I knew what the mortals would do to him. But they're the ones who did it, not me! And now there's this fast-talking Italian sophist, Galileo. She's getting too close. She might win the bargain with either one of them – I had to do it!"

Footsteps echoed in the temple from behind him. Julian risked a slight turn of his head, hoping to glimpse his master. But the footsteps stopped and resumed only when he put his head straight and down again.

That is not the reason I summoned you here, said Zeus, his voice seemingly coming from everywhere in the temple, and from high above it in the sky.

Julian sat up a little straighter. "So, I was right to have them killed?"

Your mistake is that you think our enemy is a man, and so you have been looking for a man to kill.

Julian grinned. "Of course, I understand now. Our enemy is that scuff-bearded battering ram, Prometheus –"

Our enemy is an idea! Zeus growled at him, his voice punctuated by another distant roll of thunder.

Kill a man, and another will rise to take his place. Kill an idea, and men will no longer think about rising.

"I understand, my lord," said Julian, his head bowed.

Do you? I shall be watching.

The footsteps moved away. When the temple was silent again, Julian turned to look, and found himself alone.

§ 64.

In his office in a palace in Rome, Robert Bellarmine, now blessed with the red cap of a cardinal, thumbed the pages of Copernicus' book, *De Revolutionibus*. Its leather-wrapped covers gave a weight, not only to the physical volume, but also to its ideas.

"As you can see," said Julian, "the majority of the book is composed of long columns of numbers. Diagrams. But taken together, all these numbers assume the astonishing claim that –"

"I'm aware of the contents of this book," said the cardinal. He leaned back in his chair. Sunlight from the window behind him streamed on to the desk, spotlighting a page with a diagram of the solar system, and diffusing on to the cardinal himself.

"But are you aware of how fast its ideas are traveling?" Julian said. "People are talking about it in marketplaces, guild halls, army barracks– they're beginning to doubt the infallibility of Scripture."

"A little bit of doubt is healthy," Bellarmine dismissed it. "But most people soon find that without the guidance of Holy Mother Church, they are left with only emptiness and despair. Then they come back to us. I never worry for long about our prodigal sons."

"Brother Giordano was unrepentant to the end," Julian reminded him.

"Yes, well," said the cardinal, "He was not nursing his doubts in private. His heresy endangered the souls of others."

"You're going to see more and more such men in the future, if this book," he tapped the open page of the book with his knuckles, "is not suppressed."

"Very few people read this book," said Bellarmine. "Fewer still understand it. And of them, most can see its intrinsic absurdity.

Suppressing that book will only make it interesting to our enemies. Better to ignore it. Let it disappear by itself."

Julian shook his head. "Are you hearing what the Protestants are saying about it? And about the Church, for not officially condemning it? Look..." he took a pamphlet from a satchel, "Martin Luther himself condemned Copernicus in writing."

Bellarmine took the pamphlet and read it out loud: "'There is talk of a new astrologer who wants to prove that the Earth moves and goes around instead of the sky, the sun, the moon, just as if somebody were moving in a carriage or ship might believe that he was sitting still while the earth and the trees walked and moved. But that is how things are nowadays: when a man wishes to be clever he must invent something special. But as Holy Scripture tells us, Joshua bid the sun to stand still, and not the Earth.'" He dropped the pamphlet on his desk and smirked at it. "I'll say this for Luther: he had a talent for wordsmithing."

Julian enjoyed the joke with him. Then said, "Still, people are saying the Protestants are more committed to the Bible than we are."

Bellarmine leaned forward again. "Well. We cannot have that," he said.

"No, your Eminence, we cannot."

Bellarmine closed the book, then rose and held out his hand. Julian rose and kissed the cardinal's ring, though he kept his eyes up, meeting Bellarmine's gaze.

§ 65.

Padua, Republic of Venice, 1609.

"For all the problems in mathematics that Doctor Copernicus has solved for us," said Galileo, as he opened his copy of *De Revolutionibus*. "Still, he did create some new ones. The one that troubles me is that nobody can account for why all planets orbit the sun, and yet the moon still orbits the Earth. It never comes closer to us, nor dallies further away. During an eclipse it covers the sun almost perfectly, every time. Why is the moon the odd one? What do you think?"

Brendan Myers

His students sat around his dining room the table, looking at each other.

"No one has any idea?" said Galileo. "Or is everyone waiting for someone else to speak first?"

His students chuckled, and Galileo grinned. "There is no shame in admitting you do not know something," he said. "I once heard Giordano Bruno say as much, and he had the best mathematical mind of anyone I have ever met. The only shame, he used to say, would be in not trying to find the answers out."

"I heard that they burned him for heresy," said one of the students. "Is that true?"

"They did," said Galileo, as he sat down. "Which is why I host these classes here in my home, in secret. Our republic owes nothing to Rome. You all know that they excommunicated the Doge and the senate – all the same, critics of Rome are not safe here. Not more than two years ago, a gang of footpads attempted to murder our friend Paolo, for denying the doctrine of the Divine Right of Kings. Right here, in La Serenissima."

Paolo Scarpi, sitting among the students, brushed back his hair so that others could see the scar on his right temple and cheek.

"So, mind who you speak to about these meetings," Galileo concluded. "Someone tells you he's a Protestant: what should you do?"

"Get it in writing, you can't trust anyone," the others answered together, and they grinned.

"If there are no other questions?" said Galileo. Seeing none, he said. "Then goodnight and be safe to your homes."

Galileo moved to the door of the dining room, to collect his student's fees as they left. Paolo Scarpi remained at the table, pouring himself some wine in a delicate long-stemmed Venetian glass goblet. "You don't mind?" he asked.

"Not at all, help yourself," Galileo offered, and poured a glass for himself. "It's not every day that an advisor to the Doge pays me a house call."

"You were teaching Copernicus. There are rumours going around that the pope is soon to place his works on the Index. I wanted to know what the fuss was all about, while it's still allowed." Then Paolo produced a letter for Galileo and said, "I also come bearing a commission from the Doge, for ten more of your geometrical compasses."

Galileo grinned and took the letter. "Tell him I'm happy to oblige! I can give you one of them right now." Galileo jumped up and took out of a nearby cabinet a small metal device resembling a quadrant, with arms that could be opened or closed, an arc between them, and several inscribed lines and moving cursors.

"Marvellous things. But I haven't the head to figure how they work," Paolo said.

"Here, I can show you –"

"Not tonight, but thank you," Paolo said.

Galileo handed him the calculator and sat down again. "I can invent for you a thing to tell what angle to point your guns so you hit the enemy ships before they can hit yours. I only wish I could invent a thing to see the look on the captain's face when we sink him."

"Oh, there *is* such a thing – I forgot to tell you," said Paolo. "A merchant from Holland passed through Venice recently. A maker of spectacles and lenses. He told a story about how he was looking through two of his lenses at the same time, quite accidentally, and they made the house across the road from his workshop appear close enough to touch. So he put two lenses on either side of a long tube, one lens bigger than the other. You look through the smaller lens and point it at something. Instantly, it's there in front of you. I think he called it a spyglass. The most astonishing thing I've ever seen."

Galileo remained in silent thought for a moment after Paulo finished describing the Dutch merchant's device. When Paolo grew uncomfortable, he said, "Hello?"

"It was a tube, with two lenses? That was all?" Galileo asked.

"Yes, I believe so."

"Concave lenses or convex? Or one of each?"

"I'm afraid I don't know the meaning of those words."

"Did the glass bulge out of the lens like a ball, or curve into it like a cup?"

"Ah. Like a ball."

"Convex, then. And how long was the tube?"

Paolo held out his hands to the width of his shoulders. "About this long."

"How wide the bigger lens?"

"Like the palm of my hand, perhaps? I didn't look closely, there was a sort of hood, or shade, around it."

"And the smaller?"

"The size of my eye."

"Perchance did the merchant sell one to the Doge that I can examine?"

Paolo sighed. "Not to my knowledge. The merchant said it was a children's toy. A curiosity."

"It is nothing of the sort at all," Galileo declared with authority. "A man with such a device would be the first to tell whether a distant ship is coming for war or for trade. He could be the first to raise the alarm. Or the first to meet it at the dock and bargain for its goods."

Paolo slapped the table. "By God, you are right! Why did no one of us think of that, at the time?"

"Perhaps the novelty of holding it in your hands?" Galileo suggested. "I suppose I would be as curious as a child, myself, too. But even so: Venice must possess this device. It may turn out to be more important than my compass."

"I will recommend it to the Doge myself," Paolo said. "You are proving quite indispensable to the republic, master Galilei. Especially to its arsenal."

"Thank you, kindly," Galileo grinned, "I shall remember you said that the next time my contract at the university comes up for renewal."

Paolo laughed. "No need; I myself shall not forget it." Then he rose and picked up his hat. "And now, if you don't mind – I have never entirely recovered from the attack," he tapped the stab wound on his face, "and I need to find my guest house and sleep in it. Sometimes I feel like I could sleep for two whole days at once."

Galileo rose, and handed Paolo his coat. "I have felt the same, ever since the night I caught the chill," he said.

"Goodnight, professor. Thank you for letting me join your meeting tonight."

"*Mio amico*. Come back any time."

As Paolo left the room, Urania entered through another door. She wore a servant's uniform and carried a small tray of damp cloths. She picked up the two long-stemmed Venetian glasses that Galileo and Paolo had been drinking from."*Khâîre*, master Galilei."

"Leave one of them, please; I'm going to take my tonic soon," Galileo asked her.

"Yes sir," she said. She began cleaning the other glass. "I heard you talking about the spyglass," she said.

"Fascinating device, yes. I would pay good money to have one," said Galileo.

"Well, sir, it seems to me, you could use it to look at *anything* that's far away. Ships at sea, distant mountaintops, *the moon* –"

"The moon!" Galileo burst out. "Perhaps the view through a spyglass would be the nearest thing to walking on it. I've often wondered what that would be like. How much of tonight's meeting did you hear?"

"Almost all of it, sir," Urania told him. "And I was thinking... if Copernicus is right, that the orbits of Mercury and Venus are inside the orbit of the Earth, then they would have phases, like the moon. And if you had a spyglass –"

"Then I could see them and that would be the *proof* that Copernicus was right!" Galileo gasped. He leapt up from his seat, almost breaking his wine glass; Urania caught it in time. He ransacked a cabinet for some paper, an inkwell, and a quill. "Bring me some more paper, and more ink. I'm not waiting for any Dutchman to return to Venice. I'm going to design and build my own!"

Urania grinned.

§ 66.

Galileo sat on a rooftop terrace, with his new spyglass balanced on a three-legged stand, so that its smaller lens was nearly level with the height of his eye. A wooden board lying across his lap served as a desk, on which he sketched an image of the half-moon as he saw it through the telescope. Urania stood nearby, looking at the same moon in the sky, smiling.

"I see mountains on the moon – white mountains, and shadowed valleys, round like lakes. Isn't that the most extraordinary news you have heard all year? Mountains on the moon!" Galileo exclaimed.

"There are mountains on Mars, as well," Urania told him.

"Hmm. This device cannot bring me close enough to see them," Galileo said, as he turned his instrument toward the bright red beacon of Mars, his thoughts still transfixed by the night's revelations. "I must build a larger one. Mountains on Mars – what makes you think so?"

Urania smiled. "If the Earth and the moon can have mountains, so can other planets."

"I noticed something about Jupiter," Galileo said, re-orienting his spyglass again, as he was too excited to stay on one thought for long. "It's too far away to see if there are any mountains. But I did see four new stars, very close to it. Jupiter is brighter than them, by far and away. But these four others… there's something about them. It is as if Jupiter is not one planet, but five."

Urania put his hand on her shoulder. "Give those stars close attention. Map their positions relative to Jupiter on every clear night. I think they will surprise you."

"How so?"

Urania shrugged, and smiled. "They might solve a problem you described to your students last month. Have you looked at Saturn yet?"

"Not yet. Is he in the sky tonight?"

Urania pointed at a dim yellow light near the horizon.

"There he is," Galileo grinned. He pointed the spyglass to it, looked in, and then pulled his head away, as though the view had suddenly gone black. He cleaned the lenses with a pocket cloth, and looked back in. "What am I seeing – Saturn has *ears*!" he said.

Urania laughed. "Ears? May I see them?"

"By all means!" Galileo got up and let her take his place.

Saturn was too distant to get a clear image of its disk through Galileo's spyglass, but what did show through was two hazy wedge-shaped spots on either side of it.

"Oh! Haha – you mean the rings!" she said.

"The what?"

"Saturn's rings," Urania grinned. "I often wondered how you would describe them the first time you saw them."

"You're speaking in riddles tonight," Galileo said. "As if you knew about them years ago."

"I did," she told him.

Galileo blinked. "You bought one of those merchant's spyglasses? And you didn't tell me?"

"No, I don't need one."

"Then how did you know about Saturn's ears?"

Urania answered him with a mischievous smile.

Galileo said, "I gather that the new Greek-speaking serving girl in my household was not always a serving girl – am I right? Don't answer that – I already know that I'm right. Well, if the sky can be full of surprises, then so can people."

"That, I can tell you, is quite true," Urania smiled.

Galileo touched her shoulder and said, "Let me have another look in there."

Urania gave him back his seat. He examined Saturn in silence for a while, though occasionally making noises of astonishment.

When he sat up again, Urania said "There's something else I would like you to see." She pointed the telescope to the Milky Way and gestured for him to look.

"You're pointing the telescope at nothing," he said.

"Not at all. Look!"

Galileo looked. His jaw fell. His breath held in his breast. When at last he found his voice he said, "Stars... the Milky Way – thousands, thousands of stars!"

"Two hundred thousand million of them," Urania said.

"The sky is a deluge of stars – brimming with them, flooded with them!" Then he looked up to Urania.

"How did you know?" he asked.

The moonlight on the terrace came down at the right angle for Galileo to see the stars that flecked in Urania's hair. She smiled but did not answer.

§ 67.

**Venice,
1611.**

"*Sidereus Nuncius* – The Starry Messenger," said Galileo, as he distributed a pamphlet-sized book to several members of the Venetian senate, and some of the Doge's advisors, Paolo Scarpi among them. They stood in a circle around his spyglass on its tripod, near the quayside of the Piazza San Marco.

"These copies are so new from the printing press, the ink is still wet," he boasted, with an impish tilt of his head. "And may I draw your attention to page twenty-three, where I discuss the four stars that surround Jupiter. A friend of mine – at first, she was my maidservant but she was clearly qualified for higher things – she recommended that I study these stars with close attention. And, so I did. And the most astonishing thing – they travel together with Jupiter. See how they always remain close to the king of the planets, like children clinging to their father? They are moons – moons of Jupiter, and they solve the problem of the Earth's moon."

"Which problem?" asked Paolo.

"That all things in the sky orbit the – ha ha, well, they *appear* to orbit the Earth, of course," he grinned. "But where the moon has no retrograde motion, the five planets do. They appear to squirrel around – sometimes going backwards, then going forwards again. It leaves the question: What makes our moon so different, so special? Now, I know the answer: Nothing! Other planets can have moons of their own, as well. And so our universe revealed herself to be stranger and more wonderful than anyone ever imagined."

Paolo touched the telescope and said, "May I see?"

§ 68.

Florence, Tuscany, 1611.

"Indeed, please do!" Galileo encouraged the young Cosimo de Medici, and he oriented the telescope for the duke.

"Astonishing – Jupiter is a *disk!*" said Cosimo, after a moment of slack-jawed awe.

"It is," Galileo confirmed. "And I am a witness to Venus, Mars, and Saturn exhibiting a disk in my lenses, as well. I dare say the planets are probably spheres, like our Earth."

"And these four stars beside it – they are moons, you say?"

"I watched them every night for a year," Galileo grinned. "They move with Jupiter, and around him. They are not fixed to the firmament, like the rest of the stars. Oh, and since I discovered them, I'm claiming the right to name them. And so, I name them the Medicean Stars. In honour of your noble self, and for your three good brothers, too: Lorenzo, Carlo, and Francesco."

Cosimo grinned. He said, "You would not name them for the Doge of Venice? Were you not in his employ when you made this device?"

"I am a professor, in his university in Padua," Galileo explained with a nod. "But I do not wish to remain in Padua forever. It is not my home. I am much happier in my native Tuscany."

§ 69.

**Rome,
1611.**

"And you named them the Medicean Stars, in order to court the Grand Duke for a patron, I suppose?" said Pope Paul the Fifth. He and a circle of cardinals, clerics, and monastics gathered on the roof of the Castel Sant'Angelo for Galileo's demonstration; a site which offered an excellent view of the evening sky.

"Your Holiness is most insightful," Galileo confirmed.

The pope said, "We are pleased to hear that you have found a home in a more amenable state. With a more God-fearing prince upon its throne."

Galileo grinned, and hoped the pope would find his smile authentic. When Bellarmine looked up from the spyglass, Galileo re-oriented it and said, "The book I have just given you does not include my most astonishing discovery, because I am preparing a separate publication for it. But I should like to reveal it to your eminent selves tonight. Prepare yourselves to witness... the phases of Venus! Your Holiness, please, be the first to see!"

As the priests and cardinals gasped and muttered among themselves, the pope looked into the telescope. "That's Venus? But it's a *crescent*!" he exclaimed.

"Just like the moon," Galileo confirmed with a smile. "We didn't know about this because we needed a spyglass to see it. But now we have one. And now we know! Isn't that exciting?"

"How is this possible?" said the pope, as he stood and let Bellarmine look next.

"When Venus, the Sun, and the Earth make a right triangle," Galileo explained, "we see it as a half-moon – pardon me, ha ha, it's a half-Venus. When it swings closer to us, it makes a smaller angle, and we see it in crescent. When it is closest to us, we do not see it at all, of course because the sun illuminates its far side, and its dark side faces us. And when it is full, its bright side faces us but it appears dim, because it's on the other side of the sun, and too far away. But the important matter here is the implication. The phases of Venus are the evidence – the observable, universally available evidence of the truth of the new Copernican system, and the wrongness of..."

Galileo found himself confronted by a circle of frowning faces.

Bellarmine stood up from the telescope and said, "To say that the sun is really fixed in the centre of the heavens, and the Earth revolves around it, is a dangerous thing. Not only irritating theologians and philosophers, but injuring our holy faith and making the sacred Scripture false."

"But you see the evidence for yourselves. And the implication, surely, is logical," Galileo finished.

"So are the Scriptures, my son," said the pope.

Bellarmine added, "The phases of Venus could be evidence of the Tychonian system, where the Sun orbits the Earth, and all other things orbit the Sun."

Galileo opened his mouth, then thought better of what he was going to say. "That is a possibility," he conceded.

Bellarmine said, "But thank you for demonstrating your device to us, master Galilei. What did you call it again? A telly-scope? Well. Let us retire to warmer chambers. This cold night air must be hard on your fragile health. And we have much to discuss."

§ 70.

"You said *that*? To the *pope*!" Urania howled at Galileo.

"I am from Tuscany; we are an excitable people," the old scientist defended himself.

She paced around his lens-grinding workshop as if she owned it, and Galileo sat on a stool by one of the work benches, clenching and unclenching his fists. Kynisca leaned on a door post, her eyes moving from one side of the argument to the other.

"Didn't you think of the consequences?" Urania asked him. "Have you already forgotten what they did to Giordano? For saying nearly the same thing?"

Galileo's fists lost their tension; his shoulders drooped. "No," he said.

"I was there when they killed –" she said, almost shouting. Then she fell in a chair, looking away, to avoid imposing her grief upon him.

Galileo turned to Kynisca, asking with a gesture if she was there too. Kynisca nodded, and closed her eyes for a moment.

"Can you tell me," Galileo asked, "was he brave?"

"The bravest of them all," Kynisca said. "He preserved his integrity, to the end."

"I met him only once," Galileo recalled. "He had a lively mind. It felt like a privilege, that he shared some of it with me. But if you don't mind me saying so: I do not fear the Inquisition. The Holy Father has now seen with his own eyes the Medicean stars, the mountains on the moon, the phases of Venus. In Giordano's time no one knew of those things. But now, everybody knows them. If I am accused of anything heretical, if I am put on trial, all I need to do is invite the judge to see the evidence for himself."

Urania, listening to Gallileo's confidence, imagined him bound the the same pyre as Giordano. It was not a prophetic vision: it was a kind of love, like teachers have for their students, and a fear that another of her students might be taken from her.

"Your best defence at an Inquisition court is not to be charged in the first place," she told him. "So keep your hands on the reins of your mouth. And mind what you *publish*, too."

"I've no argument with that," Galileo agreed. He picked up one of his nearly finished telescopes and examined the fit of the lenses in their frames, and the frames in the tube. "Doesn't it seem curious to you that a simple change in the way we *see* prompted such a radical change in the way we *think*. We know our place in the universe now. We are no longer guessing about the nature of the world. Only sixty years ago Copernicus imagined the cosmos with the sun in the centre. Today, we can see for ourselves the proof. In the same vein – today we can see the mountains on the moon... perhaps someday, we shall walk upon them. And look down upon the earth from up there, see how small and silly all our conflicts are, against the curtain of infinity."

Urania reached to him and said, "Would you like to see it?"

Galileo didn't notice her hand. He looked out the window through his scope and said, "Then perhaps we shall visit all those other worlds that Bruno says orbit the other stars. I should like to see a day when there is no place in the cosmos we cannot go, or cannot see. No darkness where we cannot bring a little light."

Urania closed and opened and closed her hands, drew a breath to speak and then remained silent.

Kynisca whispered to Urania, "Shall we tell him who we are? I think he deserves to know."

Urania gave no sign that she heard what Kynisca said. Her eyes, still glistening with coming tears, fixed on the jovial and wide-smiling man at the window. She clasped her hand over her heart, as though Galileo's words were a stone that pressed down upon it. Then she left the workshop without saying anything.

* * *

You know, I think I loved Galileo, too. And not because he might win my father's bargain for me. But because of the kind of man he became. Jovial, generous, fun loving. A mind as quick off the mark as a greyhound. And the curiosity of a child. I wanted to show him he was right. I felt that he deserved to see with his eyes what he had so far only imagined in his mind. But in his telescope, he had already seen it.

He didn't need me.

Prometheus had warned me such a day would come. He said that the gods were destined to give way to humanity. I began to wonder: if I win the gamble with Julian and my father, will I lose my home all the same? Or will I be locked away in it, where no one of the outside world can find me?

Not only me, but Kynisca? My sisters? My mother? And all the Hidden World?

§ 71.

Cardinal Bellarmine handed the large scroll to Pope Paul the Fifth, who sat on his throne in the Papal audience chamber, surrounded by his cardinals.

"Your Holiness, this is the order to amend the Index of Forbidden Books, to include *De Revolutionibus Orbium Coelestium* by Doctor Nicolaus Copernicus. The only remaining legal requirement is your signature and seal."

The pope unfurled the scroll and read it. An acolyte placed a small writing table in front of him; another supplied an inkwell and quill.

"We are satisfied that the legal process has been conducted properly," said the pope, as he took the quill and dabbed it in the inkwell. "And we are pleased to sign the order." He signed the document. An acolyte poured a dab of hot wax on the bottom of the page, and the pope pressed his ring into it. "As of this moment, this work by our son Nicolaus Copernicus is forbidden to all mankind, on pain of excommunication."

Bellarmine took back the signed scroll and displayed it for the cardinals, who applauded the deed. Then he waved for his assistant to come and take it.

"Send this proclamation to every bishop in Christendom," he said. "And arrange for every copy of the book itself in every library in Europe to be burned."

Julian, serving as his assistant, took the scroll and said, "Your Eminence, I have already begun."

§ 72.

**Pisa, Republic of Venice,
1616.**

With a train of admiring students following closely behind him, Galileo strode over the cobbles of Pisa's wide streets, smiling like a king on his coronation day, and waving to his friends who he passed in the shops and tavern patios.

"And last month, they translated my *Starry Messenger* into Chinese. Chinese!" he trumpeted to his parade. "I had no idea that it was now possible to get there and back again in less than one year. What an age of wonders we live in!"

"Do you have a copy with you? What does Chinese writing look like?" asked one of the students in the train.

"They write from the top down, instead of from left to right. And they don't have an alphabet. Their letters represent whole words!"

A woman, carrying a folded and sealed paper, caught up with him. "Father, there you are – you're never at home. A letter came for you today, from Prague!"

"Thank you, my dear Ginny," said Galileo to his daughter, and he broke the seal on the letter and opened it, slowing his walking pace as he read. His students drew closer, to read over his shoulder. "It's from Kepler," Galileo told them. "He says he is still plotting the Rudolphine Tables, but progress has slowed down as he must devote time to defending his mother in court. It seems she has been arrested for witchcraft, the poor old dear – oh, here he says that the telescopes I loaned him have arrived, and that he has now seen the Medicean Stars for himself! And so has the Emperor! Ha ha – wonderful stuff!"

His students applauded. Galileo passed the letter to his daughter, along with a few coins. "Buy some fresh mutton for dinner tonight, if you please. I feel like celebrating."

"Where did this come from?" said Virginia, as she accepted the coins.

Galileo grinned. "I was going to announce this once I signed the paperwork – that's where I'm going right now. But today is such a beautiful day, perhaps there's no harm in announcing it immediately. My friends and fellow travellers: I have been appointed chief philosopher and mathematician to the Grand Duke of Tuscany, with permanent effect, and a salary of a thousand crowns a year!"

His students cheered and slapped his back. Virginia hugged him. Then she asked, "What about the Doge of Venice?"

"The Doge never delivered the raise that he promised me," Galileo explained. "So, since he failed in his side of our contract, I feel no obligation to hold up mine."

"Mother wishes to remain in Padua," Virginia told him.

"Yes, she told me," Galileo admitted. "She has lived there all her life. And I who am so glad to return to my hometown could not find the heart to demand she should abandon hers. But Padua is not so far away, if you ever want to see her. And I do hope you come to love Tuscany as I do. It's here in my beloved city of Pisa, that I hope to stay to the end of my days."

Someone among the train of students said, "We got him back!" The other students cheered, laughed, and patted Galileo on the back again.

Arriving at the palatial villa that housed the university's administration offices, the front door opened before he had a chance to knock on it. Standing in its frame, and holding a copy of Galileo's pamphlet sized book, *The Letters on Sunspots*, was Cardinal Bellarmine.

Galileo's grin immediately dissolved away, as did the cheerfulness of his students.

"The Copernican system is *heresy*, Master Galilei," said Bellarmine.

"Your Eminence," said Galileo, as he kissed the cardinal's ring.

"Please come inside," the cardinal invited him. Galileo glanced to his daughter and his students, opened his hands in a gesture of helplessness, and stepped inside.

§ 73.

In the hall, Bellarmine said to Galileo, "Before we go further, I want you to understand a few things. I have been sent to you as a personal representative of His Holiness Pope Paul the Fifth, to tell you that you must not hold nor defend the Copernican system. If you cannot do this, then I will be required to impose an official warning upon you, in the presence of the notaries and witnesses of the Inquisition. An official warning is a step in the direction of excommunication, and possibly... much worse."

Galileo did not need a reminder of what might be worse. He studied Bellarmine's demeanour, looking for a sign of friendship, or animosity. Then he said, "The Inquisition is here?"

Bellarmine nodded. "This is not a formal trial. But there are some men in the next room who would like nothing better than to see you follow our son Giordano Bruno to your perdition. Follow my lead, and hopefully you will *avoid* an official warning. And then you can continue using the Copernican system as a mathematical device – provided you always frame it as heresy whenever you mention it, and you give no one any sign that you personally believe it. That, I think, would be best for everyone. God knows, including me."

"But I have *seen* the proof – and so have *you*," Galileo protested.

Bellarmine put his hand on a door half-way down the hall, but did not open it. "What you and I have seen or not seen will not matter to the men on the other side of this door," he said.

Galileo grimaced. "I was warned that something like this might happen."

"By who?"

"It doesn't matter. Let's get this over and done."

The cardinal opened the door. A gauntlet of grim-faced, grey haired men in black clerical robes stood on the student benches, looking down on the path from the door to three chairs on the lecturer's stage. Bellarmine gestured that Galileo should sit in that chair, and he and Julian sat on either side of it. The grey-hairs in the benches stayed standing as Galileo lowered himself into to his seat.

"Master Galilei," said Julian, his legs crossed and his hands animated as if in casual discussion. "We have read your recent publication, *The Letters on Sunspots,* which includes a description of your observations of the planet Venus. Is it possible that some of what you claim to have seen in the heavens is not the way things are? But instead, are the products of optical illusions generated inside your instrument?"

"That was my first thought, when I saw the Medicean stars," Galileo said. "The lenses might not have been as perfect as I had hoped. I might have been looking at sun motes in – or, ha ha, star motes – in a crack in the glass."

"So, you admit you may be mistaken about everything you wrote in your books?" Julian accused.

"Not at all," Galileo replied. "Because I tested my devices to rule out exactly that kind of possibility. I pointed them at candles that I placed on my neighbour's rooftops. Church towers, ships at sea, anything at a distance that had a lamp in the window – anything that could have appeared similarly distorted. None of them – I say again, none of them appeared with a spread of extra lights."

"And you say that Venus has phases, like the moon. Is it not also possible that your lenses might have distorted her shape into the crescent, depending on the angle of your telescope to the sun, instead of the angle of the planet?"

"Were that the case, sir, I should see through my telescope all things bent into a crescent. Including your head!"

He grinned, but Bellarmine leaned into his ear and said, "Please remember... none of these men have a sense of humour."

Galileo saw the grimaces on the faces of the lawyers. "Of course," Galileo whispered back.

"We are not accusing you of blindness, master Galilei," said Julian, folding his arms. "We are concerned that you do not properly understand what you have seen."

Galileo waved his finger at the ceiling, and the sky beyond it. "What is there to mistake about the Medicean stars, the shape of Saturn, the crescent phase of Venus – all those things I wrote about in my book?" he howled. "Hundreds of people across Italy have bought my telescope and seen them for themselves. The Holy Father himself has seen them, and so has Cardinal Bellarmine here –"

Bellarmine did not much enjoy being drafted into Galileo's cause. He said, "The Holy Father and I have seen those things, yes. But he and I know not to apply an erroneous *interpretation* on what we have seen."

Galileo raised a finger, ready to dispute the point, but he calmed himself and said, "Sir, the easiest way to answer these and any other questions you may have is to borrow one of my telescopes and look for yourself. I don't have one with me at this moment, but I have several at home –"

Bellarmine said, "The Holy Father acknowledges that the planet Venus does exhibit phases. That the moon has mountains. That the Milky Way is composed of myriad thousands of stars, all too small to be seen individually. That the planet Saturn is oblong in shape. And finally, that the planet Jupiter has four moons of its own. All of these having been confirmed by the Church's own astronomers."

Galileo breathed in and out, and smiled. "Thank God – the Holy Father is on my side," he whispered.

"But the scriptures are not," said Julian. "And the words of Scripture –"

But Bellarmine interrupted him, "require expert interpretation, which you, deacon, are not qualified to offer. Now we are all friends and good Christians here. And our purpose is to teach and to guide one of our wayward sons, before we have to *warn* him of the dangers that lie in the side roads."

"Yes, your Eminence," Julian acquiesced, and he sat down.

"Master Galilei," Bellarmine said, "if there were a true demonstration that the Sun was in the centre of the universe and the Earth in the third sphere, and that the Sun did not travel around the Earth but the Earth circled the Sun, then it would be necessary to proceed with great caution in explaining the passages of Scripture which seemed contrary. And we would rather have to say that we did not understand them than to say that something was false which has been demonstrated. But I do not believe that there is any such demonstration. Do you have one, Master Galilei? One which rules out the system of Tycho and all other possibilities, and definitively proves the system of Copernicus?"

Galileo felt the prick of stiletto daggers in the eyes of all the lawyers and clerics among the witnesses. Julian was the only man smiling, but it seemed to Galileo he was imagining a pyre in a Roman square, and himself holding the torch. But most of all, he heard the coded message in Bellarmine's words. He said, "Your Eminence, I do not have that demonstration at this time."

"Thank you," Bellarmine smiled. Then he stepped closer and said, "There is one other thing these witnesses need to hear you say. I believe you already know what it is."

Galileo nodded, then stood up to say it. "I am as good a Christian as any man here. And in all matters of faith and of the Christian religion, I defer to the appropriate authorities."

Bellarmine smiled. "Very good, my son, and thank you." Then to the witnesses in the hall he said, "Gentlemen, I think we need not detain the good professor any longer." With a gesture he invited Galileo to leave with him.

But Julian snatched Bellarmine's copy of *The Letters on Sunspots* and pushed it in front of Galileo's face. "Yet in this book you published your support for the Copernican system, knowing that it is heretical. And I quote..." he flipped a few pages to find the text he wanted, "'I say to your Lordship that the emergence of the horned Venus agrees in a wondrous manner with the harmony of the great Copernican system, to whose universal relations we see such favourable breezes and bright escorts directing us.' Well, master Galilei, there on the page is the evidence of your contempt for the doctrines of Holy Mother Church. What have you to say about that?"

Galileo inhaled to speak but Bellarmine nudged him and said, "Don't say anything." Then to Julian he said, "I am the ranking cardinal here, deacon Augustus. So when I say we need not detain Master Galilei any longer, it means the meeting is over. No more questions."

"But – Your Eminence," Julian protested, "he is the most famous philosopher in the world. His endorsement of the Copernican heresy –"

"Need not come before an Inquisition court, since he has accepted the authority of the Catholic magisterium. In the presence of all these witnesses!"

"Then he should be willing to put it in writing," Julian insisted. One of the clerics among the witnesses handed him a scroll. Julian thrust it into Galileo's hands and said, "This is your formal renunciation of the Copernican heresy, and your sworn oath to never teach it, nor *speak* of it, on pain of excommunication. Sign it."

"Don't sign anything," Bellarmine ordered Galileo. He took the scroll and said to Julian, "You and I shall soon discuss why Pride is a deadly mortal sin." Then he pulled Galileo by the collar out of the lecture hall.

§ 74.

In his workshop, Galileo finished his beer and plunked the goblet on his table. "I worked with Inquisition censors for years on those letters, before I published them. Years, I tell you!" he complained. "So, to be dragged in front of a battery of clerics like that, and accused of rejecting every Catholic doctrine since Christ himself taught the Sermon on the Mount... it's more than a man my age can –" his words were broken off by a violent bout of coughing.

"Sit down, Father, please," Virginia implored him, as she guided him to a chair. "You are fifty-two years old; this kind of excitement cannot be good for you."

"It's the vapours," Galileo said. "Something that was in the air... came from those caves beneath the cottage... two of my friends died of it –" then another round of coughing disrupted him.

Urania finished mixing his tonic, and brought it to him, but he waved it away.

Cardinal Bellarmine asked, "Has he suffered like this for long?"

"For almost fifteen years," Urania answered.

The cardinal blessed him with the sign of the cross. "Well, I have dismissed deacon Augustus from my service, and written a letter to the Holy Father with a true account of today's meeting. He is quite fond of you, since you demonstrated your telescope to him. So if anyone disputes what happened today, he will certainly look favourably on *our* version of events. With any luck, by this time next year everyone will have forgotten about it."

"Thank you," Galileo gasped.

"But one thing was said today, that rang true for me," Bellarmine recalled. "You probably *are* the most famous philosopher in the world. Any number of people out there would love to see you make the smallest mistake. So, I trust you will avoid saying or doing anything that could bring this circus of stupidity back on your head?"

Galileo, coughing again, then wiping the phlegm from his mouth and chin and wheezing through a constricted throat, could only nod.

Bellarmine took his hat and moved to the door. "I must go. God bless you and keep you, my friend," said the cardinal, his hands on Galileo's shoulders. Then he swept out of the workshop, leaving Galileo to recover.

§ 75.

The cardinal arrived at his guest room in the bishop of Pisa's palace that evening to find Julian sitting in his chair by the fireplace.

"*Valeo*, my friend," said Julian.

"Deacon Augustus – what the devil are you doing in here?" Bellarmine said. "I already sent you away!"

"You should not have come to Galileo's defence," said Julian. He tapped the cardinal on his forehead and said, "Give me the letter you wrote to the pope about today's meeting."

Bellarmine, dazed with surprise and with magic, handed over the letter.

"And now you will write the pope a new letter, declaring your intention to retire from your duties with the Inquisition. Then you will go home, and find some interesting way to die," Julian ordered him. Then he left the palace, with Bellarmine staring upwards as if its ceiling was ten miles high.

§ 76.

"I told you that Galileo would see the cosmos the way you do," said Prometheus, as he poured the wine for his guests. "Had your work with him begun sooner, we might have avoided that encounter with the barbarians."

Kynisca and Catherine drank; Urania smelled hers, then put it down.

"They are people, not animals," Urania corrected him.

"They are instruments of the forces of ignorance," Prometheus replied.

Urania shook her head. "They can learn, they can change. Galileo is teaching them."

"But if the Inquisition silences him before you are ready to test him," Prometheus said, "then you will lose your way back to Olympus. Kynisca and Catherine can protect him from other Olympians. But now you need him protected from other *men*. It's why you're here, isn't it?"

Urania nodded.

"The Inquisition tried to silence him only because Julian was controlling them," Kynisca observed. "So, all we need to do is keep him away from the mortals, until Galileo is ready to be tested."

"We have laws about that," Catherine noted. "We can't confine him to the Hidden World without a good enough reason."

"He broke his promise not to interfere," said Urania. "Is that enough?"

"It's enough for me," said Prometheus, as he stood up and moved to the far side of his belvedere. He leaned into what appeared to be a copse of thorn bushes which grew on the other side of the railing and whispered something. A moment later, the head of a giant vulture reared up. It blinked in the sunlight, then took to the air on wings that were big enough to knock down a horse.

Urania said, "Is that the same vulture which –"

"Yes, he is," said Prometheus, patting his belly, above his liver. "It seems that your father *forced* him to do what he did to me. And he felt regret, the whole time. A most unusual way to make a new friend."

"Where did you send him?"

"To find Julian," said Prometheus, "and to bring him here."

§ 77.

Julian was asleep in his villa on the Palatine Hill in Rome, when the great creature found him. Its claws crushed part of the roof of the villa, awakening everyone in the neighbourhood and scattering them in panic. Julian rose, stepped over the rubble outside his bedroom door, rolled his eyes at the mess, and scanned the sky through the hole in the ceiling in search of the cause. Another crash collapsed more of the roof and revealed the monster; Julian laughed at it.

"Well, aren't you a beauty? Bend your head down here, let me get a look at you," he told it.

The vulture reached its head down and took Julian in its beak and then launched into the night sky again. Julian howled out with surprise and pain, and tried to pry the creature's beak open or punch at its eyes. But the vulture transferred him to his claws, where he could not reach any vulnerable part of its body. They flew east, toward Prometheus' villa in the Caucasus mountains.

§ 78.

The following morning, the vulture dropped Julian on Prometheus' belvedere from a height that would have broken several bones in an ordinary man's body. He rolled across the ground, protecting his head with his arms, and crashed to a stop against the wall of the villa. The vulture circled around its nest, then settled into it, and disappeared.

"*Khâire*, Julian Augustus," said Prometheus.

Julian staggered to his feet. "You're going to regret doing that to me," he threatened.

"What will you do? Chain me to a mountain?" Prometheus smirked. He pulled a chair from his belvedere table. "Sit down," he ordered.

Julian shook his head but sat down.

"I understand you broke your oath to Urania, to no longer interfere in her work," Prometheus said. He leaned over Julian; his head was almost as wide as Julian's shoulders.

"A promise to an enemy isn't a *real* promise," Julian justified himself.

"Urania is not your enemy," Prometheus said. He leaned across the table and said, "I am."

Julian shrank backwards, doing his best to hold his nerve.

Kynisca, Catherine, and Urania emerged from the villa; Julian folded his arms at them. "So what is this? You want to renegotiate our bargain again?"

Kynisca said, "We're here to enforce the bargain you already agreed to."

"What does that mean?"

"It means," said Catherine, "that you are going to stay here with the old man until Urania decides she is ready to test someone."

"You can't hold me here! There are laws – the laws of Zeus."

"I do not care about the laws of Zeus!" Prometheus bellowed. "I am the last of the greatest race ever to rule the land of Hellas. Zeus and his Olympians pushed us from our seats by trickery and deceit. Every day since his treachery, I have sworn an oath to throw him down the same way!"

Birds on nearby crags startled and took to flight, as Prometheus spoke. A faint echo of his words returned from another mountain. Julian scuttled backward in his chair, hitting the railing of the belvedere. Urania and Kynisca shared worried glances.

Brendan Myers

"You will stay here as my... my dishonourable guest," Prometheus told Julian. "If you wander more than a league from my door – if you are not back before nightfall, every day – if you talk to anyone but the four of us, in any way – the vulture will feed you to her children." He nodded in the direction of the vulture's nest; the great bird leaned its head on the edge of the nest, watching Julian, and not blinking.

"It seems your queen has trapped my bishop in a corner," said Julian. "But while your eyes look to my queen on the left, my pawns threaten your king from the right. Human nature will win the bargain for me. For if that vision-trick of yours doesn't break Galileo, it *will* break everyone around him."

"Not this time," Urania retorted. "This time we have the telescope. Everyone will be able to see the truth for themselves."

"They'll look straight at it, and they still won't believe it," Julian argued. "Their nature is their destiny, Urania. And their nature is to take aim at the highest targets and to miss. So, you can hold me here for a century or more – it doesn't matter what I do, or what I don't do. You can't fight against human nature – you will always lose."

"Then why do you keep interfering?" Urania demanded.

"Because you still don't believe me," he declared.

"No, that's not the reason," Urania told him.

"Oh no? What is it then? Tell me."

Urania studied him for a moment. "Not sure yet," she said.

Julian leaned back, and smirked like he had beaten everyone in a game no one else knew they were playing. "Well then! I wish you luck with your next student. Though when it comes to human nature, there's really no such thing."

Urania glanced at Prometheus. But his face was unreadable. She threw her himation over one shoulder and her satchel over the other. She marched around the villa to mount her fairy horse, and rode away.

* * *

196

Julian is something of a genius, isn't he? To blame human nature for the death of Giordano – a death that he intended and arranged – it takes a genius like him to see the logic in a bull-headed contradiction like that.

Catherine reminded me that with Julian out of the way, we could test human nature directly, and not Julian's ability to interfere with it. I would have a fair trial at last. It is good to have clear-thinking friends like her. So, I shared my time between Bohemia and Tuscany, helping Johannes with his star tables, and Galileo with his books. And Tarquinia with her concerts. I went to La Rochelle sometimes, joining dinner parties with Catherine, with all the important local poets and writers and thinkers as guests. She called it her 'salon'. One of her best ideas.

Not much else happened in the world during that time. Germania started a war with itself, over something to do with religion. The Thirty Years War, historians would later call it. Catherine was caught in it, too. A Catholic army attacked La Rochelle, and arrested all the Huguenots, my dear friend among them. Your history says she died there a few years later. Our history says she used the occasion to let go of her last ties to mortal society and make the Hidden World her permanent home. The timing was right: the war could cover her tracks, and her family started to notice that she wasn't growing old. What else? The pope died, and his successor happened to be a patron of Galileo's: a man named Barberini, who took the Papal name of Urban the Eighth. Kepler finished his Tables, and wandered Europe again, looking for work. He wrote a novel about a journey to the moon – perhaps that night in Prague had some good influence on him after all. Oh, and nine years after Julian had his mother arrested for witchcraft, they dropped the charges, for lack of evidence. Let that fact speak for itself.

What else? Crops were sown and harvested. Seasons turned. Life carried on. Eighteen years was a heartbeat for me. Though for Galileo, the same heartbeat was almost a fourth of his life. Time does not mean the same thing for us, as it does for you.

I am sorry for it.

§79.

**Rome,
1624.**

"Human nature is a curious thing," said Pope Urban, as he wandered around the maze of wooden scaffolding that filled much of the interior of St. Peter's Basilica. "Here in the Eternal City, men have come together to raise the greatest dome in the world, to the glory of God. While north of the Alps men hack at each other like butchers and burn their neighbour's houses down, praising the same God all the while. Everywhere else, they're talking of comets, and the phases of Venus, and mountains on the moon. Not only men but women, children, bankers, merchants, peasants, even the most wretched beggars, planting their eyes in those long wooden tubes with the glass plugs in each end. Talking of the wonders of God's creation without mentioning His Holy Name at all! These modern times: what can a man of faith do?"

Galileo walked beside the Holy Father, admiring the height of the basilica's columns, and imagining the dome that would someday cover the view of the open sky above. "If I had an answer to that one, Your Holiness, I might have written a book about it now," he said.

"Ha ha! I believe you would have," said the pope, slapping Galileo on the back. "You've written a book about nearly everything else under the sun. But therein lies the reason I wanted to speak to you."

"Ah, you *do* want me to write theology," Galileo guessed, with a grin.

"Not quite," the pope clarified himself. "Our situation is this. Men are putting their faith in those tubes of yours, instead of in the teachings of our Lord."

"My telescopes are no danger to the faith," Galileo defended them.

"If human nature were as perfect as it was in the Garden before the Fall, then I would agree with you," said the pope. "But as it is, men are easily distracted by anything glamorous and new. Your telescope has everyone doubting the scriptures, doubting Aristotle and the ancients, doubting everything. And from there, it's a short step to believing in nothing. And so I must enlist you to help me bring certainty back to their lives."

Galileo nodded, though he was careful not to let the pope see the grimace on his face. "I am honoured to be of service, your Holiness. But I cannot tell people to disbelieve the evidence of their own eyes."

The pope chuckled. "I ask nothing as hyperbolic as that. Rather, I want you to write a book in the form of a dialogue on the two chief world systems – the Copernican and the Ptolemaic. A book that compares them, gives each of them their due, then leads the reader to the correct conclusion. Such a book coming from the great Master Galilei, the most famous philosopher alive, could do much to resolve the confusion in the minds of men."

Galileo grinned. "I never aimed to be a *famous* philosopher. Only a wise one," he said.

Pope Urban grinned. "Good man. I shall expect the manuscript to come straight to me, when you finish it."

"Then I shall write it," Galileo agreed. "I'd rather deal with you as my censor, than some anonymous cleric who cares more for his career than for the truth."

The pope held out his hand, for Galileo to kiss his ring, and Galileo kissed it. Then he added one last remark: "It may take me a few years to finish, but it will be glorious."

Pope Urban, who was looking at the unfinished dome above him instead of Galileo, said "Yes, it will."

§ 80.

**Rome,
1632.**

After a tedious day of hearing confessions from his priests and bishops, Pope Urban sat by a fireplace in his private chambers and let out a long and satisfied breath. The side table next to his chair carried several books, several candles to read them by, and a Venetian glass goblet half-filled with a claret that glowed ruby-red in the firelight. A blanket lay over his lap, and in his hands a copy of Galileo's *Dialogue on the Two Chief World Systems*, the private reward he had saved for the end of long days like today. He smelled the spine before opening it and smiled.

"The longer you wait for a pleasure like this, the greater the pleasure it is," he said aloud, as though the scientist was in the room to hear. Then to his majordomo he said, "Cancel everything I have for tomorrow, except for morning Mass. I want to spend all day reading this book."

The majordomo bowed and left the room.

The pontiff, stretched out in his chair, skimmed the first several pages, reading a few lines here and there, chuckling in places, laughing without restraint in others. But a few pages later his smile diminished and was replaced by a serious frown. Something was wrong. He turned the pages faster. Something was very wrong. He skipped ahead to the next chapter. Then he slammed the book shut and shouted for his majordomo. When the man appeared, the pope ordered: "Summon the Grand Inquisitor! Tell him to arrest Galileo Galilei!"

§ 81.

Catherine de Parthenay strode along the Via Sacra, once a grand ceremonial procession into the heart of an empire, now a gravel path that ran between its broken ruins. Night had fallen; the stone facades of the newer buildings that surrounded the forum glowed orange in the light of lamps and torches carried by people going by. No moon gave any more light, and though Catherine was accustomed to the darkness of night, neither did she feel safe in it – especially in the centre of a city like Rome. She kept her lamp held high and wondered if she should have brought a friend.

Passing under the Arch of Titus, she found Urania sitting on a crumbled wall, reading a book. She saw her friend and jumped up to meet her.

"Catherine – we have to move fast. They're going to put him on trial for heresy!" Urania reported.

"I know; I got your letter," Catherine said. "You want me to summon the Secret Academy again."

"Would you?" Urania pleaded. "Giordano never got his chance. They killed him before we could rescue him."

"You know what the professors are like," Catherine reminded her friend. "And how hard it is to assemble them."

Urania handed Catherine the book she was reading. "They don't have to come here to Rome. They just need to read this book."

Catherine flipped through the first few pages. "This is the reason he was arrested, isn't it?"

Urania nodded. "And it's banned now. But we can make our own copies."

Catherine considered this as she read a few lines from the text. "Another Copernican," she surmised. "You have a *type* in men, don't you?"

The muse grinned.

"But it's not just his ideas that the professors need to examine," said Catherine. "It's also his character. We cannot admit someone into our Academy if he is not *right* for us. If we accept him, we will have to live with him for centuries."

"I promise you, Galileo is the right man," said Urania. "And I know how to prove it."

"How so?"

"The Church is going to put him on trial," said the muse, "where they will almost certainly ask him to admit that his beliefs are heresy. They will remind him of what happened to Giordano, to make him afraid. But he won't be afraid. He will stand by his integrity. Even while his life is in danger. You will see."

"If he can do that, he *would* be the right kind of man," Catherine admitted.

"I have already asked some of the professors to come to the trial, to see for themselves," Urania told her friend.

"Really? You do know that's my job –"

"I couldn't wait," said the excited muse. "And they haven't replied to me yet. Would you mind prodding them with a stick for me?"

Catherine sighed, and found a place to sit down. She read some more of Galileo's book, then asked, "Why did you want to meet me here, in the old forum?"

"I used to come here when it was still new," said the goddess. "It was a good place to meet people."

"What was it like, back then?"

Urania looked around. She pointed to a copse of trees and said, "There was a man who used to stand right there, with his market cart, and a kind of portable stone oven. He would buy the bad cuts of meat from the butchers, grind it into a kind of mash, mix it with eggs and olive oil, and cook it right there. Then he would wrap it in some flatbread, maybe add some salt. Delicious."

"When I was learning philosophy," Catherine related, "my tutors always said that Rome was the source of all things great and good. Law, literature, engineering, political order. Civilization."

"I am Greek," said Urania, "so I am obliged to have a different opinion."

Catherine laughed. She waved her hand at the ruins that surrounded them. "And now, all that remains of the greatness and the glory of ancient Rome, is this *mélange* of pillars and walls and sand. Urania, is this what will become of us some day?"

"No, no, not at all; we of the Hidden World have always been here," Urania replied, without hesitation. Then after a moment's thought she added, "But why do you ask?"

Catherine looked around the forum, inhaling to speak and then pausing, searching for the right words. "The professors have been talking about you," she said, after she thought she could no longer keep Urania waiting. "Some of them think that your teachings are causing humanity to advance its knowledge too quickly."

Urania shifted in her seat slightly away from Catherine. "Tell me they're not siding with the Inquisition. Or with Julian!"

"Not at all," Catherine reassured her. "But they have been wondering. In this new world you are creating, is there any room for us?"

Urania had been avoiding that question. She looked away from her friend, to hide the discomfort of having to face it. "I wondered that, when Galileo saw the moons of Jupiter without my help," she said.

"What if, someday," said Catherine, "these people become as powerful as we are, without the need for an Awakening? What if, without our help, they discover how to see the face of God?"

Urania got up and took a few steps away but did not speak. She turned her eyes to the stars, where she always found the answers to her questions. Tonight, they twinkled down in their ethereal beauty as they did every night, self-assured in their eternity, otherwise saying nothing.

"They need an answer," Catherine said, "Or else they will not help you."

Urania turned back to her friend. "Tell them – tell them –", she said, struggling to think.

"*Oui*? Tell them what?"

Urania closed her eyes, breathed, and looked at the stars again. The familiar shapes appeared before her: Sagittarius and Scorpio, to the south, and low to the horizon; Virgo setting in the west, Aquarius rising in the east. Saturn shone from the south, and brightly; no other planets were above the horizon this night. Saturn, who in Urania's own language was known as Kronos. One of the first of the Titans. The father of Time.

"Catherine," she asked, "When you were Awakened, did anyone tell you about the war between the Titans and the Olympians, back in the Mythic Age?"

"Of course," Catherine answered, puzzled.

"Did anyone tell you how it started?"

"No, but I didn't ask," Catherine said. "Why does it matter?"

"Because – it never really ended."

* * *

The more they learned, greater they became in body and mind and spirit. In time, some of them became the beings whom the old stories call the gods.

The first and greatest gods of the Greek world were Mother Gaia, who knew all the secrets of Earth and Sea, and Father Ouranos, who knew the powers of Sun and Moon and Sky. They fell in love and had two children together: a son called Kronos, and a daughter called Rhea; the first of the Titans. Ouranos and Gaia taught their children all they knew. Then they went away, still restless for knowledge, but now seeking it together. And so the Titans, their children, became the rulers of the Greek world.

The Titans had children of their own: the greatest of them was called Zeus, the first of the Olympians. He was strong, and clever, and beautiful: everyone loved him, and he loved everyone.

And when he thought the time had come, he called upon the Titans to share the knowledge and power that Ouranos and Gaia had given them. And to share a place in the world that he and his Olympians could call their own.

But the Titans, fearful of change and hardened by pride, said No.

A terrible war was fought, all over the earth: Titans against Olympians, the old gods against the new.

They called it The Titanomachy.

With Zeus as their war leader, the new gods defeated the old, and buried them in the coldest and darkest prisons, deep beneath the earth. And so the Olympians came to rule the Greek world.

Then the gods had children, and their children had children. And so, things continued, like the turning of the seasons.

* * *

Urania let go of her friend's hands, gently returning her to the present moment. Catherine opened her eyes and saw Urania in a new light. Stars twinkling in her midnight hair; the gold of the sun and the silver of the moon in her eyes.

"That's why the gods went to war?" she said.

Urania nodded. "And every generation after that war lost another part of the knowledge those first philosophers had found. The gods were people, once. Mortal women and men, no less than anyone in this city. Would you deny them the chance to progress in knowledge, and to someday Awaken, as our oldest ancestors once denied us? Would you hold them back from realizing who they really are?"

Catherine, her eyes astounded at the sight of every ordinary passerby, whispered, "No, no, no."

Urania smiled. "Write to the professors."

Catherine nodded her head, to show she would do as her friend asked.

"Thank you," said the muse.

The two friends shared a warm hug, in the starry darkness of the ancient city.

§ 82.

The only light in Galileo's prison cell came from a metal grill above the heavy wooden door. He had a bucket for a toilet, a pile of straw for a bed. And no view of the sky. He had been allowed a Bible and a few other books to read, but even at the height of midday there was not quite enough light to see by. He spent the time writing his next book in his head, repeating the important phrases and arguments in order to memorize them, and sometimes weeping.

The heavy bolts unlocked, and the door swung open. "Visitor," said the guard. Urania entered. Galileo stood to brush off his clothes, but his muscles were weak. He braced himself against a wall; his trembling hands grasping for the last shreds of his dignity. The guard laughed at the sound of Galileo groaning in pain, then clunked the door closed.

Urania helped him raise himself to sit on a wooden block that served as his pillow and his chair. From underneath her dress she took out a small burlap pouch, that had been tied to the back of her leg. She unwrapped it, revealing a few simple gifts: a bottle of medicine for his chill, some stubby candles, a flint-and-steel to light them, and a few letters from supporters and friends.

"I see that you have brought me the means to escape this prison, in mind if not in body," sad the old philosopher. His voice wheezed with effort: the dust and the cold air bringing fresh pain to his old afflictions.

"Your trial before the Inquisition begins tomorrow," she told him.

"Tomorrow," Galileo repeated. He drank the medicine, then held up the bottle to the light, thinking about it. "You know, this is the first thing of green that I have seen since they put me in here."

"You will see green again," Urania promised. "Fields and forests of it."

"No," Galileo said. "In this cell, I can't even see the blue of the sky. The damned tower is in the way."

Urania shifted closer to him. "I need you to do something for me," she said. "When you're in the middle of that trial and the prosecutors are making hay of your books, remember what you saw in the sky. Remember that you're right."

Galileo examined the earnest woman who faced him: the slight flecks of star light in her hair appeared sharper, like distant bell-chimes, in the semi-darkness of the prison cell. "On the night that I first saw the rings of Saturn, the mountains on the moon, the many stars of the Milky Way – you already knew about those things. And you never did tell me how you knew."

Urania said, "I couldn't tell you. Not back then."

"Who are you?" Galileo asked her. When she didn't answer immediately, he said, "More than thirty years I've known you. And in that time, you haven't aged thirty days. Who are you?"

Urania could tell there was no further avoiding the question. She said, "I'm Urania."

Galileo grimaced at her. "I know that's your name, but who are you? You're certainly not –" then he caught himself, and asked, "Perhaps you really are."

Urania smiled for him. Stars twinkled in her black hair.

A broad grin possessed the aged philosopher. He looked to the ceiling and said, "I give infinite thanks to God, who has been pleased to make me the first observer of marvellous things! The mountains on the moon. The phases of Venus. A child of the time before the expulsion from the Garden," he said. But then the further implications hit him. "But how is it that a creature of flesh and blood like you can live so long, and stay so young? And what of the other muses? Are they flesh and blood, like you? What of the angels? Does Christ still walk among us? Or does the Adversary?"

"After the trial," Urania said. "I'll tell you everything, I'll *show* you everything. But first you have to win the trial."

Galileo let go of her hands. "The only way for me to win is to recant. But that is also how I lose."

"Then refuse to recant," Urania told him.

"And that is how I die," Galileo reminded her, with a stern sorrow. "What are you asking me to do?"

Urania paused again; her face anguished by all the things she wanted to say but felt she couldn't. "In thirty years of friendship," she said, her words stepping carefully, "have I ever done you wrong? Have I ever caused you harm, or steered you into sin?"

"By following your lead, I did end up here," he said, and he waved at the prison cell walls.

Urania felt the weight of Galileo's truth as though she, too, had been thrown in prison for the crime of trying to do right. Tears grew in the depths of her eyes. "All I can tell you right now," she said, "is – when they put you on trial, if you stand by the truth of your discoveries, no matter who stands against you – if you can do that." She spoke no more and let the pain on her face make her apology for it.

Galileo nodded. He closed his eyes and made a few deep breaths. Opening them again, he said, "I shall trust you to do the rest."

Urania nodded, wiped her tears clean, and squeezed his hands.

§ 83.

**Rome,
12th of April, 1633.**

Urania pushed her way through noisy and excited crowd of people in the square before the courthouse, all clamouring for a space to hear Galileo standing trial. Kynisca, being taller than Urania, pushed a path through the mob for Galileo's daughter Virginia. Although some in the crowd stepped aside for them, seeing that Virginia wore the habit of a nun, most were too absorbed in the passion of the trial. Some held copies of Galileo's books, and some carried his telescopes. Others started a fire in the centre of the square, to burn them. "Telescopes are tools of the devil" someone shouted. Another: "Every one of them is possessed by no less than twenty demons!" A third fanatic proclaimed: "They'll make you go blind – they'll suck out your soul!"

When Urania was close enough to the doors to reach out and touch them, she found a heavyset man wearing a Papal coat of arms, blocking everyone's path. He grabbed someone whose walking stick carried a pair of shoes, and heaved him away, saying "No Protestants – true Christians only!" To a curly-haired and bearded man he shouted, "No Jews!" To a third person who wore an academic gown, he shouted, "And absolutely no philosophers – get out of here, you pagan!"

When he saw Urania approach, he made an effort to grab her from behind, shouting "No women – this is a court of Christian law – no women!" But Kynisca bent his arm behind his back and shoved him to the side. The crush of the crowd prevented him from taking his former place. Urania, Kynisca, and Virginia found a place near the back, where they could stand on a bench to see what was happening. The pope himself presided as judge, seated behind a high desk. A prosecutor in a Jesuit's black robe and mini-cape paced around him. He stood a head and shoulders above Galileo, whose witness box was sunk deep into the floor.

"There he is – look at him!" Virginia cried, when she saw her father in the dock. His once-proud professor's cloak carried thick smears of dust from the prison floor, as well as some new tears and patches of dried urine.

Urania found the scene too familiar. Her knees weakened. She reached out for Kynisca's hand, to steady herself.

"What?" asked her Spartan friend.

"There was a time when people *wanted* to hear what philosophers had to say," said the muse. "They sought us out, asked our advice. They respected knowledge."

"You're thinking of Nicolaus?" Kynisca said.

Urania nodded. "And now another of my philosophers stands before a powerful man, but this time, in a prisoner's dock. Charged with the crime of seeing reality for what it is."

"Is this too hard for you to watch? Do you want to go?" her friend asked.

"No," said Urania. "I want Galileo to see us. I want him to know that the three of us, if no one else, are with him." She reached out to Virginia, to add her hand to the chain.

Virginia looked Urania in the eye and said, "Thank you. Truly."

The prosecutor called for silence in the court room with a thump of his ceremonial staff on the floor. Then he addressed himself to Galileo: "In the matter of the place of the earth in God's creation, the words of the Bible are abundantly clear. As are the words of the Papal Bull declaring the books of Copernicus heretical and forbidden."

Kynisca leaned to Urania's ear and whispered: "That prosecutor... isn't he –"

"Of course it's him," Urania whispered back. "How did he get away from Prometheus?"

Julian, leaning over the prisoner's dock, sensed their conversation. He winked at Urania and returned his attention to prosecuting Galileo.

Virginia tugged on Urania's sleeve. "You know the prosecutor?"

Urania nodded. "But we are not friends, I promise you."

Galileo, meanwhile, would not let himself be intimidated by a prosecutor who looked like he was only half his age. "And yet some of the words of the Bible also clearly contradict the evidence of the senses," he retorted. "And I do not feel obliged to believe that the same God who has endowed us with senses, reason, and intellect has intended us to forgo their use."

Annoyed murmurs arose among the audience. The prosecutor leaned over the railing of the witness box and said, "Do you wish to imply, sir, that we forgo the use of reason when we read the Bible?"

Galileo said, "Not at all. I wish to imply only that nature is inexorable and immutable. She never transgresses the laws imposed upon her or cares a whit whether her methods are understandable to men. The Bible, however, is not chained to conditions as strict as those which govern nature. Nor is God any less excellently revealed in Nature's actions than in the sacred statements of the Bible."

"We all know that God gave us two books by which we may know Him: the Holy Bible, and the book of nature," Julian said. "Yet surely, as you are a good Christian, you see the hubris in the belief that anyone could understand either of those books by human reason alone, without the light of faith, nor the guidance of the Church?"

The aged philosopher said, "These two books are authoritative in their separate spheres. To quote a cleric of eminent degree: The intention of the Holy Ghost is to teach us how men may go to heaven, and not how the heavens go."

A few voices in the audience laughed but were quickly silenced by their stone-faced peers. Julian's cheeks flushed red. Galileo gave the audience a quick smile, to thank those who laughed with him. He saw Urania and Kynisca had enjoyed his joke. But Virginia offered him a pained smile; she expected the court to judge against him. He put his hand over his heart, and bowed his head to her.

Virginia tugged on Urania's sleeve again. "Why is he making fun like that? If he keeps that up he will lose."

"The trial, to be sure," said Kynisca. "But he might win the *argument*."

Virginia let her hand drop from Urania's. "That won't help him if they burn him at the stake."

"I have made arrangements," Urania said to Galileo's frightened daughter. "There are some very important people in the gallery today, here at my invitation, to see for themselves how strong your father is." Urania directed Virginia's attention to a few select people standing along the side of the room, a bald and tan-skinned man wearing a desert tunic; a white-bearded man with matching white scarf and embroidered skull cap; a woman wearing a maroon peplos fastened with gold clasps, and silver cords bundling her hair; a woman wearing a black dress of French design, and a conservative neck-ruff.

"Who are they?" asked Virginia.

"Professors, from a secret academy," the muse explained. "They are the real judges here. If your father remains true, he will be protected."

"Does he know?"

Urania shook her head. "He has to think that this trial is real. So his words will be real."

Virginia nodded, though she did not fully understand. She squeezed Urania's hand, and did not let go.

Galileo was still addressing the court. "But let me answer you more seriously. The passage of time has revealed to everyone the truths that I previously set forth – the shape of Saturn, the Medicean stars that orbit Jupiter, and others of which I have committed my life to study. Men who were well grounded in astronomical and physical knowledge were persuaded almost immediately. There were others who remained in doubt only because of their novel and unexpected character, and because they had not yet the opportunity to see for themselves. These men have by degrees come to be satisfied. But some appear to find pleasure in remaining hostile – not so much toward my discoveries, as toward their discoverer." He patted himself on the heart. "No longer being able to deny the facts, these men now seek to damage *me*, personally. As if by doing so, they could damage the facts, too."

The few members of the audience who supported Galileo cheered to hear this. They heckled the prosecutor, accusing him of having a personal vendetta, and of not truly caring about the law. Others, as if in confirmation of Galileo's assessment, heckled the defendant, calling him a variety of ugly names. Virginia, still craning her neck to see over the heads of the people in front of her, caught Galileo's eye. He summoned his strength to sit up taller, straighten his tunic, and make a weak smile for her.

The pope silenced the courtroom by standing up and reaching out with his hands. Then he gestured to Julian: "My lord Inquisitor, do continue."

"Is it true, master Galilei," said Julian, "that in the year 1616 you were officially warned by Cardinal Robert Bellarmine, a prince of the Church, never to hold, defend, nor teach the Copernican system?"

Galileo said, "No, sir."

The court rumbled in surprise at this answer. The inquisitor gave him the kind of look that a parent might give to a belligerent child. "And yet we have a written statement signed by several witnesses, stating that you were warned never to hold, defend, or teach Copernicus," he said, brandishing a large document, with a dozen signatures on the bottom.

"I was *never* officially warned – here, let me see that!" Galileo demanded. The prosecutor handed him the document.

"Look here – the cardinal didn't sign this. And neither did I. And some of the people who *did* sign it were not there that day!"

The inquisitor turned to the pope and said, "The man is desperate, Your Holiness. He'll tell any kind of lie, to save himself."

"There's another account of what happened," Galileo argued. "Cardinal Bellarmine wrote a letter to your predecessor, Pope Paul the Fifth, which will confirm *my* version of events. I know that he is in heaven now, but the cardinal's letter is surely among his papers –"

"There is no such letter in the *Archivio Segreto*," the prosecutor said. "We searched most thoroughly, looking for it."

Julian grinned, and winked at Urania again.

"Then summon the cardinal himself as a witness – he will tell this court what happened," Galileo demanded.

"Cardinal Bellarmine is dead," said Julian, and a smirk appeared on his face.

For the first time that day, a slump appeared in Galileo's shoulders.

"In fact he has been dead for thirteen years," Julian added.

"No one told me," Galileo lamented. "No one told me."

"And now," said the prosecutor, "may it please the court for me to read a selection from Master Galilei's most recent published work, as follows." He opened a copy of the *Dialogue of the Two Chief World Systems* and read: "'*What is more vapid than to say that the earth and the elements are banished and sequestered from the celestial sphere and confined within the lunar orbit? Is not the lunar orbit one of the celestial spheres, and according to their consensus is it not right in the centre of them all? This is indeed a new method of separating the impure and sick from the sound – giving to the infected a place in the heart of the city!*" Julian slammed the book on the judge's desk and said, "You heard his use of words like 'vapid', 'impure', and 'infected'. As if someone who rejects the Copernican system has the plague! Is this not clear and obvious proof of Master Galilei's endorsement of the Copernican heresy, despite the warnings he had been given by numerous authorities on numerous occasions?"

"The passage you read is only a flutter of rhetoric," Galileo said, his voice softer now, less confident. "There is a more direct logical demonstration elsewhere in the text – and besides that, the entire point of the book was to compare the two systems – the *two* systems, and I cannot do that without giving both –", he interrupted himself with heavy coughing, "both systems a fair explanation!"

"Yet the character in your dialogue who speaks for the true geocentric system, you named him Simplicio – the simpleton, the idiot – and the character who speaks for the Copernican heresy is called Salviati – the saviour!"

"Those are only the names of characters in a play – it doesn't matter what names I chose –" Galileo's words were lost in another sudden fit of coughing. His breath became short.

"Is it not true that Salviati is the character who stands for *your* point of view, Master Galilei?"

"He stands for the Copernican view, that is all," Galileo struggled to say, as his lungs heaved for air.

"And Simplicio is the clown who stands for The Holy Father himself?"

"No – he only stands for –" Galileo choked, and spoke no more.

Virginia shouted, "Give him time to breathe!"

Many in the audience agreed, although a few muttered something about the scandal of a woman in the courtroom. The pope silenced them all by raising his hand.

Virginia grasped Urania's shoulder. "Can't you help him?" she pleaded.

"He has to do this on his own," the muse replied, though with less confidence in her voice.

"Your Holiness," the prosecutor addressed the pope, placing the book on his desk, "I believe you have already read for yourself his persistence with the Copernican heresy. And may I remind the witness," he turned to Galileo again, "what happened to the last mathematician-philosopher who refused the love and guidance of Holy Mother Church in matters of his own salvation? Do you remember his name?"

Galileo, still suffocating in his own chest, squeaked out the name "Giordano –"

"Brother Giordano Bruno, of Nola, in the Kingdom of Naples," Julian repeated. "He was forty-five years old, still fit and strong, when he was arrested. He survived corporeal re-education for seven years. And he remained committed to his heresy until his soul was freed from the prison of his body. But you, master Galilei: how old are you now? Sixty-eight? Sixty-nine? Have you ever seen a man suspended in a strappado? His arms tied behind his back, then hoisted by his wrists up twenty or thirty cubits in the air? Then dropped to the floor again, with the fall arrested less than a palm's length before he hit the stones, thus breaking both of his elbows? Or sometimes, they let him hit the stones whence he might break one of his knees, or crack his head. Have you ever seen a man stretched on a rack, his wrists and ankles pulled in opposite directions, until his arms popped from their sockets? Unable to stop his confessor from laying a red-hot iron on his breast, tracing him with the sign of the cross? From his shoulder to shoulder, and from his throat all the way down to his... navel? Or have you heard the pleading and the crying to come from a man strapped to the rim of a wheel, his body turned over a fire – or perhaps turned over a vat of water, where he might drown if his confessor does not turn the wheel again, and so lift him out in time."

Galileo's coughing subsided, but he chose not to speak. His white hair and grey beard attested to his age; having been reminded now of Bruno's final years, the slump of his shoulders deepened.

"But there remains a chance to save you, body and soul," said the prosecutor, a broad smile growing over his face. "Confess your heresy, repudiate the pernicious lies of Copernicus, and swear to obey Holy Mother Church in all things."

Galileo did not move nor speak, and nor did anyone else in the courtroom.

"Your Holiness," said Julian, a note of victory in his voice, "I believe the defendant has nothing more to say."

Pope Urban rose to his feet. He grinned wide enough for all to see his jagged and yellow teeth, and he held his hands up to heaven, revelling in the ability to hold the silence and the anticipation of his audience in his hands. He said, "We pronounce, judge, and declare, that you, Galileo Galilei, have rendered yourself vehemently suspected by this Holy Office of heresy, that is, of having believed and held the false doctrine that the sun is the centre of the world; also, the false belief that an opinion can be held and supported as probable after it has been decreed contrary to the Holy Scripture."

"That's it," said Virginia. "My father is officially a heretic." She buried her face in Urania's shoulder.

"That's only what the court says," Urania consoled her. "What matters is what *he* says."

The pope, still grinning like a proud boy with the biggest stick in the schoolyard, continued his declaration: "Yet it remains Our pleasure that you be absolved, provided that with a sincere heart and unfeigned faith, in Our presence, you abjure, curse, and detest, the said error and heresies, and every other error and heresy contrary to the Catholic and Apostolic Church of Rome."

Galileo did not move. The Inquisitor placed a scroll in Galileo's hands. Then he placed an inkwell and quill, and a copy of the Bible, on the ledge of the witness box. "Read your confession out loud, and sign it, and you shall be saved," he said.

Galileo opened the scroll and read it silently to himself for a while. His hands trembled. The audience in the courtroom held its breath, awaiting his choice. Urania and Kynisca grasped each other's hands.

Galileo read the words on the scroll. "I, Galileo Galilei, son of the late Vincenzio Galilei of Florence, aged seventy years –" he coughed before continuing, "I swear that I have always believed, I believe now, and with God's help I will in future believe all which the Holy Catholic and

Apostolic Church doth hold, preach, and teach."

The Inquisitor closed his eyes and put his hand on his heart. The audience let out a relieved sigh.

Galileo coughed again and cleared his throat before continuing. "And now," he read, "wishing to remove from the minds of your Eminences and all faithful Christians this vehement suspicion reasonably conceived against me, I curse and detest all my errors and heresies, and every sect that is contrary to the Holy Catholic Church."

"Don't sign it," Urania whispered, as if Galileo could hear.

"Don't sign it, don't sign it," Virginia prayed.

But Galileo signed it and dropped the quill on the floor.

Julian took the scroll with Galileo's signed confession and handed it to a court clerk. The pope descended from his bench, took Galileo's hands in his own, and said, "Welcome back to the fold, my prodigal son." Then he embraced Galileo with both arms.

The audience applauded them. But Catherine de Parthenay led the other Secret Academy judges out of the courtroom, pausing only to shake her head at Urania, disappointment and exhaustion in her eyes.

Virginia collapsed on her bench. She wiped her eyes with the cowl of her habit. Urania sat next to her and tried to hug her. But Virginia threw her arm away.

"You could have done something," Virginia accused. "You could have warned him, or done something!" She got up and walked away. Urania reached for her, but she threw her hand away again.

Galileo lumbered toward the exit, his head down and his shoulders drooped, through a gauntlet of applause, blessings, back-slaps, and congratulations. When he reached the door, he stopped and turned to face the pope again. The pope was receiving his courtiers who kissed his ring and praised his patience, his wisdom, and his mercy.

The Inquisitor was standing next to him. "You had some last thing you wanted to say?" he asked.

Galileo closed his eyes and said, "No."

Virginia ran to him, and he leaned on her arm as he walked away.

§ 84.

"You broke him!" Urania howled at Julian.

"And I didn't have to touch him to do it," Julian grinned, holding up the fingers he often used to give orders to suggestible minds. "That's how pathetic he was."

At Prometheus, sitting in his chaise-longue nearby, she shouted, "And you were supposed to keep him out of my way. Instead, you sat here like a giant slug, drinking the whole time. How can I ever trust you again?"

Prometheus winced at the shrillness of her voice and drank a pitcher of water. "Not so loud, please," he asked her.

"It's not his fault," Julian crooned. "There was something in the wine that night. It put him to sleep for three whole days."

Urania didn't want to speak to Julian. To Prometheus she said, "You let Julian trick you into letting him go? And why didn't your vulture stop him?"

"Because I killed it," Julian told her.

Urania paused to take this information in. She knew that Julian was willing to lie, cheat, and steal to get what he wanted, but she did not know he could kill. She rounded on the titan again: "And now, because that *malakas* carved his name in your ass, they're burning all of Galileo's books, and keeping him prisoner in his own house! Did you and your magic foresight see that coming? And why are you letting him get away with it?"

Prometheus shook his head and smiled on half of his face. "You are still young. You do not yet see the deeper movements of things. Galileo's life and work will soon inspire another man, who has not yet been born. That man will revolutionize human thought more radically than Copernicus. Then his work, in turn, will –"

"That's what you said about Tycho!" Urania snapped at him. "When will it end?"

"It ends now – because Urania lost!" Julian proclaimed, stepping in between her and the titan. "The bargain is over, and she lost. She agreed that Galileo would be her last student –"

"No, I didn't," Urania insisted.

But Julian ignored her words. "And I agreed to stay out of her way. And I *did* stay out of her way – well, I didn't do anything an ordinary man couldn't do. So the contest was still fair. And now we see the result of it. Galileo saw the cosmos and then denied what he saw. You could put him in front of the Secret Academy and he'll deny it again – you know he will. He's too terrified now to speak the truth. You lost the bargain, and that's the end of it."

"You are not the one to judge that," Prometheus retorted.

"And *you* are? You couldn't judge a drinking contest, you lumbering old ox!"

Kynisca joined the argument. "Boys, boys, boys! No one here is judging anything. We all agreed that the Secret Academy will judge the bargain, and we can assemble them in Florence in a few days. Urania, would you be willing to –"

Urania had left the belvedere. They looked down the mountain trail and saw her trotting away on her faerie horse.

Kynisca turned back to Prometheus and Julian, and said, "You two are real gentlemen, did you know that?"

* * *

I suppose you might imagine that as I left the mountain that day, my thoughts were on Galileo, and how to help him make another great discovery, so that he could find his courage again. But if you must know, my thoughts were on where I might find the next Galileo. It didn't have to be someone formally educated. It didn't have to be some Great Man who would go on to change the world. It only had to be someone with the right mix of intelligence and courage. Maybe a librarian in some small provincial town, reading one of Galileo's books? Maybe an apprentice glass blower somewhere, who built his own telescope? Copernicus published his Revolution a hundred years before: so there might be thousands of people now, who call themselves Copernicans. Or Galileans.

Then I thought I could go down the Nile and into the desert. Or down to that cold continent on the south pole. Or anywhere at all, where I could forget about my bargain with that smooth-talking Roman troglos for a while. And live my own life again.

But if I did that, I would be alone again. Back when this whole thing began, all I wanted was someone to understand me – and still, there is no one.

My mother once told me that some of the oldest of the gods – Inanna, Kali, The Morrígan – lived for more than twenty thousand years, then left the world altogether. Some went deep into the earth. Some, into the ocean. Some, to the stars. I wondered what stars they chose? I wondered how they got there? It seemed obvious to me why they left us. Time could not mean the same for them, as it means for me.

For a moment, I wondered why my father Zeus didn't go with them.

And I wondered… if I left for the stars, would anyone on earth miss me? Would my sisters miss me? Would any of them want to come with me? I wanted to be alone, but not to be left alone – does that sound strange to you?

Before I went anywhere else, I went to Greece again. I stayed in a guest house in a town close to Mount Helicon – as close to home as I could go, before my father's lightning strokes would chase me away. I found a hilltop with a good view of the night sky, and I opened my mind to the stars. I saw a great island, on the western edge of Europa. And a great telescope in its midlands, a leviathan of a machine. Almost as long as a trireme. Was it England? Was it Éiru? I wasn't sure. So I went to England; the closer of the two. Anyway, the continent was swimming in the blood of the Thirty Years War. And England was far away from Rome. Almost far enough to be comfortable.

I might have kept going to Éiru, and then to Turtle Island. But I met a boy in a farm in Lincolnshire, and everything changed. Again.

Brendan Myers

Book Six: Isaac

§ 85.

Lincolnshire, Kingdom of England, 1665.

England's country roads were rough and twisty, and its fields bounded by sturdy stone walls and clipped hedges. To Urania's feelings it was more fertile and green than the rocky plains of her home in Greece, yet with fewer patch-forests and hedgerows than Italy or Germania, making the country seem more like the work of human hands than any other she knew. It was pleasant to her, yet at the same time strange; beautiful, but its beauty was more cultivated than natural. She knew, of course, that all of Europe was cultivated. But as this was her first visit, the contrasts called to her more quickly than the familiarities.

Passing a farm near a crossroads, she noticed the sun sinking to the west, and decided the time had come to find a guest house to stay the night. Most farms had a loft in the barn where travellers could stay. She had allowed her hosts to believe she was on a pilgrimage to Glastonbury; that story, and a few silver pennies, was usually enough to buy a dinner, a bed for the night, and some fruit for breakfast in the morning. At this particular farm, the only person she could find was a young fellow, somewhere halfway between boy and man, dressed in breeches and jerkin and a lace cravat: certainly not the outfit of a farmer. He was sitting on the ground in a cattle field, leaning on an apple tree, and reading a book. A border collie lay near him, watchful but at rest.

"*Kháìire*, young man," she called out to him.

"Eh, what?" the man called back.

"Good evening," she translated for him.

The man nodded and returned to his book.

"Have you a room for travellers here?" she asked him.

"We do," he answered, without looking up.

Urania paused, expecting him to ask how long she wanted to stay, as most farmers would do.

"Well, can I take it for the night?" she asked.

"Not my room," said the man. "You'll have to ask me mum."

"Where can I find her?"

"Don't know."

"Is she away? Is she coming back soon?"

"Don't know."

Urania shifted her weight from one leg to the other and burned her gaze into him for a few heartbeats. "Well then," she said, "how far is it from here to the next town?"

"A few miles. Listen, I can't talk, I have work to do."

"Looking after the cattle?"

The man looked up and noticed that the cattle were walking over a broken-down part of the wall, and into the next field.

"Bloody 'ell, they broke through again!" the man cursed, and he dropped the book and ran to herd the cattle back into his own field.

"Need some help?" Urania offered.

"Yes please! You come at them from the left, and I'll come in from the right –"

"It will cost you a room for the night!" she grinned.

The man rolled his eyes and conceded. "You're a tricky one! Come on, then!"

Urania hitched up her skirt as she jogged down the lane, stuffing it into her sash so that it fell only to her knees, the better to be able to run in a muddy field. She hopped over the wall into the field where the cattle were trampling the neighbour's corn. She watched the young man's gestures and words, and copied them, so to get the animals moving. As they responded to her, she discovered their different personalities: some more curious than others, some more easily frightened, some more spirited, some more playful. She laughed when the first cow finally obeyed her. Between herself, the strange character who dressed like a city student but swore like a country peasant, and his dog, the cattle were safely returned to their proper field just as the sun touched the tops of the trees in the fields to the west, to turn everything into gold.

Chasing the cattle, she realized, made her laugh, for the first time since the trial of Galileo.

"Me name's Isaac," said the young man, as he invited her to follow him back to his tree.

"Urania," she replied, and shook his hand.

"You've never worked a farm before, have yeh?" the man observed as he closed the gate on the cattle.

"No," said Urania, "I usually work in an observatory."

"An observatory! None of them round here – where you from?"

"*Hellas* – Greece."

Isaac regarded her with a cocked head. "That's kind of far – what brings you to England?"

"The lovely weather, of course," Urania grinned.

"Try Scotland for that," Isaac laughed. "They can have all four seasons in the same day." It was the first time Urania saw him smile.

"I might do," said Urania. "I'm here to find somewhere quiet, some place where there's not too many people. Where I can do my own thinking. Some place with a good library, perhaps."

"I would recommend Cambridge. I'm a student there, meself. But they have plague right now. That's why I'm back here on the farm."

"Oh, I'm sorry."

"Don't be," said Isaac. "The professors are all rubbish. They still teach the Peripatetics and the Scholastics. Can't be bothered going to class anymore. I go to the library, read whatever I want."

Urania picked up the book that Isaac had been reading. A broad and joyful grin grew on her face. "You're reading Copernicus!" she cheered.

Isaac folded his arms. "Nothing wrong with that. It's not banned here in England."

"Oh no, I'm delighted!" Urania praised him. "What about Bruno, or Galileo – have you read them?"

"All the Italians, obviously," Isaac sneered. He gestured for Urania to return his book to her, which she did. He opened it to the page with the diagram of the solar system. "But I like Brahe and Kepler better," he said. "Copernicus is pretty good, but he didn't have the Rudolphine Tables. Most accurate star charts ever made. Can't do any basic astronomy without them now."

Urania's head turned to the east, where Prometheus and his villa lay beyond the horizon. "He said they would prepare the way..." she said, then her gaze drifted back on Isaac.

"Prepare for what?" Isaac asked. He shifted slightly away from her, as though her appraisal of his posture was a net that might entangle him.

Urania shrugged it off with a pained smile. "Something between me and someone I used to know. It's not important anymore." She motioned that they should sit under his tree again, and they did. "You're studying astronomy and mathematics, then?" she asked, making conversation.

"Physics!" he informed her. "Natural philosophy. The only branch on the tree of knowledge that matters."

"My great love was always astronomy." Urania said. "It always seemed to me that to obey the Oracle of Delphi, to know yourself, you need to know the world around you. See its beauty."

"You're a strange one," Isaac chided her.

"I think it's strange if people *don't* notice the beauty all around them," Urania said. "It would be like – I don't know... sleepwalking through life."

"Don't know much about art," said Isaac. His gaze wandered to the sky, and the rising gibbous moon in the east.

"There's beauty in philosophy, too," Urania suggested.

"There is indeed," Isaac agreed. "Kepler's three laws of planetary motion: elegant, simple, *real*. Galileo's optics. Old Copernicus, too. Why anyone would swear by that clunky old Ptolemy, I'll never know."

Urania picked up the copy of *De Revolutionibus*. "Copernicus left us with a problem that no one knows how to solve. Why do some things fall to the earth, and other things go round the sun?"

"That's a monster of a problem," Isaac brightened. "He swept old Aristotle and his five elements away but gave us nothing in their place. To solve that one, it would take a new way of *thinking*, a new way of *seeing*. I do not yet know what that would be."

Urania turned her head toward him, her jaw slightly open. "I once heard a man say those very same words. He went on to write a book that changed the world," she told him.

Isaac grinned. "Ha! My ambitions are not so big. I only want to solve an interesting mathematics problem. And, perhaps, solve it before anyone else gets to it first."

As Isaac contemplated the moon, Urania looked around the farmyard. The sun had plunged waist-deep in the horizon now, and the golden streaks of his light shone through the orange and red clouds.

"I was reading Plato, Socrates, and the pre-Socratics – you know, the men who gave Aristotle his ideas," Isaac continued, thinking out loud. "And I asked myself, why *five* elements? Why not six, or ten?"

"You surely know the answer to that," Urania said. "Empedocles said all things are either hot or cold, wet or dry."

"I do know that," Isaac agreed, "but still, why not six basic properties instead of two? Why not eight? Why not ten? What forces in nature did he *miss*?"

As Isaac meditated out loud about the follies of the ancient philosophers, Urania looked up, and saw that some of the apples in the tree above them were ripe enough to eat. She made a gesture toward one of them, and it snapped its stem and plopped into her hand. Isaac's jaw gaped to see it fall, and to see how nonchalant Urania was about it. So she offered it to him, saying, "You like apples?"

Isaac took it and said, "How did you do that?"

She smiled and shrugged her shoulders. "Not magic, if you were wondering. I could tell that the apple was ready to fall, so I just opened my hand."

"What, from ten feet below, and without touching it?" Isaac marvelled. He looked at the apple as if it had become solid gold.

"It's an ordinary apple, nothing is different about it," Urania grinned.

Isaac bit into the apple and contemplated the moon as he chewed. "What if..." he said, his mouth still full, "what if there are cause-and-effect forces that can act at a distance like that?" He tossed the apple in the air and caught it a few times. "What if the force that pulls an apple to the ground is *the very same force* that swings the moon around the Earth?"

"Then the moon would not really be orbiting the Earth at all," Urania suggested. "It would be falling."

Isaac barely heard her, having already reached the same conclusion. "What if it's *falling*, just like the apple," he said, "but the curvature of its fall is greater than the curvature of the Earth? What if *everything* is falling toward everything else, all over the universe? Everything – not falling, but *flying* – everything in motion, nothing standing still."

Urania saw her new friend as though he might someday be her teacher, and not her student. She reached to his shoulder, but stopped before she touched him, as if his flesh might shock her. Then Isaac got up and ran toward the farmhouse. His dog jumped up and followed him, equally excited.

"Where are you going?" Urania called to him.

"I have the answer now!" he sang. "There's not five forces of nature, there is only one! And I have to create the equation for it – I have the answer!"

Urania picked up his dropped apple and contemplated the house into which Isaac had disappeared. She smiled and said, "And now, so do I."

§ 86.

"I'm not going to summon the professors for you a third time," said Catherine. She sat by a delicately carved writing desk, sorting through stacks of letters and documents piled almost as high as her head. "Your first candidate had no control over his own mouth. And your second lost his courage when he needed it most."

"I'm not asking them to examine anyone again," said Urania, as she mixed a bowl of gum arabic, egg yolk, and soot, to make ink for the professor's quill. "Instead, I'm asking you, Catherine, to witness something that I plan to do."

"Well, what is it?" Catherine asked, impatience undisguised in her voice. "Are you placing a bet with Caligula now? That he'll never bring back the old Roman Empire?"

§ 87.

"Oh no, nothing so obvious as that," the muse told Moses Maimonides, and Hypatia, as the three of them explored the Rialto Market, in Venice. Dozens of heady fragrances filled the air, especially pepper, nutmeg, cinnamon, and dozens of other spices, some imported from as far away as India, or so the merchants claimed in their calls to passing customers.

"But I think it is time he saw the truth," Urania explained.

Maimonides shook his head and folded his arms. "This has gone badly for you in the past."

"I agree," said Hypatia. "I think you have the right goal in mind, but I cannot say the same of your plan to reach it."

"It's risky, I know," Urania admitted. "But if it works –"

§ 88.

"Then you will certainly never be allowed to go home again," said Imhotep. He leaned over his work table, measuring delicate amounts of various liquids and gases, and mixing them together through a complicated apparatus of glass tubes and phials. Smoky sunbeams streamed into the room through a grated stone window.

"I know," Urania sighed.

"But if it's that important to you, and you're willing to take that risk," said Imhotep, "then tell me how you would like me to help."

"All I need you to do is bear witness," said the muse, as she sniffed the greenish contents of a flask, made a sour face, and put it down again.

Imhotep perked an eyebrow at her.

"And, maybe, help Kynisca to keep me safe while I'm doing it?" the goddess added.

"You think things will get rough, do you?" asked the old architect. "Well, it is not my style. But it is your life. So. Tell your friend Kynisca of Sparta that I, Imhotep of Egypt, can crack more heads than she can!"

§ 89.

**Cambridge, England,
1669.**

In one of the university's many dining halls, a host of professors, students, and their friends raised their glasses in a toast.

"To Isaac Newton," said the dean of the college. "Our new Lucasian professor of mathematics!"

Isaac was no longer as young as when Urania found him in his farmyard.

Still, he looked too young for the academic gown and Tudor cap that his friends put on him. He rose to accept the toast, grinning and clasping his hands in thanksgiving.

"Speech, speech!" some of the guests chanted. Isaac feigned stage fright for a moment, then moved to a podium near the head table, pretending all the while that he was under duress.

"Saint Augustine," said Isaac, "once wrote that God gave us two books, so that we may know him. I say he gave us three: the scriptures, the world of nature, and..." he paused to make his audience guess his next words, then looked to the ceiling and said, "the book of Urania, up there in the sky. We are all living inside of it. Just as we also live inside at least one of the other two books. Let me tell you the most important thing I have learned from studying it. Because I think we are only now beginning to read it right."

Urania, who had been standing in the door and watching her latest apprentice receive his accolades, chose that moment to depart. She waved to him and touched her heart. He returned the gesture, then continued his speech.

Outside, the moon had fully risen, bringing a quiet silver light to the university's mediaeval quadrangle. The yellow glow of candles and oil lamps in the windows diffused through the space, strong enough to light the way for the few students and staff who still moved about, to and from a dining hall or a library or a tavern. Urania counted the stars as she walked, following a comforting old habit, innocent of the peaceful smile that shaped her round and youthful face.

Kynisca jumped from the roof of the college to a grassy patch in the garden and moved to her friend's side. "He's coming," she said. "And he brought maybe a dozen friends with him."

"He took the bait," the goddess smiled.

"Exactly as you said he would," said the warrior-woman. Then seeing her friend's smile was not so confident, she said, "Try to relax. Trust the plan. It is, after all, your plan."

Urania made a small laugh. "I'll keep him talking as long as I can," she said.

"We can do the rest," Kynisca promised. Then she jogged away, into the college.

Alone again, Urania lingered by the dining hall door, to hear more of Isaac and his friends celebrating his new job. She did not wait long for Julian to appear, exactly as expected.

"The bargain is *over*, Urania," he said. "Why are you bothering with that idiot savant in there?"

"The bargain is over, yes," Urania confirmed. "And you lost. And I won."

Julian cocked his head. "I think you have that backwards."

"Oh, I understand why you believe that," Urania said. "Every time I found someone who could push the frontier of knowledge a little further, the forces of ignorance and fear pushed back. Someone started a war. The religious authorities arrested the man, silencing his voice or killing him. Or the man himself couldn't believe his own discovery. But you see: every time that happened, knowledge still won. Slowly. Painfully. No more than a single candle at a time. And sure, some of those candles were blown out and had to be re-lit. But no one blew them all out. For everything you tried to do to stop me, that candle I gave to Nicolaus still shines. And there are more candles in more hands now, shining brighter together. You failed to blow it out. You lost, and I won."

Julian pursed his lips, and took a few steps away, considering her words. Then he marched to her face again and said, "You know, you might have a point. I should never have tried to kill your students or burn their books. That sort of thing never works."

"Glad to hear it," Urania scorned. "You're learning to think like a normal person."

"What I should have done," he continued, "was kill *you*."

Julian pointed to an upper-floor window in the college quad. A man sat in one of them, armed with a crossbow. He pulled the string of his weapon on to the catch, loaded a bolt in place, then swigged from a bottle of wine.

Julian took in a deep and satisfied breath and smiled. "These modern universities have the most beautiful gardens," he said. "At the end of a busy market day, it's such a treat to come in here, sit by the flower beds, and imagine you're in paradise. This university in particular, this Cambridge – it has its own basilica. You can marvel at the gold leaf on the statues and the light from the stained glass windows, and imagine you're kneeling before the throne of God. They design them for exactly that reason, you know. To give the mortals an idea of the pleasures of heaven that await them if they live a pious Christian life. What do you think of that, Urania? Do you think the heaven of the Christians might look like this garden?"

"I'll tell you, if you send your *misthios* away," Urania told him, nodding toward the crossbowman.

"Or do you think the Franciscans had the right idea?" Julian asked, as he stole a bottle of wine from a passing student, tapping his forehead so that the student wouldn't object. "They think the Church should be poor, because Christ was poor, or some such thing. And that the most blessed life must necessarily be the simplest. The life of a country farmer, tending his fields and eating his honest bread with his family. Ah, sometimes I envy the small people."

"You won't do anything to me with so many witnesses," Urania told him, gesturing toward the open doors of the banquet hall.

"I'm tired of bargaining with you," said Julian. "We have to finish this business between us tonight."

"So *you* can go home?" the muse taunted him.

Julian did not answer, but only smirked at her. He knew she was right.

"Listen. Killing me will not stop Isaac or any other philosopher lighting more candles around the world," she told him.

"But it will show the rest of Olympus what happens when you cross the will of Zeus," he declared. He waved to his crossbowman, and the soldier took aim.

Urania stepped back and shouted "Kynisca, now!"

The would-be assassin fell back into the window, as though yanked there by an unseen hand. A heartbeat later, the crossbow flew out the window and cracked when it hit the ground. Julian gaped at the sight of it. Next, the soldier's jerkin flew out the window, followed by his tunic, and then his pants.

"Your *hamartia*, Julian, is your need to put people down; your need to feel superior, and to make others feel shame," Urania told him. "Your assassin could have killed me the moment I stepped out of the banquet hall. But instead, you had a speech for me. You rehearsed it, didn't you? You wanted me to admit that I lost. And your *hamartia* gave my friend enough time to find your assassin and stop him. All I had to do was keep you talking."

"She isn't going to kill him –" Julian gasped.

"Oh no, that's not her style. She's more like –"

A door opened in the college hall below the assassin's window, and the man himself staggered out, and fell to the ground. He was missing all his clothing but his hat and his boots. The banquet patrons across the green enjoyed a wave of loud laughter at his expense, although one of them did bring him a cape.

"More like that," Urania finished.

"He's not the only one," Julian threatened.

"Neither is Kynisca," the muse replied with a grin.

A heartbeat later, Julian saw Imhotep in one of the windows, blowing a pinch of reddish dust into a mercenary's face, thereby putting him to sleep. In another, Hypatia sat herself on the windowsill, denying a third assassin a line of sight to his target. When he tried to push her out of the way, she made a gesture that caused his crossbow to fall into a pile of disassembled parts. The sound of men shouting with surprise issued from several more college windows, all around the college green. Broken crossbow parts fell to the ground. Urania grinned and winked at Julian, as if defeating his assassin squad was easy.

"What do you *want*, Urania?" the wily Roman grunted.

"I want to talk," she answered him, "like rational, civilized people. I want you to tell my father that I don't care anymore if he shuts me out of Olympus. I'm staying here."

"What?"

"That's right," Urania confirmed.

"Olympus is your *home*," Julian said. "These mortals will never understand you. They are not like you. The Hidden World is where you belong."

"Have you ever looked at Olympus, and thought about it, for more than a minute? It's a place where the clouds are always wispy and light, the sunshine always warm. But the days fade into each other, until no one can tell the difference between them."

"Olympus is not hell," Julian countered.

"Olympus is *over*," Urania argued. "Look at what life is like in any Olympian temple. We feast and drink, we sing and dance; we reminisce about our glory days. We don't *do* anything anymore. It's like we've stepped outside of time. But here, among the mortals, people still want to know what's over the next hill; they still want to climb that hill and find out. It's not everyone, and they get it wrong sometimes – I know that. But in Olympus, nobody is curious anymore. Nobody cares."

"You think life down here is any better?" Julian shouted. "Have you not looked around? The wars of religion, the plagues, the poverty? Death everywhere? No one down here cares about knowledge. Some of them say they do, but what they *really* care about is their next meal, their next pay day, their next slap and tickle in bed. They'll cheat and lie and stab each other to get what they want. Do you know how I lost my crown? One of my own soldiers tried to murder me. I still have the scar where his spear went straight into my guts. That was my reward for trying to give my people the light of civilization. That's who they are. All of them, without exception."

"Isn't that what you are doing to me now?" Urania said, as she picked up the assassin's lost crossbow.

"Do not compare me to that coward, you smooth-talking viper!" Julian seethed.

"It's you who isn't looking around," Urania contended. "Remember what the world was like when you made your bargain with me? Everyone in Europe thought there were ghosts at every crossroads, monsters in every forest –"

"They *still* believe that!" Julian shot back. "Did you know that in a public square in this very city, they're hanging people for witchcraft?"

"But they're also pointing telescopes at the sky," Urania reminded him. "They weren't doing that a hundred years ago. They're progressing, changing – making the world less mysterious. And they're never going to stop."

Julian bowed and shook his head. "Then the prophesy of Hesiod will come true. The Men of Iron will inherit the earth; the race of heroes will die. And you and I both will die with them. You may think our world is haunted by demons but it's still *our* world. It's the only one we can live in. If you stay down here helping these bald monkeys take control, every Olympian with a sense of self-preservation will fight you. The war will never end."

"There is another way," Urania said. She turned her gaze to the sky and said, "Tell me what's up there."

"The sky. What about it?"

"Would you like to see it?"

Julian laughed. "I already know what's out there."

Urania smiled and said, "No, you don't."

"I certainly do," Julian sputtered.

Urania shook her head. "Since my exile began, I learned so many things about the world. From Prometheus I learned that the gods are petty squabbling children, and Olympus itself is nothing but a gravelly knoll. From Kynisca and Tarquinia, from Tycho and Giordano, I learned that I don't have to go back there. I have better friends here. And from Catherine de Parthenay, I learned the most important lesson of all."

"What."

"That the gods have no more of an idea what's out there than anyone else."

As she spoke, Kynisca approached Julian from one side, and Catherine from the other. They took his arms. Julian struggled, but the two women held him fast, while Urania stepped behind him and caressed his temples with careful fingers. The grass of the university green fell away beneath them, then the university itself, and then the whole city of Cambridge.

"What are you doing?" Julian demanded.

"The same thing I do to all my students. I'm showing you the world."

"I am *not* your student –"

"You are now."

England shrank beneath them as they rushed into the heavens. Urania turned him to face ahead, to the growing rocky moon, and the wall of stars behind it.

"Put me down, put me down!" Julian demanded.

"No!" said Urania. "You're going to see the cosmos the way I do."

They skimmed beneath the south pole of the moon, rushing past the round mountain-ranges of craters, following the long streak-lines of shadows, stark black and white, nearly no shades of grey in between. Then they left the moon behind, turning around only for a moment to receive the sight of the shrinking Earth, blue oceans and white clouds, green forests and yellow deserts, disappearing into the star-scattered blackness of space. Julian howled, and kicked his feet, desperate for something to stand on. Urania held his head fast, keeping his eyes open, and his mind in the moment.

"All right, I've seen enough – you win!" Julian pleaded. "Take me back – Urania, take me back!"

"Not until you understand," she told him. They approached Venus next, in her crescent glory. Its clouds resolved into wispy shapes as they drew near and faded into a bright yellow-white disk as they whisked past. The sun was larger now, its surface bubbling and churning with storms. They flew beneath a great arch of fire that burst from its surface, then sped on to the darkness ahead. They passed red and rocky Mars, a playground for dust devils and sandstorms. They passed each of Jupiter's handmaiden moons: turbulent Io, icy Ganymede, cracked Europa and rocky Callisto. Then they grazed the great red storm on Jupiter, violent and eternal, large enough to swallow the Earth entirely. Tears began to flow down Julian's cheeks. Urania only carried him further. She showed him the pearly rings of Saturn. Then she showed him worlds he had never heard of: one of them aquamarine, another deep sapphire blue, another red and white with a great beige heart on its belly and a small family of rocky grey moons. Then they carried on, their flesh pressing against their bones as they accelerated, until the sun itself appeared like another star, then it too dimmed and disappeared.

"How can you know all this and not lose yourself?" Julian sobbed.

Urania said, "By loving it."

By Urania's side, Julian saw how the stars hummed and throbbed with life: planets and moons, comets and ice-belts. On some of the planets, she showed him towns and cities where women and men pointed telescopes to the sky. On others, people pulled the levers of machines that moved great metal disks, curved inwards like lenses and bristling with antennae: metallic ears to listen to the most distant whispers of space. On the rarest of planets, people boarded chariots of metal and glass, which lifted them above the clouds of their world, and carried them to other worlds within the realm of their sun, and then to other worlds beyond.

Julian strained his eyes shut, and hot tears grew from his eyes.

Urania released her grip on him; he blinked, rubbed his face, and found himself on the college green in Cambridge again. Kynisca and Catherine let his arms go, and he staggered a few feet away, then sat down and clasped the grass in his fingers. He noticed that a group of professors of the Secret Academy had witnessed his reaction to Urania's lesson: Hypatia, Imhotep, and Maimonides, among them. He turned his face away, ashamed.

"That," said Urania, "is the other way. To know where we are in the cosmos, and how small we are within it. Mortals, Olympians, all of us, as tiny as dust-motes in the ocean. And yet how privileged we are, how wonderfully blessed, that we can see that ocean, explore it, know it. The gods don't have to die if humanity takes over the world. Seen from under the aspect of eternity we are not so different from them. We are just as small as them. And living in the same enormous, endless, wonderful world."

"But how can anyone love all that emptiness... all that *nothingness* out there?"

"The earth," said Urania, as she and her friends sat on the grass beside him, "may be only a tiny candle in the sky. But it is no small thing to be a candle, when everything around you is dark."

Julian shook his head; unsure if her words were convincing, but lacking anything else to say.

§ 90.

On the belvedere of Prometheus' villa, Urania placed a bottle of wine on the table. "Tuscan Sangiovese, five years old," she named it, as she poured a cup for herself and for Prometheus.

"Sangiovese... the blood of Jupiter – not a variety of grape that I like having about my house," Prometheus said, as he sniffed it but did not drink.

"I've come to appreciate some of the things the mortals can do, when they put their minds to it," said Urania. "I have a bottle of Bohemian Slivo, if you prefer. Cheese from Belgium and the Savoy region. Bread and olive oil from our native Hellas." She placed a wicker basket on the table and laid its contents out for him to sample.

"These were all made by mortals?"

"They were," she said. From another basket, she took a long telescope, wrapped in a burlap cloth. "And this is one of Galileo's own telescopes."

Prometheus plucked it between his thumb and forefinger, as if it might break with the slightest touch. He held it to his eye, then grimaced.

"I suppose I should have got a bigger one for you, seeing as you're a Titan," Urania grinned.

Prometheus tossed it to the flagstones, cracking its lenses. "I have no need for a toy like this. And get rid of this rancid vinegar you call wine. Bring out some proper *chian* or *lemnian*, or anything at all, as long as it comes from a proper Dionysian grove."

"You don't like my gifts? I brought them to show my gratitude, for all the things you did for me."

"You can show your gratitude by winning Julian's bargain," Prometheus gritted.

Urania smiled, and shook her head. "I don't care about that anymore."

Prometheus perked an eyebrow. "No? How do you expect to get home again?"

"I don't," she said.

"You want your father to *win*?" he gritted.

"You once asked me why I persisted with Copernicus, even if it meant angering my father," Urania said. "Only now I can see – it didn't matter to you *why* I was doing it. You only wanted to know how much trouble I would cause for him. The two of you would be best friends if you weren't already enemies; you're so alike!"

Prometheus patronized her with a deafening laugh. "We are nothing like each other."

"You *are*," Urania insisted. "You both believe in fate. And you both believe it would be bad for us if humanity became enlightened. The only difference between you is that he's afraid of it, and you actually *want* it. I think you're both wrong. I think the cosmos is big enough for everyone."

Prometheus gave her another patronizing smile. "You are still very young."

Urania decided to treat that statement as a wreath of honour. "There's a way to teach people to make fire without burning down the house. I intend to find it, and I *will* teach them. And if by then you're not too old, I will teach you too."

Prometheus shook his head, as he watched her walk away.

* * *

Such is my story, so far.

I built a new home for myself on a hillside near Kynisca's training camp, in Arcadia. It was a good hour's ride from the nearest settlement: close enough to keep the loneliness away, far enough to be hard for my father and his agents to find me. And there was a good view of the night sky, here. I could not live without a view of the sky.

I continued searching the world for lovers of wisdom. Not to win any bargains, nor to prove anything to anyone. But for the more honest reason: to find my people. I never found anyone quite as spirited and as passionate as my sisters. Or any of the Olympians I left behind. I still don't know who my people are.

But I did find a few friends who cared about me, and who made the time to know me. With them, I was content.

For the first time in an age of the world, I was content.

§ 91.

Julian approached the brazier at the foot of the statue of Zeus, where normally he would place his offerings. This time he stood before it: not kneeling, not bowing, and not offering anything. The statue of the god, as imposing and magnificent as ever, seemed in his new eyes as tiny as the ants that crossed the floor beneath his sandals.

Footsteps echoed in the temple from behind him, and the voice of his master boomed out: *Kneel, Julian Augustus.*

"Not anymore," Julian said. "Never again."

A crack of thunder boomed overhead.

I am Zeus Panhellenius, the King of the Gods, Lord and Master of Olympus, The Protector, The Strengthener, The Oppressor of the Titans, The Chooser of All Men's Fates! I am the lightning that breaks ships at sea! I am the eagle that sees all things.

Julian turned around. Standing a few steps inside the entrance of the temple was a pathetic and withered old man, half as tall as Julian, draped in a moth-eaten purple cloak. His face was crevassed and pock-marked with age, his limbs were like bones with a thin parchment of flesh hanging from them. His twisted toes and claw-like nails hung over the lip of his sandals.

"You're the king of the gods?" Julian said, and he began to laugh.

Zeus shook his fists and grimaced his face. He repeated the litany of his titles. Another clap of thunder exploded in the sky above. But Julian continued laughing. Then he strode away, leaving his former master to howl and rage against the noise of his own voice, echoing from the upper vaults of the temple.

§ 92.

Vatican City, 1992.

Her court pumps clicked on the marble floors of the great hall, and her black dress swayed in the slight breeze. An usher gestured toward her seat in the gallery, among the theologians, journalists, and various members of the Pontifical Academy of Sciences. They had come to hear the formal announcement that many years of research and careful diplomacy had reached a successful end. A curtain parted and Pope John Paul II entered. His audience rose to acknowledge him, as much from the way his cheerfulness enlivened them, as from an observance of protocol.

"Thanks to his intuition as a brilliant physicist," said the pontiff, as he neared the end of his prepared notes, "Galileo understood why only the sun could function as the centre of the world, as it was then known. The error of the theologians of the time was to think that our understanding of the physical world's structure was, in some way, imposed by the literal sense of Sacred Scripture. From the Galileo affair we can learn a new lesson which remains valid in relation to similar situations which occur today and may occur in the future. That often, beyond two partial and contrasting perceptions, there exists a wider perception which includes them and goes beyond both of them."

The Holy Father blessed the assembly; they rose to their feet again, and applauded; Urania, loudest of all.

§ 93.

Los Angeles, California,
United States of America, 1994.

In the sound stage of a downtown recording studio, Urania pinned a large poster to the sound-absorbing fabric on the wall. It was mostly black and speckled with white points like dust, but several bars of red, green, and yellow light streaked across it. The brightest of them held a tiny spot of blue in its fold. A caption on the poster read, "Voyager 1 – Family Portrait – Earth."

Across the studio, a man with salt-and-pepper hair, a pleasant round face, and an orange turtleneck sweater, read a few lines into a microphone.

"The Earth is a very small stage in a vast cosmic arena," he said. "Think of the rivers of blood spilled by all those generals and emperors so that, in glory and triumph, they could become the momentary masters of a fraction of a dot. It has been said that astronomy is a humbling and character-building experience. There is perhaps no better demonstration of the folly of human conceits than this distant image of our tiny world. To me, it underscores our responsibility to deal more kindly with one another, and to preserve and cherish the pale blue dot, the only home we've ever known."

In the control room, Catherine stopped the tape and turned off the red recording light. Kynisca spoke into the comm: "That's it, Carl, we got it!"

Carl put down the text and let out his worries with his breath. He asked Urania, "What do you think – *did* we get it this time?"

Urania smiled and said, "Perfectly."

Carl wandered beside her, to admire the poster. "There was so much more I wanted to say. I suppose this picture will have to say it for me."

"It will," Urania reassured him.

"We've walked on the moon now," he said, partially lost in his thoughts. "I wonder when we will walk on Mars, or Venus, or on the moons of

Jupiter. I wonder what that would be like."

Urania smiled, took his hands, and said, "Would you like to see it?"

Author's Notes

If you know anything about Greek mythology, you probably know some part of the story of Prometheus, the hero who stole fire from the sun and gave it to the fledgling human race. You probably also know how Zeus punished him for it, by chaining him to a mountain and sending a vulture every day to torture him. The story still informs much of Western civilization's sense of itself: his theft of fire is the symbol of Western civilization's sense of its initiative, industriousness, and enlightenment. Prometheus himself is a model of the ideal civilized man, a hero of daring and of endurance under adversity, combining the features of biblical Adam, the primordial man and primordial thief, as well as Christ, the victor over death and the benefactor of humankind, and also, though it may seem a strange combination, Milton's Lucifer, the rebel angel. We put the image of his torch in the logos of our corporations and our universities. We re-enact part of his story in the opening ceremonies of the modern Olympic Games, when we light the Olympic flame.

I think we need a better symbol for who we are.

For one reason: in the full story, Prometheus has no particular feelings for humanity. He meddled with the sacrifices to Zeus and returned fire to us after Zeus took it away, all in order to undermine the authority of Zeus; he had no other reason. Various primary sources, notably the *Library of Apollodorus*, attest to this.

For a second reason: Greek mythology also provides to us an entire family of other, better benefactors: the Muses, who embody the functions of civilization rather more directly, if somewhat less ostentatiously, than Prometheus. The muses, and not Prometheus, are invoked at the beginning of the most important epic poems, the *Illiad*, the *Odyssey*, the *Theogony*, and the *Works and Days*. They're invoked at the beginning of many of the old Greek plays, too. And while Prometheus and his torch are undeniably powerful symbols for a scientific and industrial civilization, it is the gifts of the muses which activate the imagination, the artistic genius, and the scientific curiosity, which drives civilization forward. Indeed, the very notion of 'going forward', or progress, is a gift of the mother of the muses, Mnemosyne, 'memory'. For it is our ability to remember that enables us to possess a notion of progress at all. Memory is what allows us to compare our present state of life to the past, and so assess whether our lives are any better, or any worse, or at least different. And if we find that our life has become worse, we can call the muses to help us make art and so ease the misery, if not also improve life again.

For a third reason: the nine muses embody the most important fields of primary education. There are among them six writers, a musician, a dancer, and a scientist. That is to say, they are the bringers of academic knowledge, emotional maturity, artistic excellence, physical training, and cultural identity. Compare any of the martial heroes of Greece to Terpsichore, muse of the dance. She teaches a form of physical education and health maintenance which, unlike track-and-field events or field sports, is not a thinly disguised preparation for war fighting. Next to these nine women dancing in a circle, the symbol of the torch-wielding Prometheus seems to me unnecessarily aggressive, possibly vainglorious, and even rather joyless.

For a fourth reason: One can imagine any of the muses, even unhappy Melponene, singing or laughing with childlike delight to see some thing of beauty in the world, however small. One cannot imagine Prometheus laughing, unless it comes from a Nietzschean sense of pleasure in the exercise of power. (Okay, fine, you can imagine him laughing, and wearing a clown suit and juggling seven live cats, because imagination is weird like that. But it wouldn't be consistent with his character.) By contrast, the laughter of the Muses comes from pure life-affirmation, nothing more and nothing less. Between the two, I think the laughter of the muses is preferable. It can come from that thrill you feel when life surprises you with something both unexpected and beautiful. That's what inspiration is like, sometimes.

For a fifth reason: images of the muses already possess an important place in the history of western art, in close continuity from before the Renaissance and up to the present day. Raphael, for example, included them in his *Parnassus*, his allegory of the arts, which occupies an equal place beside his *Disputatio* (theology) and *School of Athens* (philosophy). And as themes of art, the muses remain mostly consistent, yet they are flexible enough to adapt themselves for each generation that invokes them. One can imagine that today Calliope, the muse of epic poetry, now works as the muse of long-form episodic television drama. One can imagine Erato teaching college students about consent culture and how to use various contraceptives. Perhaps Euterpe, the muse-goddess of lyric poetry, works with the people who design light shows at rock concerts. Perhaps Polymnia conducts gospel choirs. Prometheus, as a symbol, seems to me somewhat less flexible. He's a straight-up hero, a trickster-god, and a rebel angel; and while those are good things to be, he's not much else. His hero-energy might remain reactionary and aimless, without the vision and guidance of the muses.

For such reasons, then, I think a far better symbol for the life and identity of western civilization should be a circle of the nine muses dancing together. It is a more joyful image, to encourage a more caring, more intellectually vigorous, and more artistically flourishing culture.

So, thank you for listening to that. And now, here are some brief administrative notes.

In order to convey the voices and dispositions of the historical characters, I resorted as often as possible to their own actual words, quoting directly, or closely paraphrasing, from:

- Pico della Mirandola, *Oration on the Dignity of Man*, 1486.
- The Fragments of Protagoras, 486-411 BCE.
- Copernicus, *De Revolutionibus*, 1543; *The Little Commentary*, 1543.
- Tycho Brahe, *De Nova Stella*, 1574.
- Kepler, *Letter to Johann Georg Herwart von Hohenburg*, 1605.
- Giordano Bruno, *Opere Italiane, Dialoghi metafisici*, 1584; *Spaccio de la bestia trionfante*, 1584; *On the Infinite Universe and Worlds*, 1584.
- The text of the judgement against Giordano Bruno, and his last recorded words, 1600.
- Martin Luther, *Tischreden*, 1566.
- Cardinal Robert Bellarmine, *Letter to Paolo Forscarini on Galileo's Theories*, 1615.
- Galileo, *Letter to Belisario Vinta*, 1610; *Letters On Sunspots*, 1612; *Letter to the Christina of Lorraine, Grand Duchess of Tuscany*, 1615 and 1616.
- The text of Galileo's abjuration, and of the judgment against him, 1633.

- Pope John Paul II, *Address to the Pontifical Academy of Sciences*, as published in *L'Osservatore Romano*, No.44, 4th November 1992.

- Carl Sagan, *Pale Blue Dot*, 1994.

In most cases where characters quote the Bible, I have preferred the New International (English) Edition, which was not available during the Renaissance, but which I hoped would make a less jarring experience for the reader today.

I had to take a few liberties with the lives of the scientists featured here, in order to drive the pace of the story. For example: Tycho's sword fight with Manderup Parsberg took place several days after the argument at the wedding feast, and not during the feast itself. Galileo did demonstrate his telescope to Pope Paul V in the year 1611, but he did not cross the Inquisition until some five years later, after he published his observations of the phases of Venus. He did spend a night in a cottage full of poisoned air, but to the best of my knowledge no Greek goddesses rescued him. I hope the sticklers among the readers will forgive these and other minor artistic licenses.

A final note. Although the events in this story have no direct relation to the events of my *Fellwater: The Hidden Houses* series, readers of both may note some similarities. I consider this story to have taken place in the same world, the same imagined universe. Hence Urania's remark in this novel that the gods are humanity's ancestors. I have a sequel planned, where the continuity will continue, and so will Urania's search for her people.

Perhaps you are one of them.

Brendan Myers
Gatineau, Quebec
April, 2021

Brendan Myers